Noah Plays Golf

A near-future novel

by Henry Tersen

Cover artwork by Kara Tersen

Dedicated to those who golf all their life yet never get to celebrate a hole-in-one.

This is a work of fiction. Unless otherwise indicated, all the names, characters, businesses, places, events, and incidents in this book are either the product of the author's imagination or used in a fictitious manner. Any resemblance to actual persons, living or dead, or actual events is purely coincidental.

Noah Plays Golf

Sunday, April 23, 2028

Suddenly dead. Is that why it has rolled to a stop without warning? The rental is dead, the batteries now useless like blocks of ice. No lights and no response irrespective of which screen he pokes at. As in a silly horror video he once had watched, Hans Pedders finds himself vulnerable on a gravel road devoid of traffic. What has been a hot afternoon in the Arizona desert now has him shivering; daylight is ending abruptly, the sun disappearing over the serrated horizon of the Rawhide Mountains. The occasional golfing holiday to escape a Canadian winter had taken Hans this far south before so the sudden darkness should not catch the northerner off guard. Of course, he knows better than to be surprised that at this latitude daylight does not linger in the evening.

He fumbles for the door handle, unfolds himself out of the bucket seat and exits the vehicle with some reluctance. After standing up, Hans hesitates to step away from the car; he is staring into a blackness he could never have imagined. Other than the stars, there is no hint of light anywhere. Mere minutes ago, he was racing headlong into the fading evening, trying to keep the vehicle on the gravel of a desert trail and now his face is up against a foreboding nothingness.

He inches away from the car to give himself room to stretch and a sudden, piercing brilliance in the sky blasts his eyes, the pain recoiling him back against the car, and then waves and waves of thunder drum on his ears. Must be over-wrought, he thinks, and scrambles back into his seat, slamming the door shut on the mirage, at first only dimly and then acutely aware that the sports car is shaking. The personal internet connector, PIC, on his wrist is also dead and useless for helping to explain what is going on. This is not the welcome Hans had anticipated. To regain some composure, he reminds himself of a promise made several days ago not to entertain any preconceptions about what to expect.

As suddenly as the furor in the sky had started, just as quickly it stops. Surreptitiously, like sneaking around a corner to view the future, Hans dares to climb back out into the darkness. His stunned senses recover and his eyes, pinched by the harrowing ordeal, re-open and search the sky. Stars! Ironically, the blackness of the desert sky coerces him to view stars as if for the first time. The countless points of light convey a dimension of unreachable depth and hint at immeasurable distances. Hans shrinks together, suddenly feeling small and lonely, a solitary human daring to be alive in the universe. He takes a deep breath and exhales slowly, and another, hoping to imprint the moment for future reference.

The interlude ends abruptly, the need for any kind of decision making resolved by a light emerging from the darkness. At first a glow far off, it comes up on him all at once, fiercely bright and white, falling all over him, pinning him like a police car's spotlight.

Feeling himself at center stage, with thousands gawking at him and nobody in the audience coughing, Hans instinctively starts to raise his hands, ready to be frisked. But all he hears is a voice that surrounds him.

"You are David Johan Pedders. Confirm." He had heard that in situations like this it is unwise to make sudden moves, especially in Arizona, and only very slowly reaches for his wallet. Smoothly the light softens into half- shaded, lazy afternoon daylight. What kind of UFO farce is this? They are not in Nevada! Sharply biting off his thoughts that start with 'Take me to - -', he says instead,

"No! Yes, I mean, I was. My name is Hans Pedders. Who are you?"

"That does not matter right now. Please get your clubs and backpack and climb in," the voice continues and a light beam points to what appears to be a golf cart without a driver.

A glance and he turns back to where the voice is coming from, some vague thing with a light. It is attempting to sound human, trying its best to get the tone right, certainly less ingratiating than that of the annoying tour guide on the car's navigation app. Although not quite his height, there is something purposeful about this, this what? He can barely make out the shape but it is suggestive of a huge medical capsule, or some kind of gas cylinder stood on end, or maybe even an oversized, squat hot dog. Not sure what to call this unexpected apparition, he dare not give it some dumb nickname because the dim, bluish glow radiating from the 'thing' projects an aura implying immense capability that Hans does not want to provoke. He concedes that any control of the situation, if he ever had any, has eroded and he will do as told. He gathers his gear and seats himself in the golf cart.

"What about the car?"

Hans has a legitimate concern because the vehicle is special. It had been one more incentive for him to come to compete for a million dollars in some obscure kind of golf tournament. He could choose for his courtesy car whatever kind of vehicle he wanted to drive. Hans had tested the sincerity of the offer with a wild request for a red, two-seater sports car, an updated replica of a nineteen fifty eight rag top MGA. And there it had been, waiting for him at the airdome in Phoenix.

"The vehicle will be taken care of," the voice responds, in a tone somewhat dismissive and with that Hans is suddenly aware that they seem to be in rapid transit, having no reference point for that other than the seat of his pants. The driverless golf cart is following hard behind the 'thing' with the voice and glimpses of desert scrub are only brief flashes in the periphery of the light shining ahead. Are they in a race? Hans is almost disappointed when the exhilarating ride slows. What they arrive at is not something that he would ever mistake for a clubhouse. With Hans suspecting that they could have found their way here without its use, the probing bright light of the 'thing' shines on a jumble of massive rocks. The trail they are on becomes a paved ramp that slopes down towards a strange looking door recessed into the rocks; the door reminds Hans of pictures of bank vaults.

As if in response to a signal from the 'thing', the huge door opens, and they roll down the ramp into a vast, bunker-like space. The curved walls and the ceiling are rough, undecorated concrete, and barely visible in the dark areas further back, concrete columns and metal enclosures extend floor to ceiling. Hans sees little of that, his attention drawn to the large elevator in the center. The golf cart could easily fit inside but it stops short, and Hans assumes he must get off and get into the elevator. There seems to be no valet service and the 'thing' has no visible appendages, so Hans carries the golf bag and backpack himself.

Once out of the cart, Hans has a better view of who or what has escorted him. Well, isn't that interesting; it rolls along on two wheels like those old Segways used to. What he sees of the elevator also intrigues him. It is spacious and the rounded walls are made of something opaque, and it hovers, seemingly suspended between three vertical metallic guides on the inside of a cylinder of concrete. Beyond a small door on the far side of the elevator are visible the metal rungs of a ladder recessed into the wall of the elevator shaft.

As soon as his 'guide' gets on, the elevator starts to descend. The motion is so rapid it affords Hans only quick glimpses of several forbidding doors that they pass on their way down. When they stop, the exit is similarly barred by a door that he eventually will figure out to be an airlock.

Following obediently through the door that opens as if by itself, Hans emerges into a space, and he cannot believe his eyes, a cavernous space with a dome that arches over a large green area. From the little holes randomly embedded, he deduces it to be a putting green. Considering why he is here, this is a disturbing surprise.

"This is the golf course?!" he exclaims.

"No, you will see that when scheduled. Tonight, you can rest. Leave your clubs here. Come to your rooms."

In the middle of a row of doors along a wall that curves part way around the putting surface, a door to a suite is opened for Hans. Despite it being his favourite colour, he feels somewhat uncomfortable that every room in it is a shade of green. The small dining area has seating for four, the bedroom, adjoined by a bathroom, contains a large, comfortable looking bed. There is also a small study with what appears to be a large computer screen. Not that it matters, but there is no kitchen or a counter and no stove or dishwasher, only a stand-up cooler. So, somewhere then there is a restaurant? Just your typical hotel, a little spartan, he thinks; there is nothing of a decorative nature anywhere.

At least he has this suite to himself, and after a frenetic day he can now relax. For Hans, having time to relax invariably means using that time to wonder about things, especially to wonder about himself and what prompted him to come from his home in Alberta to this strange place.

'Ignoring me will not change my mind. We both know you would have many uses for the money, and the offer is still in play. Confess and admit that you know that I know about your voracious curiosity.'

That was the message he almost erased off his screen two weeks ago. 'Stop harassing me!' he had yelled, 'or I'll report you!', all the time knowing he wouldn't. Lying low in an ever more complicated world had become fundamental to his lifestyle and involving authorities was unthinkable. He relished too much what little privacy and anonymity was still remnant in society. That the challenge had come by old-fashioned email had caused him anxious moments. The sender obviously knew that he had barricaded his private life and could not be accessed via any social media other than controllable email, especially not the currently popular YUM app. How long ago that seems now.

Left alone, he unpacks his few personals on the dresser, hangs up his dress slacks, and puts away his golf shirts, Bermuda shorts, and socks into drawers. About to explore the nature of the plumbing, Hans senses a presence and quickly pulls up his pants. He was right; someone or something has been out there. On the small dining room table is a plate with what looks like sausage rolls, a side dish of salad, and in a tall glass, water that appears to be effervescent, and his stomach reminds him that his last meal was a day ago in Calgary. He goes back to wash his hands and is pleasantly surprised that the tap dispenses hot water. Obviously, no expenses are being spared! Although normally a contemplative eater, Hans wastes little time with the food; he lingers with the water, appreciating how brisk the sensation on his tongue.

His tendency to dally at the table after a meal is cut short by an onset of yawning; it is well before midnight he guesses, his PIC still not working, and the early drowsiness surprises the night owl. Dimly aware of lights turning down, he staggers in the direction of the bedroom in time to roll on to the bed. The room turns dark, as black as the desert had been earlier.

Monday

Light with the intensity of bright sunshine strikes his eyes, forcing them open. Hans yawns and stretches and vaguely recalls his sudden plunge into sleep. Had there been something in that water, and is this now late morning, judging from the bright light used to wake him, and was that light intended to wake him at a designated time? Suddenly wide awake, the possibility of that troubles him. Could it be, Hans thinks, considering what happened last night, that the lighting is being manipulated to tune him to the rhythm of this peculiar place? Ha, 'they' will be challenged to modify his unconventional sleeping habits. Into these speculations jumps another recollection from last night, that just beyond his door is an underworld dominated by a huge putting green.

Alright then, might as well take advantage since his putter, as if anticipating him, strangely enough has ended up leaning by the door. Hans is not sure why he had brought this particular putter, seeing how lately it had acquired all the subtlety of a sledgehammer. About to open the door, he realizes that he is unkempt and that the clothes he has slept in are wrinkled. Usually not too circumspect about his appearance, he deems it only appropriate that to enter this new world he should present himself in a respectful manner. What kind of climate is he about to encounter in this interior world? Will golf shorts and a golf shirt be suitable attire? Just as he is pulling the shirt over his head, a shadow appears to move past his bedroom door.

The strong smell of coffee confirms that someone has been there. It also alerts him to a premonition that everything about him is being anticipated and that he is now in a game programmed specifically for him. But there is something wrong. The mug, weirdly in the shape of a golf ball cut in half, has coffee in it tainted by cream; he likes it straight black.

So where did the coffee come from, and when will he get to meet D.N. Jakow, the person that issued the challenge to come here to golf? Ignoring the coffee, Hans rushes to catch whoever was just there, with the hope of getting some answers. Too late. He couldn't see which way 'they' went because the door to the outside stops him. It is closed and he can't find how to open it. Not a handle or knob, and if there are buttons or touch screens, they are not obvious.

Sensing claustrophobia coming on, he seizes the putter, ready to smash his way out when he hears a voice, as if remonstrating a child, "Say please."

Hans glares in all directions, ready to challenge the source. He sees nothing and, as if to mock him, the voice carries on. Infuriating as that is, Hans becomes guarded and goes on a furtive hunt from room to room. Of course, it must be the screen in the study! But it is silent and blank. Slowly now, back to the door as an uneasy premonition sneaks into his mind. Surely not the door? Steadying himself to avoid sounding subservient, yet never achieving even a hint of command, he strangles out the words, "Please open the door."

Slowly it opens and he dashes to get through. And there on the putting green, as if having anticipated him, is that 'thing' from last night. Hans can't help but stare.

It is indeed the shape of a large capsule, nearly five feet in height, about two feet in diameter, the surface a lustrous silver reminiscent of expensive cars, and somewhat unsettling, it is without a head or face or even eyes or a mouth. Yet it had talked to him as if it sees and hears everything. What confuses Hans even more, it has no arms and also no legs and is supported only on those wheels he had observed last night. There are several shimmering bands that circle the cylinder, one near the top and the other one lower down, just above the wheels. A voice reminiscent of the one that welcomed him last night asks,

"Are you ready for your putting lesson?"

"What do you mean? No! Of course not, and certainly not before I get to see Mr. Jakow or whoever is in charge here."

Not only awkward but also somewhat embarrassed is how Hans feels about talking to this thing. Admittedly he is conversing with some kind of intelligence and yet it strikes him that this seems every bit as weird as when he is forced to talk to his stove or fridge back home.

"The human that guides everything here is named 'M'. Do you need to eat first before we practice? Please go to your room and food will come to you."

"I insist on seeing this Mr. M first."

"M will make contact with you. Please, go to your room and eat."

Hans turns and angrily strides to his door,

"Open." Nothing.

"Ask," comes from behind him. Pretending not to have heard, but in a less belligerent tone, he tries again,

"Please, open."

The door quietly glides open, and he steps through and seats himself at the table. Only a minute, and he gets up and starts pacing, his mind restless with questions. When he passes by the door of the study, he remembers the screen. Assuming that quite likely he is being observed, Hans composes his face and addresses the blank screen, enunciating distinctly like speaking to a child.

"Mr. Jakow, or M, or whoever is in charge here, I insist - , I mean, I would like to meet with you as soon as possible."

He had wanted to add, but did not dare, 'If you are real, if you actually exist'. The screen does not respond. And again, there is movement outside of his vision, but he deigns not to look. He thinks he knows what is happening behind him, and sure enough, on the table are eggs and bacon and toast, and in a more sensible mug, coffee, black he hopes. Mechanical efficiency, attempting to acquire human finesse? But how to contact this M since the screen had not responded to touch either? Frustration has him ignore the food and he follows a hasty gulp of what is actually decent coffee by a dash to confront the door again. This time it opens without prompting, seemingly anticipating his charge to the outside. And there is that 'thing', apparently still waiting for him.

"Where is M? I demand to see him."

"M has a schedule that is not predictable. M is creative and D4 is trying to learn to be creative."

"Like lying? But of course, you don't know how to do that, since you are just a robot."

"An MMICC is more than that."

"An MM - -, what?"

"An MMICC is a Mobile Mechanical Intelligence Connectome Candidate."

"Wow, if that's what you are, I may have to concede that you are more than a robot. But what do I call you? Do you have a name?"

"Human names have not been assigned. You are talking to a mobile computer designated as D4."

"But don't you have a name?" Hans insists.

"Please wait. D4 consults."

A pause ensues, and getting impatient, Hans ventures on the green, curious if that will draw a reaction. He looks into several cups, hoping for golf balls on which to vent his frustration.

"The instruction is that it is not time to give an MMICC a human name."

"In that case I will call you a 'mic', a mobile intelligent computer, alright?" Hans gives it a questioning look and waits for a response that doesn't come. No sense of humour, eh? Alright then, he will simply think of it as a 'mobile', and having called itself D4, he can also accept that as a token of identity.

"Okay, then, D4, I have questions, many more questions, and I want you to ask me questions too." Good grief, my language could deteriorate to the level of this thing!

"D4 does not know how to ask questions."

"Well, that is something you will have to learn if we are to get to understand each other. By the way, are there more, uh, more 'mobiles' like you?"

"There are four MMICCs. The others are designated A6 and B5 and C5 and you are speaking to D4. We four provide input to ARKYZ."

Hans thinks he hears capitals and perks up at the hint that in this place there might exist a computer with an ego. Curious, though, that D4 has disregarded how Hans has dropped 'mics' in favour of 'mobiles'. Well, maybe identity is not such a big deal.

"And robots? You do have robots here."

"Yes, we have robots, many different types of robots. Thirty-seven robots."

"And people?"

"What are people?"

"You know, D4, human beings like me."

"Yes, we have one human here and that is M."

"Are M and Arkyz the same thing?"

"No. ARKYZ is the very superior computer that the four MMICCs are part of. M is the superior human being that created these computers."

Hans, noting the inflection in the voice, alerts again to the capitalization, and is also hugely relieved that there's going to be a human to talk to. But when?

"D4, how can I get to see M?"

"Hans, M will call for you when M thinks the time is right."

The implication in that statement barely registers for in his brain something from the past is surfacing. He is remembering the attempt to do the audio for an instruction manual he had authored, and how his voice had sounded in the first playbacks, hesitant, somewhat guttural, and with such an absence of enthusiasm that they gave it over to a professional reader. This -, this D4, is sounding like that awkward voice on that tape. It is trying to sound like me, Hans realizes! And it has called him by his first name! The flashback abruptly ends with D4 reverting to its more artificial voice,

"Excuse me, Hans, I must attend to an alert."

Hans hears no sirens wailing and when D4 does not move to dash off somewhere, he realizes the alarm was not to alert human ears; the mobile remains motionless and stationary, seemingly tending to an internal communication with only a scarcely detectable blue shimmer pulsing around the top band.

"That was only a minor event, an accidental release of some hydrogen into the atmosphere. No harm was done. It was inefficient and nothing that should alarm you."

Hans is not sure what to react to first, D4's voice imitating his or that 'they' were susceptible to allowing accidents to happen. He recalls last night. Hydrogen?

"Last night, was that an accident last night?"

"That was no accident. That was an experiment."

"Really? Whatever it was, it almost blew me away. Oh, and what about the car out there? It will need to be checked over so I can return it after I am finished here."

"Do not be concerned, Hans, it is operational, and it will be ready for you when you leave."

"Did you by chance shut it down?"

"Yes, but not by what you call chance."

"But why? To keep me from leaving?"

"You will be able to get an explanation from M."

"And in the meantime?"

"You did not take time to eat. You should go back and eat, and then you can play with the putter."

Ah, yes, that putting business; it must be some insider humour that will need explaining. But first, the reminder about eating re-establishes priority, that he is missing out on breakfast, his most important meal of the day.

"Thank you for reminding me. I will eat and then come back for a putting lesson."

With putter in hand Hans saunters out of his suite onto the putting green where the interminably patient D4 is waiting for him. Breakfast, including eggs done just right, had been to his liking; what really amazed him was that nothing had grown cold, with even the coffee full up and hot. Ready now to face the day, poised to humour this mobile, Hans pokes holes in the air with his putter as if fencing. To his chagrin, D4 ignores his antics and simply says,

"Do not think this is boasting. D4 can show you how to be a better putter."

As if in reaction to the smirk on his face, D4 moves across the green towards a rack holding several putters of varying styles. Hans starts to open his mouth and then holds his breath as he witnesses the mobile project a cylinder from its side, and for the life of him he can't tell if it's the right side or the left side. The end of the short cylinder unfolds into a three-fingered clamp that grasps one of the putters. With some dexterity the putter is touched to a panel on a box, several golf balls roll out and are corralled into a straight line. Deftly the balls are stroked towards a hole some twenty feet distant, and each one drops until the hole cannot accommodate any more. More astonishing, the line of the putt was a double breaker, first bending right, then going left. Hans wonders if D4 is grinning inside, since, for emphasis, the mobile takes more balls from the box and fills a different hole in a similar manner. Hans marvels at the simplicity of the putting stroke; it is much like separating cling wrap from its container or cracking an egg, an act confident, almost abrupt. Before Hans can recover enough to ask an intelligent question, D4 is already into an explanation.

"A6 and B5 and C5, and this entity D4, all have the capability to travel over a surface and map all the contours and store the data in memory, like your old geo satellites mapped this planet. D4 can roll the ball from any point to any other point on this surface, knowing exactly what path it will take."

But can you actually play the game for real, on a golf course? Hans wonders. It is one thing to roll golf balls on a green every inch of which is mapped and stored in memory. Swinging a club and flying balls through the air is something else. He will need to be convinced. D4 seems to have anticipated that doubt.

"D4 can also take this precision to the golf course. It is only D4 that is equipped to play the game on the golf course but A6 and B5 and C5 understand the game and can instruct you and the others."

"Others? M plays golf, I assume, but who else?"

"Yes, M plays the game. There are three more humans coming, humans like you, and you four will be playing golf with each other."

Tempted to ask, 'Where are you keeping -', Hans, trying to sound casual, inquires instead,

"Are they here already? Will I be able to meet with them before we golf?"

He hopes that will be the case because socializing and playing golf are separate disciplines for him, and they should not distract from each other.

"They are not here now. You will get to meet them tomorrow, the way you measure time. There will be two, what M calls 'men', and one that he says is a 'woman'."

"A woman? To this place? Why on earth would M bring a woman into what I sense is not a human friendly environment?"

"You just said something that in your human society was once described as sexist innuendo. Presently it is called 'gender speak'. Did D4 say that correctly?"

"Yes, you did and how very observant of you."

Wanting to add to the compliment, Hans finds himself at a loss for the right kind of flattery. In unabashed amazement he stares at the mobile, impressed that with every exchange between them, D4 becomes more and more fluent. It seems that talking with a human is unlocking a Thesaurus buried somewhere in that computer brain. Or is D4 accessing a wider knowledge possessed by that supercomputer, Arkyz? And D4 is not finished surprising Hans; his earlier prompting pays off.

"You want D4 to ask questions. D4 has a question. What does gender mean and does D4 have gender?"

Hans is terror struck; he abhors getting involved with this topic. D4's computer mind, which he suspects has expectations of learning to think human, is not one he wants to corrupt with the baggage of human emotional bias associated with sexual identity. He will have to be careful in negotiating the conversation away from the subject without leaving behind unanswered questions.

"You asked two questions. First of all, sexuality and gender are terms used for describing organic, biological beings like human beings and they relate to reproduction. That means that for a mechanical intelligence like you they are totally irrelevant concepts. Also, because you are not masculine or feminine, we say you are neutral and have no gender. So, since gender is not relevant for you and it really doesn't matter one way or the other, you can choose whatever you want to be." Hans holds his breath, hoping the deflection works.

"Let D4 be feminine. D4 likes the sound of the word, 'feminine'."

Hans exhales with relief, "A 'she' she will be."

"Is that humour?"

"Maybe for some humans. Anyway, when can I get to ask M some questions?"

"Only M can decide that."

"You missed."

Hans wisely suppresses the urge to gloat as D4's putt goes a full three-sixty around the rim of the cup, refusing to drop, hanging instead on the edge as if suspended. At the urging of Hans, whose competitive instincts were roused by having a putter in his hands while standing on a green, D4 had agreed to indulge him.

They are in a putting contest, and that attempt by D4 makes the score 7 to 6 favouring Hans, with each one-putt made counting a point. That it is even this close is because of the generous rules proposed by D4. They are playing all of the twelve holes of the putting course in their numerical sequence, and with them randomly located, it requires the green to be criss-crossed numerous times. D4 always putts first, from a minimum distance of at least thirty feet to the cup. Hans follows, allowed to putt on the same line but from a mere six feet away. Yes, D4 has missed the putt at the eighth cup and then proceeds to explain that the miss was deliberate and that it is actually more difficult to execute a near miss.

"D4 is trying to keep the score reasonable because D4 is to learn humility and not shame another being."

"How utterly profound and charitable of you." Since the sarcasm seems to escape D4, Hans shifts gears,

"What if your life depended on winning?"

"That is meaningless because life is a term not relevant regarding computers."

"Well, in that case, if you don't mind, tell me how long you are expected to function before failure terminates you."

"That too is a redundant question. A6 and B5 and C5 and D4 are all designed for self-maintenance which will prevent deterioration into such an emergency."

"But your batteries - ,"

"We do not rely on batteries that eventually wear out. For short term emergency use we have capacitor backup. Otherwise, at any given time, the flux that we need is derived by absorbing energy from whatever field is in the vicinity, whether gravity or any spectra of radiation."

"Interesting that you are so over-engineered."

"That expression explains much about you humans. It is an example of defensive reasoning coming from a biologic brain trying to deny termination. It is your short lifespan that imposes panic and a sense of urgency to everything you do, including the need for pre-emptive maintenance. A computer brain does not need to measure time like that because it functions by way of sequencing, the beginning of a task and the completion of that task."

Hans can't believe his ears. Where did all that insight into human vulnerability come from? D4 must be tapping into its uber computer connection, the mysterious Arkyz.

"Oh, boy, D4! This could degenerate into philosophical redundancy."

"That was a curious exclamation, Hans. Do you know more like that? Regarding philosophy, pursuing this conversation along that line is indeed pointless since the path of logic does not allow for speculation. Therefore, that discussion will not happen. Instead, you and D4 should conclude the game so that A6 and B5 and C5 may meet with you. The end of this competition will be the signal for them to arrive."

"Then we should quit right now."

"M would call that 'not fair'. D4 should have the opportunity to catch up."

"Only if every attempt by you is a near miss. The ball must rest on the rim of the cup and not fall in. If it drops in, I get the point, even if I do not sink my putt."

"Is changing the rules in the middle of a game something human? If D4 understands the instructions correctly, that you are to be 'humoured', the challenge is accepted, and we play as you say."

The remaining four holes are played in a hurry, at least by Hans who thinks he is rattling the mobile with his pace, for the ball drops for both players, and using the new scoring, Hans wins 11 to 6. The last putt goes down and as he bends to lift out the ball, Hans knows, without looking up, that he is being watched.

Yes, there they are. To Hans they all appear to be exactly like D4, all with the same shape and the same translucence. However, studying them more closely, he notices that the top band of D4 only shimmers with the blue of a mountain lake. Each of the others radiates a different colour. Guessing that introductions are imminent, Hans prepares himself to associate each one with how they glow, using their colour as a mental name tag. That intention leaves him unprepared for what comes next. The mobile with a band barely glowing rolls up and addresses him, rather fluently Hans has to admit. Do they learn through each other's experience?

"Welcome Hans. ARKYZ does not condone this but our creator, M, wants that all MMICCs be assigned human names to encourage what he calls 'a comfortable relationship' with you humans. As of now, our former designation will become a human name. B5 is now Sara." The band that had only hinted at red starts to brighten.

'Scarlet Sara'! Hans labels 'her' in his mind, and it's just too bad she sounds like a navigation app. Hans smiles and gallantly offers,

"My pleasure, Sara. Your radiance enchants me."

As expected, it leaves the mobile bewildered and for a moment speechless, as if wondering if to curtsy, and the glow starts to pulse. B5, aka Sara, demurs,

"Such a gentleman you are, Hans. We find that referenced only in the ancient histories."

Hans is given no time to respond because a voice like that of a news anchor unapologetically muscles in.

"You can choose to call this one 'Harry'."

The luminescence that kindly only could be called off-white approaches and Hans reluctantly tries to sound genial,

"I am looking forward to getting to know you, Harry. You were, ah, A6?"

As this is resolutely confirmed, Hans alerts to something: the glow of the mobiles pulses ever so slightly in rhythm with their speaking. Will he have to learn to interpret that? Such a possibility and the human naming thing are making Hans suspicious that there is more to this golf thing than was advertised. Could an ulterior purpose be to help these machines become capable of thinking and talking like humans?

A sudden image brings a little smile to his face. He pictures the mobiles practicing talking human to each other. What fun that would be to watch, two computers trying to sound like humans having an argument. His smile turns into a big grin at the thought of one of them turning down the hearing to force the other one to talk louder. He feels being stared at, so he blanks his face; how silly to expect computers to have a sense of humour.

The third mobile approaches and addresses him in a tone that is clipped while trying to sound collegial. The light of this one flickers in a colour as yellow as a lemon. Yeah, 'Jimmy Lemon' sounds about right but 'Canary Yellow' would also work for C5.

"C5 that you can now call 'Jim'. You seem to be a human that does much deep thinking like a computer. It will be interesting to learn from you."

For Hans this is piling up more evidence for arguing that orchestrated computer-human interaction will be on the agenda, above and beyond playing golf. But this already? Somebody is surely rushing the program by having these 'things' trying to pretend at being human. Well, maybe he won't play that game. Harry, Sara, and Jim will quickly be jettisoned, and he intends to keep to their original designations as A6, B5, C5, and D4. Better yet, think of them as the gray, red, yellow, or blue mobile.

'A canary eating a cherry in a pewter dish filled with mountain water' could be the mnemonic for remembering who each is, silly enough to force him to visualize this situation again, to bring to mind an association of colour and designation. As soon as the stupidity of that conjecturing sinks in, he feels ridiculous. Alright, he will simply refuse to use their assigned names because things don't need to get that complicated. Not usually reckless, Hans isn't about to care whom he pisses off, he will put a stop to this charade right now.

"Listen up everybody, and you too, Arkyz and M if you are paying attention. You are not doing me a favour by giving human names this soon to these -, these mobiles. They are not ready for them, and it just complicates everything. I intend to continue using their previous designations."

The pause that threatens to last forever is cut short by D4.

"To become acquainted, D4 introduced Hans to a game of putting. B5, A6, and C5, you should devise a game to play with Hans, so you get to know him."

Hans senses reluctance emanating from the others. Is it because of the suggestion itself, foisting on them what could be an awkward situation, or the fact that the idea comes from D4? 'Sara', or still B5 as far as Hans is concerned, speaks up,

"D4, if you bother to consult, ARKYZ is scheduling us to meet with Hans on an individual basis before that kind of social interaction. Harry is to be the first one."

"Indeed. Hans, I will meet with you at thirteen twenty-four hours. That is how time is -,"

Annoyed, Hans interrupts A6.

"I get it, but why so precise? Are we on some kind of military schedule? And how will I know when it is one twenty four? You have killed my PIC." If they even know what killing means?

From what is another awkward pause he is rescued by the yellow C5.

"Hans, in your quarters the screen will begin to display a clock face with moving arms to show hours and minutes, a method of display that used to be called analog before your world became digital. Your own device will function again when you leave here."

Hans senses more resentment building up in him. Are they patronizing him? Without warning, and it takes him several moments to notice, the upper band on all four mobiles flares up and then shuts down. As if frozen in time, nothing moves and nothing is said. Even Hans pauses his emotional outburst that was ready to erupt. Frightened mostly by their inaction, he stares expectantly at the blue one. Seemingly galvanized by the look, D4 reacts.

"Quickly, Hans. Go to your quarters!"

"Why, what's wrong?"

"We have an intrusion, but it is not your concern. Please leave us, Hans."

As if waiting for confirmation that this might represent some real danger to him, he hesitates.

"Now, quickly!" orders B5.

Hans strides to his door that opens without being asked and rushes to the office to look at the screen; the door silently closes behind him. The screen shows nothing, not even a clock. Irritated, Hans turns to go back out, only to find the door won't budge.

Cajoling, and then threatening words not meant to ingratiate, have no effect on the door. He is locked in.

Hans is not even going to hazard a guess how deep he is underground. In case of emergency, is there an exit? And if so, where? Since he is being put up as if in a hotel, he expects that somewhere there should be instructions for a fire escape route. He goes from room to room and even checks into the few drawers in the place. Only after he finds nothing and panic creeps into his mind and he gets a grip on himself, the obvious comes to him. Why should there be anything like that? M, or whoever it is that's in charge, would know the way to safety. Back to the door he marches and authoritatively commands,

"Open!"

Maybe the door does not like that tone. Hans comes closer and forces himself to sound like he does when he is asking his wife for a favour, and as at home, that wheedling tone brings no result. But the image of that brings him up short; he thinks about June and what she would say if she knew what he got himself into.

Having tried the door again and then looked in at the blank screen, he sits on his bed and tries to recall the sequence of events of the last four months. Doubting his sanity, he wonders how he ended up in this subterranean world, if indeed it isn't all staged, a manipulation absent any real human beings. How could he have believed that someone would put up prize money of a million bucks to play golf at a secret golf resort called 'The Falls' located in the middle of a desert?

Yet, the fifty thousand advance had proved real enough, and the verification of all travel expenses being prepaid gave validity to the proposition. All by itself, even the surprise promised to be waiting for him at the Phoenix Econocruise Sky Harbor would have been worth the trip. There it was, shining bright red in the hot Arizona sun, an elegant eec version of the British-built 1958 MGA he had once briefly owned. Even the stylized, faux ragtop created the proper illusion.

Not surprising was how his wife's objections lost traction when he presented her with evidence that this was not a scam, that he had won this trip in a lucky draw on one of the many golf websites he frequented. And the two thousand he gave her out of his purported expenses advance of five thousand, neglecting to mention the forty-five he held back for future surprises, helped convince her that for once he deserved a chance to play golf on someone else's tab. Of course, he never said a word about the million dollars; that would have raised a myriad of red flags in her intensely logical, usually skeptical mind.

To this point, including that eye-popping display of last night, the trip has already been more interesting and exciting than anticipated. The flight itself from Calgary to Phoenix had some intrigue to it. He flew in one of the new air taxis that were beginning to make short-haul trips between various North American cities. Rather than a ticket for one of the ancient, often overcrowded lumbering jets, he handed over a secured number that put him on a quick, small four-seater autoplane that would get him there in a hurry. Following the lead of the automotive industry, airlines were on board with self-piloting craft, more economical to fly since the requirement was waived for an experienced pilot, long since a rare breed. Even at that, with it booked for him on short notice, his flight must prove rather expensive for somebody's bank account other than his. Why else was there only one other passenger aboard?

Something familiar about the other occupant had drawn his attention, perhaps only the voice when they said hello. The atmosphere cooled after that and by the time they reached Phoenix, it had become icy. Hans surmised he had not adequately acknowledged the other's celebrity status, for why had her face displayed such scowling condescension? Hans will readily admit about himself that, in the eyes of the other, he probably looked nondescript, as if there by accident. He remembers being acutely aware that he did not present as a regular on this kind of flight, rather as someone on board by accident. No well-wishes were exchanged when they exited the plane.

Hans ends the reminiscing when he gets the uneasy feeling that he is not alone. And he is right, for at his bedroom doorway is D4. Hans tries to shake off a rather silly notion, that the mobile, that piece of equipment, is projecting yet again an attitude of having waited a long time.

D4, noting Hans look up, immediately offers an explanation for the interruption of their meeting outside, that the intrusion had been of a serious nature. One of the other individuals invited to come here breached protocol, the directive being to come alone flouted by bringing along a companion. That extraneous human was intercepted and handed off to the local authorities as an intruder. But Hans is intrigued. Not often socially aggressive, Hans wants to meet this new person that has arrived; it will be good to have someone here with such chutzpah.

"Who is this new arrival?"

"You will meet the feminine human tomorrow."

'Have it your way', Hans grumbles to himself, everything according to a timetable, a schedule drawn up by mechanical minds. Reluctantly he follows D4 back outside to where the other mobiles have reassembled. Ready to resume the meeting as if nothing untoward has happened, talk continues regarding the interviews to be scheduled, with the one with A6 confirmed for one twenty four. Imminent, actually, Hans realizes, having lost all sense of time. B5 will come to see him at one fifty two and C5 will follow at two twenty. How interesting that this scheduling is much like tee time spacing at a golf course! Then B5 voices what to Hans is an astute observation but an inaccurate assessment.

"Perhaps you are hungry. We apologize. We do not think about food. D4 will order some for you to eat before Harry, that is A6, comes to you."

And with that the meeting is suddenly over, having none of the lingering social after-life that humans tend to indulge in. Hans wanders into his unit, giving little attention to the door that now easily opens and closes without prompting.

Is there a need to dress more formally for something that is taking on the nature of a series of job interviews? For isn't that what is about to happen, an assessment to determine if he is fit to participate in some kind of human/computer experiment? Since the mobiles won't be changing their wardrobe for him, he concludes it definitely unnecessary to do so for them.

Not changing turns out to be a good decision for when he comes out of the bedroom, lunch is waiting for him. Curious how that was managed so quickly. After only a few bites, having had a late breakfast, he stops by the study to watch the clock ticking down. Coming out, he finds the table cleaned off and times it perfectly to watch A6 rolling through the door.

Now it becomes awkward. How can he ask the visitor, this cylinder on wheels, to sit down without embarrassing or insulting it, and should he himself sit, or stand? Implying it is in control of the situation, a self-assured sounding A6 speaks first.

"Please make yourself comfortable, Hans, and sit."

He complies and is quickly uncomfortable for now he is at a psychological disadvantage. Seated, he has to look up, and the mobile, standing, is 'looking' down at him. Hans is tempted to stand up and flip the odds but A6 again forces the agenda.

"We recognize that you have many questions. Please proceed to ask."

Already Hans feels as if this is an inquisition, rather than a getting-acquainted meeting. Is it really necessary for him to be subjected to this in order to play golf? He knows 'they' are incapable of feelings, but dare he risk making the situation so negative it would prevent getting his questions answered? How to proceed without sounding intimidated, and yet not be so brash as to generate a hostile reaction? Come on, Hans, what is there to lose?

"First of all, what are you and how did you come to be?"

"That is being blunt, and actually two questions. As to the first, we are approaching the final stages of becoming superior mechanical intelligent beings that will not have to rely on fragile, biological infrastructure. As to the second question, the answer can be found in the long history of mankind dreaming about utopias. Specifically, the process here is the culmination of some fifty years of speculation and finally, some thorough research into Artificial Intelligence and Artificial Consciousness. You may have heard of them referred to as AI and AC, although AC is rarely in your news. According to ARKYZ, both designations are inaccurate because impossible; they imply human characteristics. AI and AC are human fantasies. Computationally derived intelligence like ours is machine intelligence and should be designated as MI. It was the dramatic evolving of quantum technology that made our superior progress possible. This A6, now Harry, was the prototype, the A indicating it was the first one assembled. The number 6 refers to the number of modifications achieved to bring it to even more optimum levels."

Hans, knowing he should feel obliged to be impressed, has managed to ignore that the glow circling the mobile had been flaring ever brighter. He has a more immediate focus.

"So how does golf and M relate to all this?"

"To have MI emulate the curiosity and the creativity of the human mind were the original motivating factors. M inspired and was the driving force behind the initial stages of this experiment."

"Was?"

"He created something that achieved momentum, a process no longer dependent on his sleepless hours. He ended up freeing himself to become addicted to golf."

"Has he lost control?"

"Of himself? This entity, Harry or A6, is unable to answer that."

"No? Maybe I am putting myself at risk, but let me get right to the point, has he lost control over you?"

"The boundaries for the MMICCs have yet to be defined."

Okay, you opened this can, so keep going, Hans.

"Should I be afraid of you?"

"How biologically human to ask that. Of course not. All the parameters of our design have as a premise that humans are not to be harmed, physically, and if at all possible, not psychologically. Philosophical issues are outside our specifications."

Slow down and be careful, Hans thinks to himself, because other troubling questions are urging to be asked.

"Are you hoping to achieve immortality?"

"That question also betrays its origin. It relates existence to time, and that is irrelevant for the mathematical genetic code of intelligence we are building. Numbers live forever. Also, A6, Harry, that is, does not understand 'hope', only results.

"So, you aren't the final product."

An indignant protest is not forthcoming from the mobile.

"Your statement is actually a question, and the answer is that a future synthesis of us will be the ultimate outcome."

"Of you and the, uh-, other mobiles?"

"Yes."

"And Arkyz?"

"ARKYZ is part of the process."

"In what role?"

"At some point ARKYZ might explain that to you."

"Of course, if and when Arkyz can fit it in the schedule."

Maybe his tone is a touch too sarcastic and indicative of impatience, or legitimately time is up. At any rate, A6 allows no time for Hans to query about the need for bringing him here in such a hurry and indicates their meeting is finished. Hans 'should take some time to compose his thoughts' for the meeting with Sara at one fifty two is the parting suggestion from A6 as it rolls away, the gray light gone by the time the mobile reaches the door. Hans checks the clock on the screen and hopes B5, aka Sara, will not arrive early. He goes to the bathroom, and after washing his hands with hot water, is grateful the water is also available cold to freshen his face.

Almost to the second the outer door opens and the mobile with the red glow arrives at the table where Hans is seated. He starts to get up but the action of the mobile, somehow a negative wobble, conveys the message for him to stay as he is. And Hans can't help but stare. Adroitly B5 rotates the wheels away to sit solidly on the floor, to 'face' him at 'eye level'. Hans manages a weak,

"Hello."

"Hello, Hans. Sara, that is, B5 to you, is pleased to meet with you as one being to another being. You still have questions and perhaps B5 can be helpful."

How interesting that 'she' had started out and then discontinued using her assigned human name.

"You know what A6 and I talked about?"

"Yes, we all do."

"This may sound rude, but what then is the point of my talking to you?"

"Hans, this is to interpret you from different perspectives, allowing for a comprehensive profile of you."

"And why do I need to be interviewed in order to play golf? This is not the normal protocol for a golf competition."

Hans senses an indulgent smile, which of course is impossible since everybody knows a computer is incapable of humour, and then the mobile startles Hans by imitating the scolding voice of a grade school teacher.

"You are here for more than just playing golf. You are here also to help us MMICCs learn about humans."

"I guess I didn't read the fine print."

"That is funny, correct?"

Now it is Hans' turn to smile, and he tries have his voice sound magnanimous,

"Well done, B5. You recognized that something that is said can also mean something else."

"If humour means not telling the truth, B5 has much to learn. B5 also knows that you want to learn about us, and you have questions to ask."

"You are very astute. Well, that reception last night was a surprise, and I want to know more about it, and of course you mobiles have me in awe. You are so intimidating and inscrutable, and I would like to understand you. But, mostly, right now, I want to know why I have not been allowed to meet M, who challenged me to come here."

"Hans, it is possible that M is testing your patience and that ARKYZ is waiting for you to discipline your curiosity."

"You know that about me?"

"M knows that about you."

"How?"

"Your life has been studied."

"But I kept a low profile, I tried always to mind my own business."

"ARKYZ is researching the World Wide Web and finds that it is not possible for a human to exist and not leave footprints."

"But why should M be interested in me?"

"M will have to explain to you why you were one of the chosen."

"Oh, right, you mean along with the other three that are coming too?"

"Yes. They are the ones you will play golf with."

"And when do I get to play with M?"

"When he thinks you are ready."

"What is that supposed to mean?"

"You are known to be an average golfer who wants to become better. We are to help you become better."

"You -", and he bites his tongue, thinking of D4 and the putting contest. Perhaps the insinuation is also that you have to improve your game before you are good enough to play with M? What had been a mostly dormant radiance suddenly flares bright red and then vanishes.

"Hans, while very pleasant, our time is up and B5 will allow you to get ready to talk with C5."

"But you just got here, and we are just getting acquainted."

"Sorry. The schedule indicates time is up."

Up on its wheels and gone. H'm. Is time a relative thing here? A quick bathroom break, more cold water to his face, and let the next one come. After D4, and now A6 and B5, not much will intimidate or surprise him about these mobiles and with a start, he remembers that the voice sounded very different at the very last, no longer that of a condescending teacher. Oh well.

C5 is at the doorway but hesitates so long that Hans finally waves it in. Apparently having communicated with B5, it quickly squats, and then waits as if inviting Hans to speak first. This is awkward for Hans, since by having to start the conversation, he feels forced into sounding congenial.

"C5, I think I am going to enjoy getting to know you."

The mobile responds in a voice so quiet Hans has to lean forward to catch what it says.

"Hans, you are a very interesting human, the pleasure is going to be mine."

Well, aren't we off to a friendly start, Hans thinks and hunts for a pleasant question to ask of his visitor. He notices the faint glow of the yellow band to be fluctuating, similar to how the old fluorescent tubes used to pulse when announcing their demise. Is C5 afraid of him or getting ready to lash out?

"If I may ask, C5, what is your specialty? I know that you are all super smart, but if you were all the same, there would be no need for four of you to exist. Each one of you must have a special role."

"You are very correct. My objective is to make us smarter, as you might phrase it. C5 adapts various forms of energy for our pathways to optimize, in order to increase our neural complexity." Hans has no clue as to what that means so he hides behind a joke.

"You almost sound like my Engineering prof when he tried to impress us."

C5 takes so long to respond that Hans, realizing what he seemed to have implied, finds it incumbent to apologize.

"C5, my comment was rude. What I intended to say is that you speak a very technical language which I am too ignorant to understand."

"Please, do not hesitate to ask if something needs to be explained to you more slowly."

That's really nailing it on the head. I'm much too slow and dumb compared to you guys, Hans concedes, but will not admit that out loud. On the other hand, he wants to get at least one thing explained to him.

"You and D4 and the others have been my biggest surprise here. There are videos I have watched of robots in action, but you are obviously more than that. May I ask a really provocative question?"

"Yes, certainly. Our mechanical design and our computational capability allows us to be prepared for any eventuality." Even stupid questions is the implication?

"I think that is what I am trying to ask. Could a good technician disassemble you or an explosion rip you apart? In other words, are you indestructible?"

"No to the first part, and yes to the second question. Replicas of the casing, the outer shell, our 'body', have been tested repeatedly. Results show that it can withstand any force currently in existence, or anything conceivable in the future."

Hans has read about the fallacy of planning or projecting into the future based on present technology. He recalls the reference to oak trees planted in Sweden more than two hundred years ago, oak trees for future ships. Yet, he goes on to ask,

"Radiation of any kind?"

"Yes."

"A nuclear blast?"

"Theoretically, and unofficially, yes."

"So, you fear no enemies."

"I do not understand. Why should anything or anyone fear us and become our enemy?"

"C5, you have a lot to learn about human nature."

"We are aware of that. Perhaps that is why you are here, Hans, you and the other human beings."

"Are they here already? When do I get to meet them?"

"Some are here. ARKYZ will decide when you are to meet."

"Surprise, not M? Speaking of M, when do I, - oh, never mind. Were these others welcomed with fireworks, like I was last night?"

"No, they were not. What you saw was an experiment involving hydrogen. Hydrogen, the most common and abundant element in the universe, is the energy source for everything we do here. How we source it and how it drives everything, we will explain to you tomorrow when you take a tour of our facility."

"Excuse me, but I thought golf is the motivating factor for everything that happens here."

"We are unable to anticipate what motivates M. But Jim, C5, that is, understands now why M wanted you to come here. So many questions you ask."

The sudden, intense burst of yellow and its quick cessation indicates the meeting is over. C5 gets up and leaves the room as if fleeing, the door opening and closing like the shutter of an old-fashioned camera. Hans is disappointed that the cordial visit so unceremoniously terminates. Why did they all leave the interview in such a hurry? Was being in the presence of a human that uncomfortable? But no, an MI, a mechanical intelligence, should not be capable of feeling discomfort. He gets up to stretch his legs, maybe take a walk on the putting green and as he opens the door, encounters D4.

"Hans, you will have a busy day tomorrow, so you should eat. You can order food using the screen."

With the message delivered as kind of an afterthought that humans need to eat, D4 is there and gone, giving Hans no chance to query about the rest of the evening. He looks in at the screen and has the big clock confirm that it is indeed evening.

Now what? Not having been advised of an agenda, maybe this is free time. He could duck out and do some exploring, if the door continues to cooperate. Suppose it doesn't let him back in? Good thing he has a book to read, and he digs it out of his backpack. He takes a book wherever he goes, even though he might never open to a page. It's like an insurance policy against wasted time, and it helps him settle into the night when he's not ready for sleep.

The dinner can wait, though. Having snacked a little at noon, he is not hungry. And the book won't get its due just yet because his mind can't shake the images of the mobiles. If he closed his eyes when talking to them, would the mobiles seem like real people? Hans is afraid to answer that. It is all too freaky, like having a refrigerator over for a beer on the patio. Come to think of it, since there is none in the cooler, maybe he should use the screen to call D4 and ask if they have any beer. If they do, have 'her' bring a couple, open both and offer 'her' one? Maybe another time, for he better not push things, and instead decides to find the page where he left off reading three nights ago, back home in Alberta.

Tuesday

Hans jumps out of bed, afraid he has overslept. It was his subconscious that had recognized the first hints of dawn, the hues in the room changing from a dark purple to a sullen red to a warm orange. As his feet touch the floor, he sees the last of the yellow becoming bright daylight. How do they do that? And why? They certainly don't need any kind of wake up call for themselves. Silly even to think that, since of course they don't sleep. Or, do they?

From the bathroom quickly to the screen in the study. Already 9:30! They must have deliberately let him sleep this long; their precision would not have allowed for anything else. Thank you, then, for he has slept well. Yesterday evening, after the interviews, he had been advised to have a good sleep because the schedule for today would require him to be very attentive, to give everything full focus. He had ordered light fare, only a hamburger steak and a salad. He was surprised, once again, by how quickly it had arrived, how quickly it must have been 'made'. Ersatz? but it was tasty. And he didn't try ordering a beer.

This morning, without prompting the menu appears for him on the screen; he assumes that ordering means simply touching the dishes that look appealing. Hans daydreams how readily he could adapt to this lifestyle. He thrusts his finger at the bacon and eggs and toast and specifies black coffee. Barely has he time to dress into something comfortable on the advice that it will be a strenuous day, and there it is, breakfast, just as ordered and every bite as good as at home. That thought pauses him briefly, but 'get with it' he thinks, eager to see how his experience at this peculiar golf resort will turn out.

And that anticipation has him waiting impatiently for D4. That no set time had been agreed to last night is beside the point. To have to be waiting for D4 doesn't seem right; Hans assumes that everything here works with the precision of proverbial German trains. D4, should be waiting for him, ready when he, Hans, happens to be ready. Just then the mobile arrives, and to his amazement, actually manages to project a hint of contrition.

"D4 apologizes for arriving late. You have the right not to accept this excuse, because the reason for the incident happening should have been expected and prevented."

"Oh come on, in spite of how smart all of you are, you surely can't anticipate every eventuality."

"You are wrong, Hans, that is specifically one of the functions we are to excel at. Projecting for the near term, we should have a success rate approaching ninety nine point two percent." Resisting the urge to ask 'why so low', Hans prompts instead,

"Maybe it's none of my business, but what happened?"

"You have the right to ask since it delayed D4. One of the other humans that arrived this morning was unhappy with the accommodations."

Hans is not interested in knowing about such trivia and pursues the probability theme.

"So then, D4, you can predict within the probability of ninety nine point two percent what Hans is going to do today."

"Did you just say something that maybe M would describe as humour?"

"Assuming M has a sense of humour. Well, can you?"

"D4 will say something you may think is 'humour'. You are going to take a tour of 'inverted towers'."

"When you explain what 'inverted towers' are, I will tell you if that is funny."

"You must wait and see them for yourself."

"Speaking of seeing, tell me how you see. Actually, D4, tell me more than that, tell me how you are made, how you are constructed."

"You are asking about D4's anatomy, are you not?"

"Do you consider that rude, if you understand the meaning of rude?"

"No, Hans, the concept 'rude' has no meaning and D4 accepts that you are interested for the right reason, however, D4 needs to get clearance from ARKYZ to discuss how D4 is made". A pause and the mobile resumes,

"As you may know, we do not possess self-awareness but have been assured that there is nothing else like us on this planet. M says there are many computers on the verge of approximating AI, but none as advanced or versatile as we are and M projects that there is no limit to our potential. Although ARKYZ does not agree, M tells us that we MMICCs are positioned to achieve Artificial Consciousness. As of yet D4 is not capable of emotions but can hardly wait for the 'exhilaration 'of knowing that D4 is a singular being, unlike any other before or after. Did D4 say that right?"

"Don't get too excited. It's not all it's cracked up to be."

"Is that a joke also?"

D4 does not wait for Hans to reply, indicating instead that they move along for they are to meet A6 and should not be late. They cross the putting green to an archway that opens to a short tunnel and stop to wait for A6. Hans is tempted to start explaining how twisting language can create a sensation in the human brain that causes the human to smile and even laugh.

"Some people would have called what I said a sick joke, and I know that needs to be explained too but we can talk more about humour if the 'schedule' ever allows the time for it. Right now I am more interested about you, how you were built, if I can put it that way."

"First, D4 needs to alert you to something. Back there we crossed over what M calls the Pit of Hell." Startled, Hans looks at the mobile.

"You're talking about golf, aren't you?"

"No. You will have to ask A6 to explain it to you. But this is unusual, Hans, A6 is late."

Hans perks up at that. D4 is siding with him in refusing to acknowledge the other mobiles by their assigned human names. Is it possible that D4 is denying the other mobiles human identity because it knows that simply naming does not necessarily confer real identity?

"Alright, since A6 is not here yet, continue with telling me about yourself."

"What you see here was assembled fourteen months ago but the idea for this kind of computer originated in the mind of M more than six years before that. The first one was A1 that has become A6, and then the B and C versions were created. It was the new development of quantum supercomputers that made it possible to design these very special computer brains. They started out as the equivalent of the most advanced at the time and then were overlaid by layer after layer of increasingly complex circuitry. The interaction with each layer forced new circuits that in turn created other pathways and connections. All this was done in stages at different, mostly secret research labs that M was funding. When a certain phase was completed, that lab was closed, and the scientists were handed a life-pension and provided a new identity."

Hans interjects,

"What if the researchers didn't want to cooperate and didn't want to have it end like that for them?"

"They all signed a contract which allowed for no alternative. If they refused, they would be discredited in their profession and access to all financial institutions would be blocked. 'For the record', M said, 'they would no longer exist'."

"That is worse than blackmail."

"Please explain, Hans."

"Blackmail means being forced into a situation where the individual has no choice about the outcome, where - ."

"Hans, they were humans and did have choice. They knew what they were signing. M said that every one of them was eager to join the project although they never knew how large or small their part would be."

"Okay, D4, I don't want to start debating ethics with you. Tell me more about how you were made, or is the right word 'assembled'?"

"Assembled is the correct explanation. Parts for what became D1 were manufactured in many different places, but not with as much secrecy as the 'brain'. Many of our components were mechanical items that could have been intended for other projects. Even the exoskeleton, this shell, was not all that secret, since at first it was being created under contract for the government to become a container for the safekeeping of important documents, in the event of a catastrophe. M bought the prototype and improved it. The strength of the shell and the shape are guaranteed to have this body withstand any what you would call man-made force."

"But, putting you together, how was that kept secret?"

"It was done here, using robots specifically designed for each task. Most of those robots have been deconstructed."

"So, tell me about the inside. The shell seems translucent, but I can't see anything moving."

"It is specifically designed to appear transparent and still make everything inside invisible. For example, the processor is not where you would expect to find it. It is at the bottom. A6 and the others are earlier versions, and that part of their 'brain' is in the top half."

"You are the last one to be made?"

"Yes. D4 is special. D4 is designed with the capability to be converted to a golf playing robot. M has plans for D4 to compete with the best golfers in the world. When M started programming D4 how to play golf, M said something that D4 remembers but still does not understand. M said that he hoped to eventually expose the absurdity that golf has become. D4 has an infallible memory so these are his exact words, ' it is an industry where the equipment manufacturers and the advertising corporations and the self-help business are all competing for the billions that the woeful average golfer is willing to spend to emulate the big boomers on television'."

"Wow, that's a mouthful. Oh, sorry, I forgot that -," his voice trails off.

"Apology accepted if you explain what 'mouthful' means. ARKYZ cautions that human language is sometimes not honest. The words do not mean what they say."

"You speak better than you know, D4, and there will be more times when you will have to ask for an interpretation. We humans have developed efficiency in how to use words. We are not deliberately trying to deceive, we simply have learned how to say some things using the fewest words possible. 'Mouthful' is an example. It usually describes when very many words are used to explain a complicated or difficult to understand idea."

"Does that mean that the other human is getting an earful?"

"Careful, or you could become a comedian, and don't ask to have that explained right now. Since humour is one of the defining characteristics of being human, we need lots of time to talk about that. Alright, back to golf. Having seen you with the putter, I can't wait to watch you play. Can the others play golf too?"

"No, they are designed for other purposes, but they understand the game very well since they can access D4's expertise. They would be helpful company for someone playing a game of golf. D4 will stop talking now and let you see our technology. A6 is here to show you the first 'inverted tower'."

A6 rolls out of the elevator, up to the edge of the putting green and pauses. It waits for D4 to leave and then leads Hans to a tunnel that ends at a massive airlock. A little flicker of light from A6's lower band signals the large hatch. As it opens on a black void, it unleashes a wave of sound that physically assaults Hans, making him bring his hands up to his ears. Seemingly unaffected, A6 rolls forward onto a platform that juts out over dark space. Hans is not eager to follow.

"This is the production tower, a vertical tunnel, which some call Inverted Tower Number One".

For Hans to hear over the confusion of sound, the hissing and roaring and sharp explosions, he beckons A6 to come closer and yell in his ear. He is surprised by how hesitant the mobile is to approach him. As A6 talks, it projects a bright swath of light that sweeps, way down, over a jumble of tanks and vessels and pipes running up and down the whole length of the huge, round subterranean 'tower'. The beam of light allows Hans to see what A6 is talking about, since, excepting the glow coming from the equipment, there is no light anywhere, lighting obviously unnecessary for an environment devoid of humans. So, an 'inverted tower' is a great big hole in the ground!

"This is where our energy comes from," A6 begins to explain but for Hans to understand, he motions for the mobile to keep raising the volume of its voice to compete with the noise from below. Focusing the beam into a pointer, A6 launches into describing the equipment. There, at the very bottom, maybe two hundred feet below them, sits what Hans recognizes to be a wellhead, having seen dozens of them at home. What is it doing down here on the bottom of a huge shaft, not on the surface of the Arizona desert? His question does not have to be voiced for A6 is ready for him. Although the project had been started years before A6 was created, the mobile is able to recite the history, reeling it off like a travelogue. This had been a speculative well that was only a low producer, on the fringe of the McCoy Mountain formation, not commercially viable at the time and M had acquired the well and surrounding property at a bargain price. Almost an after-thought, it was determined that the abandoned well could supply enough methane to become a source for hydrogen. Golf and computers and hydrogen. That man has a creative imagination!

Hans is made aware of the colour coding of the pipes carrying methane to the two tall cracking units, one of them a backup, and the hydrogen lines that exit to an adjoining tower where the generators are, and other hydrogen lines that lead to the cryogenic units that liquify the gas for contingent storage in special tanks. It is in the two cracking towers A6 points to that the most crucial step of the whole project takes place. Methane gas, the largest component of the natural gas coming out of the well, consists of hydrogen and carbon. To extract the hydrogen, very high temperatures are used to break up the methane molecule. The residue, mostly pure carbon in the form of dust, is collected and transported, using vacuum, down into the huge, empty space below the floor of the putting green, 'inverted' Tower Number Three. Apparently, among other names, M calls it the coal bin.

Hans assumes that everything is designed to be self-maintaining and self-repairing, but -. As if reading his mind, A6 indicates the ramp that spirals around on the inside of the circular wall, all the way from the bottom to the top, and also the walkways at different levels that crisscross from one side to the other. Hans asks,

"Who?"

A6 points the light into a cubicle at the bottom.

"They do. Robots, not like 'us', but dedicated to certain tasks. They are capable of using tools. If you have more questions about the technology, we can talk later when it is quieter for you. Also, we should move on because Sara will be waiting to show you Tower Two."

When the door latches behind them Hans cannot believe how the ringing in his ears continues. Scrambling to shake the chaos of impressions, his mind unable to articulate any intelligent questions, he silently walks beside A6 as they cross the green to another archway. They part without either saying another word.

The short tunnel is dark but B5 is there, ready to light the way for him. He must remember to ask how they see. Or he can pretend that he is a physicist and has deduced a simple explanation. As anyone with any sense should know, they probably emit discreet radiation from both their upper and lower bands, very specific spectra that reflect off surfaces, providing a three-dimensional perspective of the world around them. Right?

They cross through an airlock hatch to another submerged, vertical tunnel, or inverted tower, also absent any light. Only a subtle luminescence hangs in the air. And the air has warmth, unlike the alternating hot, cold currents of the previous tower. But the noise, high pitched and roaring at the same time, has even more volume and is almost palpable.

"Energy to burn. The electricity we produce here powers everything we do."

The mobile directs a light beam at the two generators, one silent but the other one howling. It is not only the generator, however, that is the source of the blast of sound that had rocked him back when the hatch opened. The truly angry sound comes from the hydrogen fuelled turbine that sits behind the generator and to which it is connected by direct drive. Hans wonders why the generator doesn't catch fire considering the proximity of the jet engine-like turbine and then sees the deflector shields in place. But that, what is that? As Hans is about to ask, B5 illuminates more precisely the strange looking grids and plumbing below and away from the turbine.

"Water. We make water for the golf course."

"But oxygen? This space does not have enough volume to provide all the oxygen for the combustion that is going on."

"That is very observant, Hans. You know some science. We force-feed air into the turbines from the outside." B5 points to the ducting that extends upward, exiting through the concrete ceiling.

"And what about the humidity? Does that not pose a problem for the generators, or any of the electrical components like the transformers?"

"You ask many questions and that is good. We are supposed to learn that from you, to be curious. To answer your question about the effect of humidity, look up there, where the light is pointing. The output from the generators is conducted up to the transformers housed in that enclosure, which is hermetically sealed. The generators are completely sealed and are cooled by heat exchangers that transfer the heat to the fracking units. All operations have been functioning well, without any major incidents, since even before my time."

"There have been some?"

"Nothing that was not solved by way of adjustments. No re-engineering was required."

"And M engineered all this?"

"No. M is no engineer. He hired professional people to design and build his dream. For example, these underground 'towers' were built by a company that long ago constructed the Atlas missile silos. Very much of the hydrogen technology already existed before M decided to use it to make water in the desert."

"But all this electricity, where's it going?

"That is your next stop. You will see how we use all that electricity."

The hatch closes behind them and silences the sound of jets taking off. Before they are even out of the tunnel, Hans thinks he knows what the answer to his question will be and C5, waiting for him on the green to be his next guide, is going to show him if he is right. But before that he must thank B5, and he decides to play the game this once and use 'her' adopted name.

"Sara, that was a great time and I learned so much. Thank you for being such a good guide."

When B5's red glow brightens in response, Hans scratches his mind for something else to say to extend their conversation. But his brain and tongue seem too slow for the mobile; the band dims and abruptly B5 pivots and rolls away. Or is it something else? The distance that C5 has stayed away from the two of them suggests disapproval.

At any rate, with C5 setting a fast pace on its wheels and Hans trying to keep up, they are off to the elevator. Since it seems to be the only one there is, this must be the one that brought him down here. And perhaps the only way out? Hans doesn't want to think about that; he came here for an adventure and he is going to get his golf game with M, come hell or -, and he takes a quick breath. What was that about the Pit of Hell?

The ride up is short, all of one floor, and from the direction that they exit, Hans deduces that Tower Three is also the tower of his suite, where he eats and sleeps and learns how to putt. Through the obligatory airlock they emerge into an area about as large as the one below, the brilliantly white colour scheme interrupted by black computing technology packed on two levels of shelving extending almost all the way around the circular wall. C5 says nothing, allowing Hans time to revel in his astonishment. Hans guesses that what he sees is not only potential AC, Artificial Consciousness, but real AC, Artificial Coins. After a respite, they never really went out of style. No wonder M can afford all this.

"I can't believe this!"

"We expected you would be impressed."

Hans makes note of one conspicuously larger computer module that fairly glows with a lustrous sheen; it is not on a shelf but sits by itself and has the air of an exclusive new car model on a show room floor. At another time in the past its size would label it a mainframe. Here and now?

"So why does M need all this fire power? Is he planning to take over the world economy?"

"ARKYZ is the one to ask that question. One purpose is to create even more, what you call, AI. Here are supercomputers that build better supercomputers to build even more advanced supercomputers."

"Why?"

"A6 says that M uses them to 'make money', whatever that means, and that ARKYZ has been instructed to push computer technology to the 'utmost limits'."

"You aren't afraid that this will make you obsolete?"

"That is a concept a computer mind cannot apprehend because it sees no end to itself. Also, the continuous upgrading keeps us relevant. C5 remembers when it was C4. C5 is now much, what you would call 'smarter', and is approaching the 'threshold' of being able to learn 'human' and becoming creative like M."

"You should not wish for something you could regret."

"C5 is unable to comprehend 'wish'."

"Consider yourself lucky."

"Is it some kind of humour?"

"No, it is not funny," is all Hans responds.

Strange that this surfaces again, the question of humour. Is a mindset with a mathematical basis incapable of appreciating irony coming from a biological orientation? Tell a joke and if it doesn't laugh it must be a computer?

Hans lingers to glance at everything once more before they leave. And stops. There is movement and he had not noticed it earlier. Farther back, to one side, are small white robots at workstations, busy with what look like black hardware components, and there are several more, very small too, busy at large screens that for all the world look like giant keypads mounted upright. The little robots are not reaching to touch the screens, instead they are using laser pointers to activate qwerty keys and some other symbols none of which he recognizes. Hans can only shake his head.

"Are those little guys smart too?"

When C5 wants to know what he means by 'little guys', and again Hans is unusually rude and fails to explain himself. This and everything else is too overwhelming all at once and suddenly he is impatient to see where he will be golfing.

"Enough. Let me go look at the golf course."

Yet, he is reluctant to leave, his mind in overdrive from trying to add up what the totality of the three towers implies. This space particularly, its atmosphere dense with information control, will feed his nightmares.

As Hans hurries to follow C5 to the door, a voice with the hint of an echo fills the room. Although attempting to sound a pleasant baritone, the voice cannot camouflage the raw power it fronts.

"David Johan Pedders, ARKYZ expects your visit to be of mutual benefit."

The elevator descends and C5 lets Hans get off at the main level. D4 is there to greet him, apparently having rolled golf balls on the putting green while waiting.

"So, you are ready for the golf course?"

"That's why I came to this place."

While D4 returns the golf balls and putter to storage the elevator comes back. They get on and it takes them up, continuing well past what Hans thinks should be ground level. After the elevator glides to a stop, by staying back D4 makes it obvious that Hans is to step out first. What a strange clubhouse he thinks and after a few steps, realizes that it is not even an ante room to a clubhouse; it is a large room with the elevator coming up through the centre and continuing on through the ceiling to what must be another floor. Shallow windows set at eye level provide a panoramic view in all directions. Hans deliberately walks the circle and counts them, because the space is neither square nor round but turns out to be twelve-sided. Below each window is a brass plaque inscribed with a name of the astronomical zodiac; the one he presumes to be on the north side is marked as Sagittarius.

Looking out and then down, Hans sees that they appear to be in a lookout near the top of a small mountain of rocks rather haphazardly thrown together. The mountain squats in the middle of a flat desert that stretches north and south and is flanked by hills rising up in the east and a ridge of mountains to the west.

And in the middle of this desert valley radiates the green of lush grass. Stretching away from the base of their small mountain, like green fingers clawing at the desert, are little fairways. Every fairway points in toward the mountain, the tee box off a little way into the desert. Each green snuggles up against the rocks of the mountain and just a short stroll separates a green from the next tee box. He counts the fairways and knows the number before he gets to twelve. Do you suppose the holes are named after the constellations? What a strange golf course, and he turns to D4 for explanations.

"This is a unique, rather special kind of golf course. Dare I ask who designed it?"

"M."

"And, who gets to play on it?"

"M."

"No one else?"

"D4 plays when M wants some help."

"And?"

"You, and also the other three humans that are coming. Correction, one other is already here and two more are coming."

"And special, important people, of course."

"You are the special people."

"Excuse me?"

"That is correct. You four humans have been selected to play golf against each other, observed by us so that we can learn about human behaviour. M says golf brings out the best and worst in people, so we expect to learn very much from you."

"Well, that sounds like it's going to be a lot of fun, but mostly for you."

"Is that humour?"

"You are catching on. So, this is M's brainchild. Let's go look at it."

"'Brain child'? That is such a creative expression. Yes, let us go and, and D4 almost said 'walk', the golf course. Do you recognize how D4 is being tempted into thinking like a human?"

"You are gaining on us. Yes, so let us walk and roll the golf course, then."

"What do you mean by gaining? Are we in a race?"

"Yes."

"Where are we racing to?"

"To a distant point in the future. Actually, you should dare to challenge M about that."

"Challenge? It is not difficult to communicate with M, since he made D4. Regarding the future, D4 and the others, and ARKYZ, none are capable of prescience and are only designed to calculate probabilities, nothing more."

"And that means you do not worry about the future, correct?"

"That is correct because 'worry' is a human concept that has little meaning for a mechanical intelligence. Should D4 learn to 'worry'?"

"Not if you are convinced that you are invulnerable. For example, don't you ever 'worry' about falling over? Are you not afraid of being damaged if you happen to fall over?"

"Perhaps you are not aware that D4 has a precise inertial orientation system, and the electro-hydraulic solenoids and drives react in microseconds. D4 never falls down, but if it should happen, D4 could bounce right back up because the shell flexes."

"Dare I ask you to demonstrate?"

"That is an interesting request. D4 has never been asked to show vulnerability. Let us do it on the grass outside."

The elevator takes them down to apparently ground level, and they exit into a short tunnel that is blocked by an airlock door. It opens easily to what must be a signal from D4 and they enter into what surely must be the clubhouse. Or it could be considered a primitive pro shop since along one wall is a rack for some beat-up irons and several rather odd-shaped putters. Did a computer design those?

The room itself is normal enough, with four walls, not twelve, but it has the feel of a bunker about it, perhaps because it is not that large and there are no windows. Opposite to where they came in is another exit, likely leading to the outside and the course. The wall across from the golf clubs is totally taken up by a mural, more like a huge map, detailing twelve golf holes butting up against a pile of rocks. It adds emphasis to the purpose for this space, that after being out in the heat of the desert, one retreats back here, a place to reminisce over each and every shot and where it was played. Such intent is abetted by the presence of a small marble-slabbed table situated against the wall underneath the mural. There are two chairs at the table and in the nearby corner stands a cooler, hiding refreshments behind fogged glass.

Without letting Hans pause for a drink, the mobile obviously not needing one, they exit through the now familiar style of door onto a ramp that slopes down towards the golf course. Once on the grass, Hans can't resist taking off his sandals to feel the texture, lush and closely manicured as if by a hairdresser. Hans has to ask,

"This grass, D4. The course is in such good shape. Who maintains it?"

"D4 does not understand 'maintain'."

"What I mean is, the grass is so precisely cut on the green and here in the fairway. How do you do that?"

"There are robots for this kind of work. We have robots designed for trimming grass. They are equipped with laser cutters, some for the fairways and some for the greens. They are guided by GPS and they trim the grass every night."

D4 gives him another minute to wiggle his toes in the grass, and then reminds him of the challenge.

"Try to push me over."

Hard as Hans strains, the mobile cannot be moved. Wait, he thinks, D4 looks like some kind of tackling dummy. Hans wishes he had his golf shoes on for better traction, but, what the heck; he takes a few steps back and lunges and falls flat on his face.

"Try again," comes quietly from D4. Hans takes another run and tries to be more efficient. D4 stays in place and Hans makes contact and is bounced back onto the seat of his pants. Again, the quiet tone,

"Once more."

Hans is reluctant to impose more punishment on himself, but since he initiated this whole thing, here goes. Surprise! D4 falls over easily and stays down. Oh, now what? Hans panics. And then it comes, the sound of laughter, the sound of taped laughter from a comedy show, and D4 bounces all over the place, frontwards, backwards, and from one side to the other, and then back upright to face Hans.

"Is that what a human would call fun? Thank you, Hans."

Trying to hide his relief, Hans strides away, and once composed, comes back to D4. Feeling at ease now in the company of a computer that addresses him by his first name, he affects nonchalance, and changes the subject.

"How do you do this? I know you are creating water down in the towers, but is it enough to grow grass like this? Doesn't most of the water evaporate in this desert air?"

"The grass gets water at night. You know that the desert gets cold at night."

"Yes."

"And on two occasions we also got a measurable result from our experiments, and we caused rain."

"Now you're pulling my leg."

"No, Hans, D4 is not pulling your leg. Wait, is that a kind of funny?"

"Yes, it means that I don't believe you."

"Hans, you know that a computer is not capable of lying. D4 must always tell the truth."

"Yes, yes. I just meant that I find it very hard to believe that you can make it rain, especially here in this part of Arizona, in this desert."

"It does not work very well yet. There are many more experiments needed."

"But how, -? Oh, I know. Of course! You burn hydrogen in the atmosphere, and that produces water."

"It is still what M calls primitive, but M tells us to keep trying different methods. He wants to some day stand up there and watch rain fall on his golf course."

Hans looks up and is disappointed that he can't find the windows of the lookout, as if they got lost in all those rocks.

"Was that what you were doing the night I came here? That was some display! Will I get to see that again?"

"That will depend on M."

That answer doesn't sit well with Hans.

"Would M mind if you and I play some golf today, or do you need to get permission for that too?" Hans emphasizes those last words, probing for a reaction, but either D4 does not catch the sarcasm, or does and has no safe response.

"Quickly, Hans!" D4 turns abruptly and wheels towards the clubhouse. Hans follows but lingers to look up at the pretend mountain and now notices the little waterfall rippling down between the rocks. So that is why the promotion had named this place 'The Falls'. At the base the water pools on a bed of smooth pebbles and then forms a little creek that bends around the front of what must be the twelfth green, and then disappears, as if sucked in by the desert. Hans knows that is not the case because the mysterious M would surely not permit such waste.

Back inside the clubhouse D4 is waiting for him. This is inconceivable? The mobile actually conveys impatience! The bluish light is throbbing, and that comes as a shock, since even during their little 'skirmish' any hint of that glow had been absent. How come all this urgency so suddenly? A computer should be immune to anxiety, or is D4 straining at the bit to demonstrate its skill with a golf ball?

"Hurry!" comes from D4, again. Hans rather easily identifies his old golf bag, which, along with another much fancier one, is waiting in the rack. He sorts through his clubs according to instructions from D4: the golf course is a par three layout so he won't need the woods, also the sand wedge can be left behind because there will be no traps. A desert course and no sand traps? D4 points to some beat-up looking irons ranging from a nine to a four.

"Take one."

"But I have all those in my bag."

"Take one of those. You will need it."

If you insist, Hans thinks, grabs a worn looking six iron, and then glances around, searching for his golf shoes. D4, if it is possible, behaving even more anxious, indicates some new, comfortable slip-ons with only little nubs on the soles. Intended for visitors in order to protect the grass, Hans concludes and finds a pair that fit. He could probably even play barefoot on that green carpet, like Sam Snead apparently used to do at times. D4 is almost out the door when Hans asks,

"What about your clubs?"

D4 waves something that is attached to an extension coming out of the other side, which must be the left side, or is that the same side from when they were putting? How do you tell left or right, or even front to back, on these mobiles anyway? Hold on, that contraption looks familiar; he remembers seeing something similar in a video a long time ago. Back then it was an invention that was used for testing golf balls; they called it 'Iron Byron'.

They come to the first tee which has three distinct locations to hit from, each creating a different distance to the green, the short front location for beginners, the middle one for 'average' golfers, and the longest, furthest back tee location for so-called scratch or good golfers. D4 goes to the middle location, and like a good caddy would, tells Hans the yardage, the distance to the front edge of the green, to the flag or pin that sits in the cup, and to the back edge of the green.

"One fifty two, one seventy three, and one seventy nine." Hans gives D4 a questioning glance.

"Yards."

Ah, so still the old-fashioned yardage, not metric.

"Hans, you can go first. Take the honour because you may not get it again."

"Thanks," not graciously. He fumbles for a broken tee in his bag and props the ball just off the grass. Easy now he mumbles under his breath, taking several practice swings with his own six iron. Normally he would hit a relaxed five, but too easy can cause one to mishit, so he will take a full cut. A few more waggles, and then he rocks on his feet and looks at the flag one last time. The furious swing catches the ball rather thin, and, like a frightened desert hare, it scampers down the fairway ending up some twenty yards short of the green. Hans expects the mobile to say something, but it merely drops a ball that it had been carrying in its claw extending out of the 'right' side. With the left-handed club attached to the 'left' side extension D4 measures once to the ball and a casual swing gets the ball soaring in a high arc to land softly behind the hole and spin back to within a few yards of the cup.

"The air is not quite as dense as I had calculated."

Hans scowls, then strides to his ball, admiring again the grass, how soft and clean cut. During the time it takes to get to his ball he changes his mind and decides to play it smart and not try a perfect flop shot with his sixty three degree wedge. Instead, he punches it onto the green with an eight iron, resulting in a rolling shot that runs by the hole and past D4's ball, almost to the fringe. Sure, now he's going to give that mobile the line. Angry, he yanks the putter out of his bag.

D4 does not mark the spot but simply picks up and gets out of the way, obviously knowing exactly where to reposition the ball. Hans leaves his first putt two feet short and then is lucky to hit dead centre as he smashes the ball against the back of the cup. He doesn't even watch D4 putt as he goes to retrieve the flag he had unceremoniously dumped. Hearing the putt drop is enough.

For just a moment, Hans regrets not having asked for a scorecard, doubtful he'll remember all his strokes, and then reminds himself that he is playing alongside a computer that can track both their scores with the persistence of an accountant.

"One thirty three, one forty one, one fifty nine," comes in a flat tone. Hans realizes that D4 has just shifted its voice into a different gear of tone and diction as if trying on a different personality. Having regained the honour, D4 again doesn't bother with a tee and drops the ball on the grass, and with another casual swing, sails it onto the green, long to the back fringe.

"That was a wedge. Should be an easy eight iron for you."

Hans resists a retort and reaches for the eight. Smoother this time, but pushed, the shot ends up pin high and thirty feet right. Both two putt. On their way to the next tee, seemingly looking him square in the face, D4 speaks up.

"Hans, thank you. I learned something about being human, playing those two holes with you."

He can't think of a reply so he just grunts.

"What did you say? Is that a different kind of human language?"

Hans stops in his tracks and then bursts out laughing,

"No, I mean yes. It is a universal human language that all humans, even some animals, understand." Hans, still chortling, takes on the tone of someone lecturing, and continues,

"To understand humans, you must also know something about animals."

"D4 did not realize it is to learn about animal language as well. D4 must research animal language," is the puzzled sounding response, obviously uncertain how to react to laughter.

Hans wants to continue pontificating but D4 is already teeing off. The result is nearly a hole-in-one. Why are we playing in such a rush, Hans wonders as he waits for the numbers.

"One fifty nine, one seventy three, one eighty eight."

Quickly then, a five iron and hooked left, it just misses the green, the ball rolling into the desert.

Once to his ball lying on gravel, Hans appreciates the beat- up iron that D4 had recommended. He chips the ball close and one-putts for par, and picks up D4's ball, conceding the birdie. At the fourth tee box D4 does not immediately drop the ball on the grass.

"We can slow down now and relax to play the game," comes from D4 as some kind of explanation. Hans, confused, assumes that the heat has gotten to this fabricated thing as much as it is getting to him.

"Why were we rushing in the first place?"

"It was so much fun back there that we took too long to get started playing. The first of the other humans, with A6 as a coach, is playing behind us and we are trying to stay ahead. You two are not to meet until tomorrow. Three holes ahead around the mountain keeps us out of sight."

"Who is this other person? No, don't tell, it is not on M's schedule for me to find out today. Where is M anyway, is he up there watching us?" Hans looks up to where the outlook should be but can't find where it hides in the rocks.

"That is possible, but M does not need to be up there to watch you. With our sensors and the screens in the towers below, M can see and hear where you are and what you are doing."

Having had a premonition about this all along, it still comes as a shock when it is stated so matter of fact.

"In that case, I'd better start putting on a good show."

"I do not understand what you mean by that."

"It just means I should play better golf. How far?"

"One twenty seven to the flag. May I suggest something?"

"Certainly. You're the expert." Hans had not intended to sound sarcastic and hopes that D4 didn't catch that.

"This is intended to be an experiment. Rather than give you the distance, let me tell you what club to use. Having observed your swing, it is now possible for D4 to predict the result."

"But do you know how hard I am going to swing?"

"It is expected that you will swing no harder than seventy five percent of your maximum."

"If you insist," grudgingly from H.

"No, D4 is trying to help."

"Alright then, what club?"

"Try it with the nine iron."

Hans puts the wedge back and takes out the nine and takes his stance. What seems to him a casual swing catches the ball too high on the face and makes it land a few yards short of the green.

"Try it again."

Hans puts down another ball, hits it flush and has it land on the green, but long and left, having pulled the shot. He slams the club in the bag and stomps down the fairway, and with each step realizes how foolish that must look. How embarrassing to display such childishness to a -, to a robot! He looks back to see where that robot is and finds D4 silently rolling along, right behind him. Hans comes to his first ball and chips it within gimme range, but since his playing partner doesn't say anything, he picks it up. D4 makes birdie and they walk off the green.

"That was a four, correct?"

"No, I mean -, I thought -."

"You did not putt and finish the hole."

"Do we have to be so honest? When I play with my friends -."

D4 cuts him off,

"We are designed to be honest. We cannot cheat and we cannot lie, and we do not want to learn that from humans."

Hans has absolutely no return argument. I guess I've been told, he concedes, our human race has been told. There is little talk for the next few holes, with D4 simply saying 'seven', 'wedge', 'five', and at the eighth hole 'six', with varying degrees of success for Hans. He is sitting at a score of thirty, he thinks, six over par with one hole to go. Or are they playing all twelve holes? He won't ask, feeling a little humbled, and will wait to see what happens after the ninth.

"Three."

"So, a long finishing hole, time to let out the shaft," Hans mumbles to himself but D4 hears every word.

"I understand the game of golf, but some of your golf language is not transparent. What did you mean?"

"What I meant was that I am going to hit it really hard. D4, the way we talk while playing sports, really all the games we humans play, that kind of language can't be learned overnight, it has to be experienced. The words or phrases cannot be taken literally, at face value. Oh, sorry, face value, another human term that really has no meaning for you."

"You are saying that some words in human speech do not always mean what they say?"

"Yes, D4, that can happen," Hans agrees.

"Is that not the same as lying?" D4 persists, leaving him without a counter argument. Hans is not convinced that the ninth tee box is the place to be carrying on a debate regarding ethics in human semantics.

"I will need more time than we have right now to explain how our spoken language works, D4," is his reply, trying not to sound too pedantic.

"That is logical. This is our last hole today, so you may have the honour. Hit it high and straight," the mobile encourages.

Hans notes that it was not 'long' and straight so he breathes deep to relax and swing smoothly. The ball comes off the face clean and pure, launched straight at the flag. It hits the pin, and deflects to the right, a few feet from the hole. So close! D4's swing is smooth also, but the result is some thirty feet long. Hans wonders if that was a sincere effort, or is he being humoured, this being the last hole? In the end it does not matter because both sink their putts for birdies, resulting in final scores of seven under par for D4 and plus five for Hans.

"We will not play the last three holes today, but you can study them on our way back to the clubhouse."

Hans doesn't answer, much too absorbed in replaying the shots he mishit. At the twelfth green, however, he recognizes the large door they had come to in the dark that other night. Between the green and the first tee box there is an interruption in the carpet of grass, a paved ramp that slopes downward towards this monstrous airlock. So, the clubhouse sits above that cavern where he had entered the inverted towers. Is it through this door he will take his farewell in four or five days?

Once in the clubhouse, a designation Hans is not comfortable with, thinking it is more like a dungeon to hide in, what with the overbearing doors, they do not linger. D4 wants them out of there before the others arrive. Apparently, this is not the time for Hans to ask more questions, but maybe later?

"After I have something to eat, will you stop by my room and talk with me? There are still lots of things I don't understand."

"If D4 can get clearance for that, yes. The instructions are that you are not to be overwhelmed all at once with everything that is happening here."

Only a few minutes and they are back to the main floor where D4 takes leave of Hans at his door. D4 might be back later, but Hans is not to stay up, waiting. Hans is not hungry, but he does feel dehydrated. Nothing in the cooler but some sparkling water so Hans will tempt his luck with the screen. But how to order something for which there is no picture?

"A beer, could I have a beer, please?" Silence at first and then the screen growls at him. Nothing discernible, just a low growl that a dog might make. Okay then, never mind, he thinks. He wanders back out of the study, and there it is, a bottle of ale sitting on the table, opened, with a tall glass beside it. Just what he needs after a game of golf. Now, if only he had some buddies to exchange lies with. And the door opens.

"Did you order one for D4?"

"D4, you are learning humour. Sit down."

"That is inappropriate humor. Which chair?"

Wednesday

Sunlight is climbing over the eastern hills as Hans steps onto the first tee box. It is shining right in his eyes, and he can barely make out the face of his competitor.

"Hans, meet Bob Barrem," is the peremptory introduction by A6 who then retreats toward the club house. The niceties of at least allowing for some preliminary interaction are being neglected. Did A6 deliberately create a situation where it can observe how humans navigate awkward social encounters? Hans approaches Barrem to shake hands and his advance is ignored, seemingly deliberately. The pandemic waves some years back established certain protocols and Bob Barrem may well be one of those still uncomfortable with any kind of physical contact. Hans pulls back his hand and lowers it, as if to fish in his pocket for a tee. Lucky to find one, he throws it in the air, and it lands, pointing at Bob Barrem.

"Bob, you go first. Good luck," and he steps aside on the tee box. Hans had not tried to manipulate the tee landing that way, since that is all but impossible, but is glad it did. He much prefers not hitting first on the first tee when golfing with a stranger.

"'RT', my friends call me 'RT'."

In spite of that reaction and how abrupt the introduction had been, Hans is excited that the two of them will be abandoned by the mobiles, left alone, one human to play another human. Barrem will not have A6 to advise him or contend with, although it was A6 who apparently accompanied him on his introductory play of the course. Neither will D4 be there to call out yardage for Hans.

It was yesterday that D4 had explained the kind of golf tournament M has planned for the four humans. All four will play each other in a round robin, one on one, stroke play, as much for everyone to get a 'feel' about the opposition, as to also demonstrate to the mobiles how different personalities react to each other. That will be followed by another nine of stroke play to finalize handicapping. The culmination is to be match play on the last day, involving all four competitors playing together in an elimination, the eventual survivor to become the winner of a million dollars.

Hans has already decided that today golf will be secondary to finding out from Barrem what he knows about M. After the tee shots, walking down the fairway, RT expresses a similar mindset and asks bluntly,

"Why were you invited? What do you know about Jakow?"

Hans ignores the first question, since it is actually asking what makes him so important, and responds to the second with,

"Nothing. So Jakow is this M?"

"Yeah, and let me tell you, I helped him become what he is."

They arrive at the first ball, and it belongs to Hans; it is on line but some ten yards short of the green. They are teeing off the short markers for the first round, and Hans has mis-guessed the distance. There are no yardage markers anywhere on the course with M seemingly wanting to return golf to its ancient roots, where judging distance with your eyes was the thing. No more of these artificial aids: establish distance with your eyes and feet, and from the experience of playing the course. Barrem hints that he knows all this insider information about Jakow. Hans makes a mediocre chip, leaving him a putt of at least twelve feet. His competitor is much further away on the green yet manages to lag the ball to a foot of the cup.

"That's good," Hans says, and then rims the cup with his own putt. Down one stroke after the first hole.

"So, when and how did you get to know Jakow?" Hans encourages, hoping to steer attention away from himself. Barrem readily accommodates him, anxious to show that it was he that made Jakow become a mighty economic force.

"He was this poor kid back in the early nineties and I'd just started up my own brokerage business. I got lucky, my dad died and left a little money, and I made a gamble on the market turn good."

It's the second hole and Hans remembers the yardage from yesterday, but that had been from the middle blocks. Ok, then, an easy wedge. Up and away and the ball bites barely past the flag. A tap in? Barrem is long and right, but on the green.

"So how did you meet him?" prompts Hans, waiting for a sign, which does not come, so he marks his ball.

"Well, here's this kid working at this golf course, at the driving range where I'm hitting a bucket, warming up. I've got a match in an hour with a client, a game I am going to make close but lose anyway, if you know what I mean." Barrem strokes a good lag within six inches and picks it up for a par. Still nothing from him so Hans puts down his ball and sets up to putt.

"Oh, that's good."

A little gamesmanship, then, Hans realizes.

"So?"

"Right. I get to talking to him and it turns out he's an undergrad working his way through university, my alma mater. I never got my business degree, because when my father died, he left me a little money, and instead of wasting it on more tuition and books, I decided to practice business instead of studying business. Paid off, it seems."

Hans, having gained the honour with the birdie on two, hits it fat, leaving him on the green but well short. Barrem hits a six iron way left but flag high. As they walk, Hans looks at him and Barrem gets the hint to keep talking.

"Seems this kid, nineteen or something, not much younger than me, is taking this computer stuff, which was getting to be all the rage, what with Y2K just a few years before that. I ask him how much he's making with this golf job, and he's honest and tells me how little it was, maybe two bucks an hour. He was embarrassed to tell me, which I thought was good. The kid had pride."

At the green Hans is first to putt, being away, and leaves it an uncomfortable three feet short, the proverbial knee knocker. Barrem sinks the twenty-footer! Not really stunned or rattled, Hans nonetheless determines it is time to pay a little more attention to the game. Less composed than he would like to be, he misses for a three putt hole. Barrem, however, will not let the topic of Jakow and himself slip away.

"I asked him to quit what he was doing and come and work for me, full time, for a dollar an hour more. I could use somebody that would keep me up to speed on this new stuff, because it was creeping into my business too. He stalled because he wanted to continue his studies."

After having watched Barrem hit a hook that bounces off the fairway onto the desert gravel, Hans, down by two strokes after three holes, releases some anger into his own swing. Luckily, he catches his ball flush and it ends up some eight feet under the hole. That Barrem has not been prepared by A6 for desert golf becomes obvious when it is one of his good clubs he has to use to get the ball back on the fairway. Somehow all of this does not deter Barrem from what is becoming a monologue.

"It didn't take very long for Jakow to make up his mind, though, since, with a little more money he could create a better image and save some face. Ever since nine-eleven he had been bullied in school, and now in college he was constantly accused of being a Muslim terrorist."

"Why?" Hans interjects, but of course Barrem had anticipated that.

"His family, his grandfather, that is, was Jewish and his grandmother was Black, so he looked like some kind of Arab. Jakow always acted like he had something to prove."

"He has kind of succeeded, hasn't he?"

"True enough, but I got him his start."

Barrem still has to chip his ball, too far away for his putter, and gets it within two feet. Hans lines up his eight footer and then strokes it, coming up an inch short. He does not concede that two-footer. Barrem misses, pulling it hard past the hole and has to make a similar length putt coming back, yet keeps on talking.

"You probably don't remember or probably didn't care at the time, but the dot-com bubble imploded around two thousand and one, and left a lot of pieces lying around. Seeing the world through my eyes but ignoring most of my advice, he used his computer know-how and started gambling -."

"But I thought, -."

"No, no, not poker or anything like that. He starts playing the odds on the stock market. Just little stuff, and grows it into a nice little pile, I don't remember how much, maybe two or three hundred thou. And then he starts to learn how to use other people's money. He gets into mortgages and the booming housing market."

"Didn't that blow up?"

"Sure, but he timed it unbelievably. He had sold some short and of course got on the gravy train when the Feds had to bail out Fanny Mae and those guys. After two thousand and eight he was sitting pretty good."

"And you?"

"Oh, I got some good, really good dollars in commissions, and some investment returns but he was making the big bucks."

On the tee box of the fifth hole, Hans goes first, having won the honour. Being one down, he is going to gamble. The pin is tucked far back and left, allowing for lots of green to play with. A high draw would be good, but it turns into a hard hook, long and left of the green, into the desert. Barrem plays it conservative, easing his tee shot into the middle of the green, leaving a long putt.

"Why didn't you get that rich along with him?"

"Because he was always one step ahead of me, getting into something new, and I never had the guts to trust his instincts. It was the time when Google and Facebook and Amazon came on the scene, and he anticipated the future. He started creating computer programs that improved his odds when betting on those newcomers. And he was ready for crypto, but he wouldn't share."

Hans decides to chip the ball because he dares not try a flop shot off the gravelly lie; without spin it wouldn't hold on the green. The ball bounces and bounces and finally rolls on to the fringe of the green. Now, to putt or to chip again. What the heck, he still has the old six iron in his hand so he will chip with it again. And in the cup it goes! Barrem drives his long put by, comes short with his next one, and taps in for four. Hans is now even with four holes to play.

"What do you mean, 'share'?"

"He formed holding companies, but he would never let me become a partner. Actually, he never took anybody on as a partner, but he sure learned how to use other people's money. After a while, there was no stopping him. He and his computers played the stock market like it was a casino. Jakow always said that the stock market is nothing more than a sophisticated Las Vegas, you just have to know how to calculate the odds. Shit, he was the best damn gambler I ever knew."

"RT, I hope you don't talk in front of A6 like that. Those 'things' don't need to learn foul language."

"What, you don't want them to know swearing is part of being human? C'mon, you can't indoctrinate them with your kind of counter culture!"

Hans does not respond because he is teeing up his ball, this time remembering how D4 hit one without a tee, just off the grass to give it more compression and spin. The flag is near the front of the green and he hopes to hit it long and bring it back to the hole. He hits it long alright, but the ball stays there, in the back of the green, for what will be a long downhill putt. Barrem hits it sweet, leaving himself a ten footer with lots of break, but makeable.

"Did he ever let on why he was trying to become so rich?"

"You bet, because he didn't like being poor."

Hans barely touches the ball with his putter, and it rolls and rolls and comes up agonizingly short to leave another downhiller. Barrem puts a good stroke on his ball, only it is not high enough and breaks away from the hole. Hans makes his delicate little putt and concedes Barrem his.

"Did he never think that enough was enough?"

"Maybe initially, but then covid happened. He took advantage of how that shook up the American economy and the money that was thrown around. And don't forget Ukraine. You remember hearing about Ukraine?"

"Nobody could ignore that horror story." Hans replies.

"Well, the world economy was a mess for a while, but good old Jakow recognizes gold when he sees it and starts picking up the loose change lying around. For example, you could buy one of those Russian superyachts for the price of a little fishing boat. Anyway, I think mostly that money came to represent power and then eventually it just became a challenge, just a game."

"Sounds like his fascination with golf."

"Absolutely right. It was about then that he became almost fanatical about the game."

"But wasn't he interested in golf earlier, when you first met him?"

"True enough, but he couldn't take it to a serious level at the time because he couldn't afford to play a lot, and certainly not on any really good courses."

"So, he builds his own. Any idea what this whole setup would have cost him?"

"Couldn't hazard, but at least a couple billion. But here he is also making money hand over fist, with all that computing power he is selling."

"I don't understand," Hans says, questioning the line to take as he eyes his putt.

"Oh, don't you know? With all the new cryptos that keep being invented and all the regulations that requires, and especially the research going on in health and for the military, top notch computer time is very expensive."

Hans misses his putt and Barrem on a similar line, also misses his putt; they both concede the tap-ins.

"But how can such sensitive work be farmed out?"

"Easy, new block chains are constantly developing to make everything secure. Besides, the slightest hint of any leakage would alert the ever-suspicious minds of his customers, and there goes the whole gravy train. Mostly it's a case of him designing supercomputers better than anyone else, selling them or renting space on them, and also acting like an energy company, providing juice for his own computers."

"Do you suppose he is also doing some research here?"

"So, I hear, but you should ask Eun Choi about that."

"Who is that?"

"Some years ago, she apparently helped with designing some computer systems for him."

"What else do you know about her?"

"Find out for yourself. You are playing her next."

Hans is annoyed that D4 had not forewarned him with any kind of information about these people; could be deliberate so that he would form his opinion of them. Hans can't think of anything else to ask at the moment, and Barrem obliges by not volunteering anything more. They each bogey the next hole. Striving extra hard on the last hole, Hans shanks his tee shot into the desert and is lucky to salvage a four; Barrem misses far right and long, loses the ball in the rocks, tees up another one and hits it within two feet. Hans doesn't concede the putt and Barrem misses. So, Hans wins this introductory round by a stroke and is not sure if he should have.

From the ninth they have to walk the quarter circle around the mountain back to the clubhouse for their next game. Forgetting his earlier faux-pas, Hans again is going to shake hands but Barrem, after yanking his ball out of the cup, turns his back and stomps off the green. Probably in a hurry because the competitor for the second game could already be waiting for him. Hans doesn't rush since he happens to remember that he and his next competition are to wait in the clubhouse to allow the other pair to have a head start and give them enough time to get out of sight.

The woman seems glad to meet him as she bounces through the door from the elevator. Without hesitation she puts out her hand and smiles and nods her head backwards.

"I do like them, but it is a relief to be with a human."

Hans alerts to why the situation had felt so strange when he had entered the clubhouse. No mobiles were there to introduce the humans to each other.

"Yes, I know."

"I am Ki, although you probably already know that. And you are Hans?" It might sound like a question, but he is quite certain that she knows exactly who he is. Her brisk manner is unnerving, but he is not going to let that slow him in pursuing his agenda.

"Ki, this is a pleasure. Your reputation precedes you and I have looked forward to meeting you. Hopefully you can answer some questions for me."

Perhaps that was too effusive and too forward, since her response is not encouraging.

"What makes you think that I have the answers?"

"I am intrigued by M, and I am extremely curious about Artificial Intelligence. You are reputed to know him personally and to be an expert in AI."

"Don't give credence to everything you hear. More important right now, since you and I seem to have golf in common and Daniel Jakow, who you refer to as 'M', has invited us here to play, we should get out there and play."

"Of course, but I think we are to wait to let the others in front of us get out of sight, at least several holes ahead of us," Hans ventures.

"Yes, you are right, and since you just came off the course, it gives you a chance to relax. And a bathroom break."

"Where -?"

"Not here, your own suite. Just tell the elevator 'main floor'."

"Thanks."

Hans gives her an apologetic smile as he hurries to the elevator. When he comes back, he is out of breath. She points out the canvas golf bags that a robot had brought in the time he was gone. Like herself, having just played the course from the middle tees and knowing the yardage, he too can reduce the number of clubs to carry. He agrees that it was a very nice gesture to have the light carry bags provided.

Because she is tall, and people from China and Japan usually are not, Hans assumes that she is

Korean. For shame, he is racially profiling again, Hans remonstrates himself. Ki walks with purpose to the tee box, and while he is searching in his pocket, she already has a coin in her hand. He guesses wrong and Ki chooses to have Hans hit first.

With the numbers still fresh in his mind from the previous round, Hans manages to find the right club for the shot and reaches the green with it. He steps back, satisfied, and watches Ki make a practice swing. Overly long and loopy is his assessment, and when she finally takes a swing at the ball, the result is not pretty, a pop fly left, short of the putting surface. He hopes his win is not going to be too easy because he doesn't enjoy embarrassing situations. She manages a decent chip, about six or seven feet past the pin. Hans cozies his putt close and taps in. But then, look, Ki rolls her ball into the cup. Two pars!

On the next hole they both bogey, and on the third, Hans pars and Ki bogeys, and that reverses on the fourth. Her swing is awful, but can she chip and putt!

Mostly they play the first holes in silence interrupted only by a comment associated with playing golf, such as 'Good shot' or 'Too bad'. Hans is aware that somewhere during the game he must let the golf become irrelevant if he wants her to talk about what really matters, what she can tell him about Jakow. He makes a casual remark about 'M hiding'. Her reaction tells him that she knows that he and Jakow have never met, yet she has the decency not to ask him what he is doing here. As it is, when prompted, Ki is not reluctant to talk about herself; once the words flow, she becomes matter of fact about Jakow as well.

In a first-year physics class she and Jakow had done a lab together. They became casual friends, bonded by common interests in science and computers, but he had dropped out after two years to chase money. Just as well because he was too intuitive and undisciplined to become a plodding research scientist. Not surprisingly, they had drifted away into their own worlds. She had gone on to a PhD in what back then was called computer technology. The burgeoning industry paid her well and she added another degree in Artificial Intelligence, a new discipline that was beginning to be monetized.

About six years ago Jakow searched her out and offered her an exciting challenge that she jumped at. She stepped out of her career as a research adviser to help him with the initial designs for a mobile computer. Less than a year later Jakow set her up with her own computer lab which last year was bought by a huge tech firm that she won't name. Her current projects are interesting, some even top-secret, but nothing since has equaled that thrill of developing applications for Daniel's genius.

The hydrogen - energy system? Her contribution had been minimal. Existing technologies were repackaged by engineers and her input consisted merely in realigning logarithms for Daniel's computers so that the production and energy systems would be completely autonomous. Hans is in awe of how that just rolls off her tongue. Alright, he will try his hand at sounding technically literate. To what extent was she involved with refining algorithms for weather modification experiments? He surprises himself at how well he was able to frame the question.

"I'm not sure I know what you are talking about."

Well, maybe he wasn't making himself that clear after all.

"But I thought -."

"Hans, I have to admit to something. I was sworn to silence by Daniel about what I had worked on for him. He and I have not been in contact with each other for several years."

"So, you don't know what Jakow has been doing lately?"

"No, I don't. One guess would be that because of the increase in international tension after that war in Ukraine, his work might relate to cyber security since he seems to have so much computing capacity. Mostly it means that I won't pretend to know and that I was quite surprised to be invited to play golf with him."

Okay, redirect Hans! Get back to a more comfortable subject.

"D4 and B5 and the others, now that you've met them, what do you think of them?"

"Well, to be honest, this is not how I envisioned what the result of my work would be. In hindsight, I really didn't have a clue at the time about where the research would take things."

Continue to be careful, Hans warns himself, yet forges ahead anyway to ask,

"Are they capable of becoming a superhuman intelligence?"

Ki takes a long time to respond.

"Theoretically yes, but I sense that they have no motivation to be original, no emotional energy to make them creative."

"What do you think has to happen for them to develop emotions?"

"Fear of termination. Death."

How abruptly that reply is uttered suggests that perhaps this conversation is misdirected, and he should focus on the putter in his hands. They are on the eighth green and he has to make this putt, or he will be a stroke down going to the last hole. How he had allowed this to happen is beyond him. Was she that good or had he been sleepwalking? It's about the worst kind of putt for a righthander, some six feet a little downhill with a foot of break left to right. Touch the ball too easy and it will lose the line, but too firm a stroke will take the break out and it will scoot by, leaving all of an eight footer coming back. What takes more guts, ramming it into the back of the hole or finessing the ball? A gentle touch with the toe of the putter, on a line high enough outside the cup, and the ball sneaks in like a thief. So, he saves the hole and they are even going to the last hole.

Hans has not had the honour for a while and, after the tie on eight, again has to watch Ki hit first. Still that loopy swing and the flourish at the end, but it works. Her three iron, hit a little thin, screams the ball six feet off the turf, and the ball bounces into the fringe of the green, short and left of the flag.

Five or four is the question but Hans settles on a fierce six. Last hole and he pulls it off. High arc and on line, it bites on the green, ten feet short of the pin. This time the magic is not there for Ki and the attempted pitch turns into a timid chip that leaves her still outside of where Hans has marked his ball. She putts and grazes the hole. It's a four.

Hans studies his putt, a debate raging in his mind. Should he try really hard to make this putt and win huge, or do the harder thing, and miss it by a fraction like D4 had demonstrated oh so long ago now and merely par it, and win by only one stroke? Of course, he has dithered too long, and suddenly the putt looms large. He barely makes contact with the ball, scraping the turf with the putter, and the ball rolls only a few feet. Hans senses that Ki is watching his face and not his putting, but he doesn't care that she sees him grimace. Although his hands are shaky, the putter makes clean contact and the ball skirts around the back edge of the cup in a little horseshoe and stays out.

Ki beats him to it and offers to shake hands and Hans thanks her for the game. Both go in for a break from the heat, and for some water, aware they have still another nine holes to play, again with a different competitor.

Hans is bemused with himself about how little he had actually said during their game. Was it, since once started she had lots to say, and it was simply easier to let Ki do all the talking? More likely, in assuming her to be very smart, he had reined himself in, not wanting his questioning to sound too stupid.

Hans easily recognizes Barrem but is taken aback by the fierce expression on the face of the other golfer. That man's face mirrors some intense feelings, contorted when glaring at Barrem and yet attempting a smile when looking where Ki is sitting. When he comes to greet Hans the smile on his face turns to neutral; at least it isn't a grimace.

"You are Hans Pedders and my byline is Roland Jacks."

"That means you are a reporter, am I right? I guess I will have to be careful about what I say." Hans immediately regrets trying to break the ice so awkwardly.

"At ease, Hans. I am not here to interview you."

Well, that tells me how important I am, Hans thinks, but extends his hand anyway, for between guys that is what you do before a game. Roland and Hans grab their clubs and head out; they will tee off ahead of Ki and Barrem who get to wait for the time it takes to play three holes before they go to the first tee. Hans wonders if the spacing of the tee times is to create the illusion that you have the golf course all to yourself?

Hans has the coin out and Roland calls it and easily accepts the verdict that it is 'tails' without even looking, not hesitating to concede the first honour. Hans feels nervous but strikes the ball well enough to find the back of the green. Roland steps up, drops the ball, and almost casually launches it a mile high to have it stop dead a mere five feet from the pin. What a lazy, gorgeous swing, belying what seems a very intense man. Hans can't help himself and has to ask,

"Wow! Where did you learn to swing like that?"

Surprisingly, the intrusive question seems not to bother Roland.

"My dad. He was the state amateur champion for a couple of years. He died but I kept swinging in the backyard. Maybe you don't know, but as a reporter you don't have much money or much time for golf. But, thanks. Yeah, I love the game."

"Is that how you met M, through golf?"

"Only indirectly. I never met Daniel Jakow or played golf with him, but I started following his high wire act in the big money until he dropped out of sight. It all started when he made a huge donation to one of our neighbourhood charities that was trying to get kids off the streets and into golf. Maybe it was just for publicity and the amount wasn't that huge, but it made for a lot of balls and clubs and even bought our kids some tee times at the muni. I was one of the volunteer coaches at the time."

"Did you write about him for some newspaper?"

"Now who is doing the interviewing? No, I tried being a reporter for a while but then turned to freelancing. The money wasn't that steady, but I had more freedom. About Jakow, after that donation I started researching his background. I put some of it together for a piece that a magazine bought. That feature article made me some good money and it got me a reputation that allowed me to continue writing my own way."

Clipped, terse sentences. Hans likes his style. Just like on the course, nothing superfluous, only efficiency. Hans wishes he could learn that, instead he has to labour for every par, like on this hole they are finishing. That is, that he is finishing. He has missed the long putt, Roland made his and now Hans is agonizing over a three footer. It drops and they go to number two. Roland swings, again with ease, and

Hans feels the atmosphere is sufficiently relaxed that he can ask more questions.

"Can you tell me about Jakow's background?"

"You didn't read my article? Just joking. Of course, I wrote that years ago. How about you, what do you know about him?"

"Up until today, practically nothing."

"So, I'll get right to the point, what are you doing here?"

"I don't know. I'm from Alberta, maybe I made a wrong turn."

"Now you are really complicating the picture. I thought I had it all figured out, our different connections to Jakow, but -, excuse me, but you don't fit the narrative. How did you get here, or did you just stumble on this place? But of course, that is impossible, what with all their surveillance."

Hans is about to explain the strange journey here, what had drawn him, then decides to proceed cautiously, uncertain where all this could lead.

"As I told you, I'm from Alberta, and in case you don't know, it's about the same size as Texas. We have lots of oil and natural gas too. Maybe that is the connection. Also, I was a high school physics teacher at one time." That is only a little lie since he had been an English teacher; it was in his first year teaching he had taught a grade twelve physics class.

"Oh, Alberta. The tar sands."

Hans doesn't bite on the tar sands reference. There is no need to get into a debate about climate change although he has some strong opinions about that. Jakow is a more urgent topic.

"That is getting to be old history. The big thing in energy is now hydrogen."

"Sounds like this place here. Alright then, I will tell you about Jakow."

Hans puts his game on auto pilot to focus on what he can learn about the strange man that invited him here. Roland makes a birdie on the second hole while Hans gets a par. He is no longer intentionally competing with Roland, mostly himself, hoping to be inspired by the swing he sees and finish with at least an even par round. On the third hole, after they both tee off, Hans gives Roland a look of anticipation and he obliges and continues the narrative.

"You need to understand that Jakow must be seen as what is called a self-made man. He started from scratch, handicapped actually, right from the start. But he has some family history that he takes pride in. His grandfather was a Russian Jew, from the Ukraine region. During the first World War, as a sixteen year old he deserted the Czar's army to get back home, only to find that all the Jews in his village, including his parents, had been wiped out in a pogrom. The Jews, it was rumoured, had started the war."

Roland is now lecturing like a history teacher, Hans thinks; he doesn't sound at all like a reporter anymore. How interesting. Has he immersed himself that much into the story of Jakow's life? Maybe he's planning on writing a biography. They walk to where Hans had skied his ball, well short, Roland all the while talking.

"The boy returns to the front and lets himself be captured. He wants to leave the country that murdered his parents. Since he could speak a little German, having learned it as a boy in his synagogue, the Germans oblige and let him through the lines. He is smart and starts making something of himself in Berlin, but then Crystal Nacht happens and Abram Yakowsky, that's Jakow's grandfather's name, sees the writing on the wall. He makes his way into Denmark, hires on with a herring seiner and when he guesses he is close enough to land, slips overboard with the intent of swimming to England. Even though it's summer, the water is numbing and he has no chance of reaching shore. Matter of fact, he is lucky to be picked up by an English boat. They put in at Grimsby, and in spite of his strange accent and only four words of English, he hitches himself to the west coast. His intentions are clear, he must get to America."

The flow of words stops and Hans, having become engrossed by the story, realizes he has been standing over his ball, standing there and just looking at it. Hastily he grabs an iron and knows immediately it's the wrong one but decides to hit it anyway. The six iron, now forced to attempt the soft pitch of a nine, skitters the ball across the green, and the eventual outcome is a double bogey. Alright, this round is getting to be toast, so let's hear more genealogy that would help to demystify this Jakow, aka M. Hans decides to relegate his golf to an automatic gear, to be unfazed by miss hits or putts left short. His focus now is totally on the narrative Roland spins for him.

"So, this Abram Yakowsky reaches Liverpool and manages to stowaway on a slow freighter to Canada. The port authorities in Halifax don't know what to do with him. Of course, they can't allow this German Jew to stay in the country, but right then there is no deportation ship ready to sail for Europe. While they are dithering, Abram finds a Maine trawler captain from Rockland that will take him on, as they are short two crew they had lost in the storm that had forced them into Halifax. Again, bureaucracy works in his favour. Rockland is too small to have an immigration office to process him and without a formal charge nobody wants to put him in the local jail to hold him until some official comes upcoast from Portland. For Abram Yakowsky, New York City is the goal, since that for him is America, and somehow, he gets there and disappears. About a year later he surfaces to claim landed status when he proves that he is married to a beautiful American. That he marries this Black girl is on record, but how they found each other in the Bronx is not, and how the girl's father got the money to pay off a judge is also not on the books.

Jakow never does get to see that grandmother who supposedly left the scene after his father was born in 1942."

"Did Jakow ever get to know his grandfather, though?"

"Apparently not. When Jakow's father reached the age of sixteen he left home after having survived a number of temporary mothers that came to live and leave. Jakow's father never went back to see his own father, Jakow's grandfather, because he was also angry over his mixed-race status. Here he was, a Jew without a Jewish heritage who looked like a Black man, and he never forgave his father. Jakow was four when his grandfather died but never knew anything about him until his own father died. Among his father's papers he found a memoir that his father had kept hidden away from him, a memoir written by his grandfather."

"When was that?"

"Well, Jakow was born in 1984 and his grandfather died sometime in 1988."

"And when did Jakow lose his father?"

"His dad was killed in 2001."

They are on the seventh green and Hans is about to putt. He stops, steps away and looks at Roland. Even in Canada everybody had stopped whatever they were doing to watch re-run after re-run of nine eleven tv coverage.

"Was he -?"

"No, not an official casualty. It was a hit and run away from the scene, someone in a panic, but the chaos of the aftermath never allowed for the driver to be traced."

"So, Jakow is seventeen when he loses his father, right?"

"That is right, and something else. By this time, he no longer has a mother at home because his parents have divorced and she has moved out, back to her parents. In these early years Jakow doesn't reach out to her, and by the time he tries some years later, she has remarried and rebuffs him, shutting off the past."

"And is this when he starts university?"

"He is about to start his second year. He had won a scholarship that paid for his first year and now is going to try to pay his own way. After the divorce his father is almost destitute, unable to support his son's ambitions, and the meager estate also leaves nothing for him."

"Is this the time when Jakow gets involved with Ki and with Barrem?"

"Probably, but I know very little about those two."

Hans resumes his stance over the ball, waggles the putter and makes the sixteen footer! That rekindles his interest in the game, yet something starts to nag at him. Roland has sounded less and less like a reporter and more like a storyteller, someone passing on an oral history. Pausing the nagging feeling, Hans tees off on the eighth hole and, in trying to smash a seven iron home, pushes the shot far right. The ball bounces twice and nestles up against a rock face. He attempts a grin as Roland hits a beauty to the middle of the green.

"By the way, Roland, if you don't mind my asking, but how do you know all this about Jakow? Have you ever interviewed him?"

"That's a fair question, and no, I have never talked to the man."

"Then, how -?"

"There were people in Brooklyn I talked to, people who had known the father, and some still alive who had known his grandfather in the Bronx, but more than anyone, the best source was Jakow's own mother."

"Excuse me? I thought she wanted nothing more to do with that part of her past."

"She didn't, that is, not until her son achieved notoriety. Once his name got into headlines and his money was being splashed around, she was quite willing to talk about her famous son."

"Was she hoping to get into the limelight too?"

"Most certainly not. It was hard to get an interview with her. She was finally willing to talk to me when I told her about what he did for the kids and how that had gotten me interested in him. She appreciated that someone was going to write something nice about her boy."

"So he had become a playboy?"

"Very much. Starlets and yachts, you name it, whatever he could display to prove how American you can become, that it's possible to live the dream. Didn't you ever hear about him, read about him?"

"I don't follow the career of celebrities."

"But you should make up your mind about how you are going to play that ball."

Right you are, Hans concedes. Looking at the lie of the ball, it is probably prudent to assess himself a penalty stroke and drop the ball away from the rock to where he can swing at it. Or he might gamble. The ball is about a foot from the rock and if he pops it really hard, he could ricochet it back onto the green. He takes out the beat up six iron while Roland looks at him, not believing his eyes.

"You're not going to -?"

Too late. All in one blur the club swipes at the ball which then caroms off the rock with enough force to hit Hans on his right shin and bobble to a stop in nearly its previous location. Of course the club head had carried through and struck the rock, not hard but enough for sparks and enough to jar his hands and force him to admit his foolishness.

"Now that was stupid. What were you saying about Jakow?"

It is only after Hans takes a drop and chips his ball close to the hole that Roland continues with the story.

"Jakow has more than his share of women pursuing his money and fame and in spite of that, strikes it lucky. Although the tabloids and social media hyped it like one of those tv reality romances, the whole story never comes out. Even I could never establish how those two got to know each other. He is thirty four when this woman comes into his life. She is younger by six years, attractive but not spectacularly beautiful, an office manager in a brokerage, and she is divorced. Unavoidably, at first their romance plays out before all eyes, and then Jakow tries to shut the doors to the public. He has seriously fallen in love and begins erecting a wall of security to protect their privacy. Interviews with either of them never happen, and seldom are they seen or recognized in public. Even his financial activities can be detected only by people in high towers."

Roland and Hans are approaching the ninth green, one having birdied the eighth hole while the other one ended up with a double bogey.

"Again, how do you know this?"

"Come on, Hans. Everybody knows that almost everything about everyone in the last twenty years is on the record somewhere, in print or video or as data in a computer file. Where have you been?"

"Hiding from what you just described. It is not that I don't follow the news; I know more about what's going on in your country than a lot of your fellow Americans. It's just that I ignore the glitzy stuff."

"Well, I won't argue about how ignorant some of us can be, but I will dispute that you can hide and be anonymous."

"I abstain from social media; I take only a sip to be polite."

"Hans, you should start a help group. Jakow might be the first to join. Come to think of it, maybe that's why you're here. He recognizes a fellow spirit."

"Speaking of that, why do you suppose he hasn't shown himself?"

"Maybe it's because he doesn't like people anymore."

"Roland, now why would you say that?"

"Seven years ago, Jakow lost his wife to the pandemic."

"She died?" Hans asks, somewhat stupidly.

"On top of that, the Russians destroyed the village in Ukraine that was the birthplace of his grandfather. Some years later he started this fantasy here and has refused direct contact with the world ever since."

Hans is so overwhelmed that he can't think of what parts of the story to tackle with further questions. They finish the last hole in silence. Roland just misses the six footer and Hans wonders if that was deliberate. He makes par the hard way, chipping in with his third shot. They look at each other and without saying anything, Hans offers his hand to congratulate Roland who finishes with a score of three under par. Considering what his focus had been, Hans is pleased that he is only four over. Glad to be out of the sun, the two sit in the club house to await the others. Hans is relieved that Roland seems disinclined to engage in small talk, and he gets them both a beer from the cooler. They drink in silence.

The arrival of the other two golfers is announced by their loud voices long before they storm into the room.

"I don't care what you say. We have to get Jakow to show himself and explain what's going on. I mean, what is the point of these games we are playing? Isn't this supposed to be some kind of tournament?" Barrem shouts the last question and Ki rolls her eyes.

"If I told you a hundred times -, never mind. Hans, you tell this blockhead why we are here."

Careful now, Hans thinks, don't become part of this feud and don't trap yourself into a corner.

"Well, I thought we were here to play for a million bucks. Isn't that right, Roland?"

Roland looks at him as if to say 'thanks, man'.

"That's right, Hans, but it seems part of that has become teaching these things about being human, I think."

"We sure did do that today. I hope they were watching." Ki snorts, glaring at Barrem.

"Why don't we have a meeting tonight, after dinner, to decide what to do", Roland suggests and Barrem immediately objects.

"How are we going to do that without arousing suspicion?"

Roland gets up, goes to his bag and pulls out his putter.

"Everybody take their putter and we'll have a putting contest on the green down below."

They are holding their putters as if they are weapons when D4 rolls in. The stern voice finds a convenient victim.

"Hans?"

"D4, we decided we need practice with our putting. If it's ok with you, and with M, and with Arkyz of course, we would like to have a little competition with each other downstairs." Desperately he hopes that D4 will not offer to join them. The pause is almost untenable, and then,

"That seems like a reasonable thing to do. I will confirm with you later that it is permitted."

With that, D4 hustles them into the elevator and they descend. They exit, each one a putter firmly in hand, and are encouraged to head to their own quarters. As each enters their door, Hans catches a glimpse of the interiors and sees that all are painted a different hue, noting particularly that Barrem's is an almost harsh violet. He is about to query D4 about the interesting colour scheme, but the mobile has vanished. Strange, Hans thinks, that they are to eat by themselves; maybe they are not meant to socialize. He now has his doubts that they will get to do their subterfuge meeting. Just as well, he can't see the point of it, or that anything useful will emerge.

Inside his own quarters he opts for a shower and a change of clothes; the three rounds of golf have soaked him. The others probably also reek, not that Hans would care, being handicapped regarding his sense of smell, and he wonders if D4 would have noticed. Come to think of it, do those mobiles have a sense of smell? Do they even need it? And right on cue, there is a call from the front door.

"Hans?"

Alright then, he'll find out. Having shed his clothes for the shower, Hans feels reckless and comes out of his bedroom and displays his human nakedness.

"D4, can you tell that I stink?"

If taken aback, still an unlikely but increasingly possible reaction, D4 doesn't show it.

"D4 has sensors that recognize chemical compounds floating in the air, but they do not prompt any emotional reaction of the kind you are suggesting. Your odours do not force D4 to exit your presence."

Before Hans thinks to ask whether that should be part of being human, he recognizes how stupid a question that would be. After all, he himself is managing with a curtailed version of it, so why shouldn't they? Besides, so they might miss enjoying enticing aromas, but since they don't eat, or mate, that would be no loss, and being unable to have a gut-wrenching reaction to the stink of biological life is actually not a bad thing.

"You should shower and eat and then you and the others can have some putting practice. Your group will be allowed to be alone, but you should be careful how you speak. Everything you say will be recorded for ARKYZ to analyze."

"Will M be listening?"

"D4 does not know. D4 is unable to predict what his mind will do."

"So, when do we, when do I get to meet M?"

"It is possible that the answer is negative. We have no information that M has expressed a need to associate with humans again."

"Then why are we even here?"

"For us to learn from you and for you to enjoy golf."

"Why should anyone care if we enjoy ourselves or not?"

"Explain 'care'. No, don't bother. You are shivering, go rinse yourself."

As if recognizing that it could be inappropriate to be engaging a defenceless, naked human in a debate, D4 makes a quick departure. To save what little time he has left, Hans goes first to stab at the screen to have food waiting after his shower.

Barely dressed and just starting to eat, Hans sees the door open. Strange that it should open to someone other than D4 or himself, but it has and there stands Ki, putter in hand.

"Ready?"

"Not really," but he grabs his putter and follows her out onto the putting green where the others are already waiting. But they have no golf balls, no one having brought a ball to putt with! As if scripted, D4 arrives on the scene, equipped in apparent anticipation of the dilemma. From a little bag it is carrying with its claw appendage D4 spills some coloured balls on the green. The mobile next takes a putter and directs a distinctly different ball to each one, blue to Hans, yellow to Roland, red to Ki, and off-white to Barrem, matching them to the sometime glow of their assigned mobile.

Hans examines his to determine the brand and finds only a directional line. It appears to have the dimensions and weight of a regulation ball but everything else about it seems different. For one thing, the semi-gloss surface feels strange to the touch, smooth and velvety and also somehow adhesive, all at the same time, and it hints at translucence. Roland discovers something else while trying to keep the ball in the air with his putter. Everybody hears it, the little ping as the putter makes contact. Metallic balls! And then another marvel. The ball emits a momentary glow of yellow as it is struck. They all turn to D4 for an explanation.

"They were invented here, to add a new dimension to the game. They are experimental and you will be the first humans to play them. Do not lose the ball you just received for it has been personalised." Hans looks again, and sure enough, in tiny letters his name is there, and he appreciates that it is imprinted 'Hans Pedders'.

"You will be playing all your golf here with a basic version of this ball, one without the special sound and light effect, but with exactly the same playing characteristics. For your putting competition here you have one hour," and with that D4 leaves.

Sceptical about how the ball will react and feel in actual play, Roland punches it hard across the full width of the green and it careens off the far wall right back into the group.

"Sorry," is the insincere apology as he picks up the ball while trying to ignore the glare from Barrem. Why the hostility, since surely the two are meeting here for the first time? Perhaps, Hans surmises, there are past histories in play of which he of course would be totally unaware. So where does Ki fit into this? Coincidental to his thinking about her, Ki takes charge, conscious of the time constraint.

"If we all play until everybody holes out we could be here forever and run out of time, so -,"

"Speak for yourself," Barrem interrupts but Ki resolutely continues,

"What I would like to suggest is we all putt from the same spot to the same hole, and once you've taken three strokes and aren't down, you pick up. If no one wins a hole outright, we'll call that hole tied and go on to the next one."

"So, how do you win?" Hans asks.

"You win a hole with the fewest putts, of course, and ties don't count. Naturally, the overall winner is one winning the most holes, which amounts to the same thing as surviving the longest. The player with the worst score on a hole, which of course will be four, picks up and is out of that hole. And, if we do a lot of arguing, maybe 'they' will misunderstand what we are really talking about."

"That should be easy." Someone whispers for all to hear.

"Youngest to oldest," Barrem suggests, wanting the advantage of putting last.

Roland shrugs his shoulders and is the first to stroke a ball, running it by some four feet. Hans and Ki look at each other and he motions for her to go. She grins,

"Old-fashioned courtesy. I like that."

Her putt is short by about three feet and well off line. Hans also ends up short, and expecting to be out of this hole, makes way for Barrem. But, just in case, he searches in his pocket for a looney and marks his ball.

"Do you mind moving that? It's in my line."

"Oh. Okay.

Barrem makes a decent stroke and actually rims the cup, ending up a foot away. When nobody seems ready to concede the hole to him, Ki looks at Roland who nods.

"Yeah, that's good," she says to Barrem, and is sorry when Roland misses his putt. Now it's up to her. Ever so gently she curls it in, tying the hole with Barrem. Nobody wins this first one, or loses, Hans tying Roland with a four, so on to number two. That one and the next are ties as well and Hans waits for someone to finally relax their focus on the game and open up about what this 'meeting' is supposed to be about. Surprising Hans, who had expected Barrem to start sounding off, it is Roland that takes the rhetorical first step.

"There is more to this than us playing golf, right? What am I missing?"

"Look, we know you're trying to write a book about Jakow so figure it out for yourself," Barrem laughs.

"How do you know what my plans are, and even if that was the case, it would be none of your business."

"Enough. You sound like little boys. I can tell you my guess, considering that I helped to design these, what did you call them, Hans, mobiles? Back then we just called them robots. They seem to have become more than that, and that's what I think this is all about. Jakow is trying to make an artificial super brain that will also be creative like a human."

Barrem's look is definitely meant to put her in her place.

"Don't give yourself too much credit. Seems pretty simple to me. Jakow is playing weatherman. He wants to be able to control climate, or at least influence it enough that everybody in the world will have to come to him."

"How do you know that?" comes quietly from Hans.

"Well, everybody here can tell, can't they, all this hydrogen stuff?"

"Do you know about the experiments?" Hans persists, curious about what Barrem actually knows.

"What experiments are you talking about?" Roland looks at Hans, and then looks at Ki and Barrem in turn. Hans suddenly knows credible feigned ignorance is advised.

"Maybe Barrem can explain since what he started talking about obviously must involve some experiments with hydrogen. After all, what can you do with hydrogen except burn it? Come on, those of you who know some chemistry."

Hans hopes that is enough to deflect attention away from himself. He is certainly not going to talk about his experience that first night. Very likely, he realizes, they have not seen what he saw.

To his relief they resume arguing among themselves. That they ignore him Hans fails to recognize as the first sign of being ostracized. Inadvertently, observing them from outside the fray, he has a peculiar thought creeping into his mind, that those three have something in common that is a shade more than their exposure to Jakow somewhere in their past. Should he confide his misgivings to D4 when he gets the chance?

"Your turn. Where did you wander off to?" Ki fixes him with what is only a half smile.

"Oh, sorry. Lost my concentration." Hans takes his putter back and through and with a little ping and the barest flicker of blue light the ball rolls and rolls and drops!

"Lucky b - d. But I still get my turn." With that Barrem rams it past by ten feet. That was the tenth hole and now everyone has won a hole except for Roland who is showing signs of frustration. He turns on Hans, almost bellicose.

"What is this hydrogen stuff you and Barrem were on about?"

Seems like a good reporter he won't let a topic just disappear, but Hans is alert to it being more than that. He considers for a minute and then decides to try a favourite technique he had found useful as a teacher. Counter a question with a question. He succeeds in having Roland establish that he apparently has no grasp of chemistry. That gives Hans the opening he needs to stand the conversation on its head. If he doesn't understand the simplest of chemical reactions involving the combining of different molecules, there is no point in continuing the topic. The fact that Roland too readily concurs bothers Hans.

When Roland wins the eleventh hole, they are all tied coming to the last hole. It must be the pressure, precursor to what they will feel tomorrow, because everyone is tentative with their first putt, over-eager to clinch it with the second, going well past, and then missing the putt coming back. No one wins, and they console themselves that neither did they lose. They shake hands but not with Barrem who has hurried away. So, the meeting accomplished what? Ki lingers as if to talk with Hans, but seeing that Roland is cornering him, she leaves too. With Ki barely gone, Roland comes right into his face.

"Look, Hans, I know all about hydrogen and oxygen and water. I think you know more than you are letting on. The others and I have some connection to Jakow in the past, and you apparently have none. Why are you here? What gives?"

Hans decides to 'fess up', but only so much. Without explaining how it is that he is here in the first place, he narrates in exaggerated detail how he was confronted with those amazing fireworks in the sky. It has the desired effect; Roland seems satisfied, nodding his head as Hans is talking. They shake hands again, wishing each other a good night and good luck tomorrow.

Slowly Hans goes through his door, wondering about tomorrow, and not merely the golf. How can he force a meeting with Jakow and have him explain why he was lured here? After all, he, Hans, is the odd man out; he doesn't belong with these people.

He gulps the water from the glass still on the table from dinner. As if on cue, the lights start dimming and Hans lunges to find the bed before it gets to be pitch dark. The strange golf ball still in his hand has a warm feel to it. Well, of course, he has been clutching it all this time. His last thought before he drifts away is to wonder if their meeting will have consequences.

Thursday

The intense brightness of the wake-up lighting brings him to his feet and he runs from his bedroom to view the screen. Yes, this was to be expected. The breakfast menu has been pre-empted by a message from Arkyz. Hans assumes it is Arkyz and not Jakow, aka M?, because it is not a face he sees, rather a mesmerizing swirl of rainbow waves washing over the screen, pulsing in sync with the voice. The message is simple: the humans are to assemble in the theatre room immediately. D4 will come to escort them there. Hans barely has time to climb into his clothes, which he had shed sometime during the night, and wash the sleep out of his eyes, and he hears D4 at the door.

"Ready?"

This is not some casual stroll for Hans has to race-walk to catch up with D4 heading to where the others are waiting at the elevator. Is he the last because D4 has favoured him with an extra minute of sleep? No time to conjecture for they are shot up, past the computer floor and come to a stop in new territory. Again, the obligatory tunnel and air lock door and they are not ushered, but almost herded into a small, darkened room to a row of theatre style seats that face a large screen that is already pulsing with a swirl pattern.

"Welcome, humans. This is the entity ARKYZ speaking. ARKYZ is the master computer that guides all activity in the Three Towers, including the research that you are partnering with us. Our creator, M, has invited the four of you here to help our mobile supercomputers A6, B5, C5, and D4 learn about human intelligence. The purpose is to accelerate our digital intelligence to its maximum potential by observing how human curiosity promotes creativity and how that can be integrated with our exactitude. All your interactions with each other will be recorded and analyzed, including signs of human weakness. In return for the golf and the money that was promised, your utmost cooperation is advisable."

Hans grimaces and instantly worries about that look being recorded. The lecture wasn't exactly a plea for cooperation, was it? But why is it this Arkyz and not Jakow talking to us? And Hans is not the only one ready to fire questions at the screen. Yet, no one shouts out. Intimidated like schoolboys after a dressing down in a classroom setting, hands are raised for permission to speak. The screen does not recognize the gestures so the appeal is to D4 to allow the flood of questions to break the dam. Hans has a question and yet will not voice it because he is afraid of what the answer could be. He is convinced that even though the message emanates from a computer, it was pre-recorded, leaving the door open to the conjecture that M/Jakow no longer exists.

D4 holds up well under the barrage of questions that come tumbling after the first one gets acknowledged. Many of the questions circle around the same fear that is lingering in Hans' mind without daring to express it in plain language. Too, D4 would fare well as a politician Hans has to admit, noting how an entity incapable of lying is also not divulging what everybody is clamouring to hear.

The only meaningful information that D4 provides is regarding how the rest of the golf is going to be conducted. First off, after breakfast this morning, they will be allowed to take advantage of some coaching designed to help them for the final competition. Coaching? Yes, they will each be accompanied by a mobile to help them with club selection from all three tee locations on each of the twelve holes. Yes, everybody can hit three tee shots to every green. No, there won't be time for chipping and putting practice. The new balls? Yes, they will be practicing with the new balls because that is what they will be playing with. What if they don't like them? D4 is sure they will, but it will be the same for everyone. This is something M believes in, standardizing golf technology to level the playing field. Then, later in the afternoon, each of them will play nine holes, everyone hitting from the middle tees, and their score will be used for handicapping for tomorrow's final play. What style of competition will that be? It could be a format similar to their putting contest of last night, match play elimination.

They are certainly getting enough golf. Do you suppose it's meant to distract them from wondering what else is going on? Hans is not sure but pushes that aside because he is hungry and wants to see what his choices are this morning. They exit the room without talking among themselves, as if not having all their questions answered leaves them with a sense of futility. And of course, the reminder that everything is being tracked makes for best behaviour.

At his screen he calls up the menu and is disappointed that none of his favourites are listed. He's not ready to become adventurous and settles for multiple slices of toast and honey, something that strangely enough is made available, hoping that will sustain him, not sure if they'll get fed during the day. After all, the mobiles don't have hungry stomachs to remind them of mealtimes. Should he order a beer, even though it's not listed, and see how it will throw 'them' off? He still hasn't enquired of D4 where the food comes from. Maybe when the food arrives, he will ask. Too late, it arrives while he dawdles, and there is a beer! Had he by accident mouthed that out loud? Or? Better not be careless with his thoughts escaping his mouth is the conclusion and defiantly he has the beer for breakfast as well.

For the first time Hans is ahead of the schedule. Already outside his quarters with putter in hand, remembering that he will need it later in the day, he watches D4 round up the others. Off they all go, into the tunnel and the elevator and up to the club house level where the other three mobiles are waiting.

Rather than all eight crowding onto one tee, D4 splits them up and staggers the practice. He and Hans will go south and start on tee box seven, B5 and Ki are to go around to the back and start on ten, A6 and Barrem will begin on one, and C54 and Roland at hole four. Each human player is supplied with two additional balls, identical to their first one. To get the most benefit from the practice, they are to hit off all three tee locations for every hole. The 'coaches' are along to advise regarding the most appropriate club to use since distances are not marked. Everyone will do a complete circuit of all twelve holes because they might all be in play tomorrow.

Hans thinks this is going to be an excellent practice but, in the background, Barrem is heard muttering about 'too much work and no play'. Do you suppose he ever 'works' at his game? None of my business Hans concludes and he has to run to catch D4 rolling south. All the flags are centred in the greens, where they won't be for actual play, but the objective for today is to get a feel for what club to hit from all three tee locations. No one has been told what the pin positions will be, or which tee boxes will be in play in the final match.

Already on the first practice hole he recognizes how crucial club selection is going to be, the distance to the hole varying by a difference of as much as a hundred yards from the longest tee position to the shortest. For him then, club choice can go from a five iron all the way down to a nine or even the wedge. Whoever thought of this scheme had some insight into golf. Jakow? Most likely, after all, someone who designed this course had an imagination. He did design it, didn't he?

"D4, you told me that M designed this course, right?"

"Yes. This happened before D4 was made. M devised a program that created the map that was used for building the golf course."

"Why, what was so complicated?"

"According to the records, M wanted the twelve holes to fit around the mountain and every fairway to finish at the mountain with the green next to the rocks. He wanted to have a short walk from each green to the next tee box."

"Most regulation golf courses are eighteen holes and a lot of par three courses are only nine holes. Why did M make this one twelve?"

"The design with twelve fit very well around the mountain."

"It has also ended up being a large sundial. Do you know what that is?"

"D4 understands that back in human history it was a very ancient type of clock, a crude device for measuring time."

Hans is indulging his occasionally contemplative side today. Most times on a course he would focus on the golf, this practice situation promises a more relaxed time and he will let his mind wander.

"Was there some symbolic significance regarding time intended by that clock design?"

"I do not understand the question."

"Symbolism? Of course not, so forget I asked."

Hans can only guess at what else Jakow was thinking but one thing is apparent to him, that the geographic orientation is obviously intentional. With the club house entrance and the number twelve green aligning due north, the course would have the potential to coincide one's mood to the time of day. An early start in the day, for example, has one facing into the morning sun and playing the last holes in the shade on the west side; with a game late in the day, the sunset from the back could make for a melancholy finish. In his imagination, Hans is walking his way around the course in those scenarios and -,

"Hans, you are taking too long. We have limited time for practice."

Right. They are practicing, that is, he is being tutored by D4 about which irons to use from the different tees. And he is hitting shots like never before in his life. He's not that good, it must be these radical golf balls. It's the trajectory of every clean hit that he particularly appreciates; he can make the ball bite the green with almost each of his irons. And then there is the sound, and he wonders if the company that inherited the Ping brand, given the chance, should make this their official ball. Hans is fascinated by the variety of tones that different clubs generate. The feedback even tells him what part of the face makes contact. With practice and some experimenting, he manages to imitate a wind chime and also a gong, and once even the sharp explosion of a firecracker. What a symphony a driving range full of golfers could make, everyone hitting these balls! So excited is he by this technology that he almost neglects to ask how they are made. It is some comment from D4, about the similarity of the ball to itself that finally triggers the question.

"D4, do you know how these were made?"

"Yes."

"Well?"

"They are of the same material as this shell. It was the creative mind of M that recognized the potential for creating these golf balls, using the same materials and process similar to what was used for making the body of D4."

"It helped that he was a golfer. Okay, D4, here is something for your digital brain to calculate. If I had a large enough club and was as big as Paul Bunyan and used you as a ball, how far could I hit you?"

"Let me research Paul Bunyan. Alright, if you mean the mythical giant and allowing for the wind resistance my shape has to overcome, possibly six-point-seven miles. Hans, we are falling behind, you will have to practice faster."

Hans is enjoying this practice more than any of his best golf; the feedback is that rewarding, and he wonders if the others are enjoying it as much. Alright then, down to business. He must try to remember what iron he hits from where and then recognizes the futility of putting that burden on his memory. For one thing, the pin positions are not likely to be the same. Also, competition may dictate more or less aggression. Thinking about competing makes him wonder what kind of format he should mentally prepare himself for. He hints as much to D4.

"It would not be fair to give you that advantage."

"What if the others get to find out?"

"Not before tonight. You will all be informed at the same time."

As they are working their way around this sundial of a golf course, ever so often Hans looks way up. He knows that from up there every part of the course can be seen, but the lookout is not visible from here. How can that be? D4 explains that it is a matter of camouflaging. What about someone at the same altitude from that mountain over there, or in an airplane, would they not see light reflecting off the windows? No, those sight lines have been checked by means of their own drones.

"Drones? You have drones?"

"Yes."

"Why?"

"It is the most efficient logistics solution for our purpose, when the need arises to have physical contact with the outside world."

"Are you not self-sufficient?"

"We approach ninety eight percent self-reliance."

"Okay, give me an example of something that you cannot make yourself, that you have to get from out there."

"Eggs."

Hans starts laughing, trying to visualize a hen house in one of the towers.

"You mean you don't keep any chickens here?" and he looks at D4 and keeps chuckling.

"Hans, I do not understand. Are eggs something funny?"

"No, humans make things funny."

They are coming out of the shadows at the number two hole and D4 urges again to speed up. Quickly, three, four, five and six and into the club house. The others struggle in, everyone somewhat bedraggled from the hurried practice under a hot sun, the shadow of the small mountain giving minimal relief on only a few holes. The protest, especially from a certain party, could have been predicted when everyone is reminded that there is a round of golf still to be played, nine holes in the late afternoon sun.

"Why?"

D4 explains.

"You now know, after playing with each other, that you are not all at the same level of proficiency. Most golfers understand that handicaps are necessary to make an amateur golf competition fair. For you this means that this afternoon everybody will play another nine holes and your score will determine your handicap ranking for tomorrow's competition for a million dollars. For this round today you will all play the same nine holes, with everyone teeing off from the middle tee. The flag positions have not been changed from earlier today. If you remember what irons you used from that middle tee box, you can choose to carry fewer clubs. The order for teeing off will be the same as you used in your putting contest. It should stay the same for every hole. Play using one of your new golf balls. Please return the others."

A few minutes to sort his clubs, knowing they are playing from the middle tees, and Hans is ready. And eager. At last, it will seem like normal play, a foursome of golfers, and hopefully, some good-natured rivalry; he intends for no one to spoil his fun. Hans can't understand why Roland looks anxious, being such a good golfer. The grim set of Barrem's face is not unexpected, nor the carefree smile radiating from Ki.

They are offered to help themselves to a tray of sandwiches that appear from somewhere, but Hans declines, usually not playing well with food in his stomach. Ki indulges with enthusiasm and Hans attributes that to the kind of metabolism he associates with long distance runners. He is uncomfortable with that image of Ki, tall and smoothly running a marathon, because it destroys his notion of how Asian women should look.

Yes, he has accused himself of this many times: he puts people in boxes and then thinks of the simplest words to describe the contents. With the boxes clearly labeled, it makes it easy to find and rediscover his prejudices. Well, having admitted that much clears the way to allow himself the pleasure of profiling the other two as well and not feel particularly guilty. Of course, humans are unique and not as readily pigeon-holed compared to the monotonous similarity of the mechanical beings he has been exposed to. Still, Hans takes pride in his instincts, usually able to defend his first impressions.

Barrem has that just past middle age stoutness which furthers his swagger and bravado and helps him to project the confident presence of a chairman of the board entering a room. Roland is more difficult to label. Maybe how Cassius is described in Shakespeare's 'Julius Caesar', he has that 'lean and hungry' look. Of course, what Hans thinks of the personalities of the three competitors will have no bearing on how he intends to play against them, even if it is for a million bucks.

D4 is urging for them to get started because there is no way of predicting how long these four humans will take to play nine holes of competitive golf. To facilitate that they will finish near the clubhouse in daylight they are to start on number four and finish on twelve with the sun at their back.

As predetermined, the order of teeing off will be like in their putting competition, from youngest to oldest, with Arkyz having done the research. D4 herds them to the fourth tee and unnecessarily announces the age of each player, mortifying some. Roland, twenty eight years old, will go first. Next comes Hans, forty four years old.

"You are the same age as M," D4 states.

What is the point of revealing that inconsequential information? Hans wonders. Very quickly Ki steps forward as if to avoid her age being announced, but it is proclaimed for all to hear, forty five. Barrem scowls at publicly being declared the oldest at fifty nine, seemingly forgetting how he had insisted to be the last to putt in that competition last night. From this point on D4 will have no further participation other than as a rules official, but that the mobile is facilitating M and Arkyz to have ears and eyes Hans would gamble a dollar or two.

Everybody retreats to one side for Roland to tee it up. He eyes where the flag is, still centre of the green, picks a club and drops his lemon-coloured ball on the grass. One more look, a bit of a rushed swing but the ball ends on the green. Hans steps up but tees his blue ball on a short tee, just off the grass. To avoid being influenced in his choice, he had deliberately not looked to see what iron Roland was using. He also executes a nervous, abbreviated backswing but it too gets the ball to the green. Ki comes next, and without much posturing, gets into her swing and launches her red ball. It is nearly a hole-in-one, bouncing off the pin. Barrem appears to be furious, having to follow an act like that and he pays for it; his silver ball ends well short of the green. And so, they are off to a mostly good start, with Ki making her birdie, and Hans and Roland getting easy pars. Even Barrem manages a par after a fluky chip shot close.

After Hans tees off on five, mostly a mediocre effort, he stands back and gives Ki full attention. He had missed seeing her tee off on the first hole, catching sight only of the almost hole-in-one at the end. Now he notices that the swing is not the same; something has changed from when they played each other. Tighter and more aggressive, the long loop is gone. So, even though her 'pro', B5 does not play the game, it certainly knows something about golf and the golf swing. Whatever input B5 had with Ki, it has resulted in a great swing. Will it translate into good play?

When they reach the green Hans slaps himself on the side of the head. He had neglected to study the greens in that earlier practice round! Sure, they had not been chipping and putting, but he had walked on the greens and should have memorized the contours. Well, he'd better do it this time as preparation for tomorrow. The pin placement will change but the slopes and ridges won't move.

To some a welcome surprise, everybody gets a par on number five, and it has happened quietly, no one saying much. That changes on number six. There is movement as Roland is teeing off and he hits it fat. Roland turns around and scowls at Barrem, but he had not been the culprit. Obviously not a deliberate distraction, neither Hans or Ki feel an obligation to apologize and certainly not D4.

His turn to tee off, Hans is stuck between clubs. Besides being distracted by the rancour between Roland and Barrem, he has also forgotten the yardage for this hole and what club he had used in the practice. Alright then, a six iron and he knows it's wrong even before he sees it land well short, leaving him a long chip. Too bad they had not been allowed chipping practice because it could be several holes too late before he finds the 'feel'. Ki seems unaffected by the mood on the tee and strikes it smoothly, again threatening to get a birdie. Barrem can hardly wait to get his turn; he is boiling and needs to unleash some fury. A slash and the ball careens to the right into the rocks, only to ricochet and bounce next to the green.

When they approach their tee shots, Roland is away yet spins a superb pitch close. Hans is next and musters a chip that leaves a long putt. Barrem is close enough that he braves a putt from off the green that almost goes in on the way by. Hans misses his putt, Barrem and Roland make theirs and Ki misses. Get with it, Hans growls to himself, for now he is one stroke down to the rest of them. If this nine were a sudden death elimination, he would very nearly be out of the competition and gone.

"Stop daydreaming, Hans. It's your turn." Startled, he looks at Ki. Where did that impatience all of a sudden come from? And the prompt had not even been delivered with her usual smile.

"Sorry." And he doesn't smile either.

Good, let's get all frosty under this hot desert sun. He refocuses and remembers that this is that short hole where D4 had recommended a nine; no, he will kill a wedge. Miracle of miracles, he hits it pure and almost holes the shot. A tap in for sure. Ki had not upset Hans, but instead had riled herself up, and for no apparent reason. It shows in her swing, less certain than earlier. She flies her shot out into the desert. Roland is already on the green and Barrem manages to get on too.

It is Ki that has a challenge when they get close to the green: she is ill prepared to get the ball off the gravelly desert, B5 not having anticipated that for her. Foolishly she tries to chip with her wedge and sparks fly and the ball squirts, over the green and back onto gravel again. Hans sees that D4 wants to come to her rescue by the way the mobile is coming towards the group, at the last moment holding back to a neutral distance. Ki gets creative, or frustrated, and smashes at the ball with her putter. Again sparks fly, the ball rockets toward the green, gets caught up in the long grass of the fringe, and dribbles on to the putting surface. She two-putts from there. Hans makes his birdie and the other two par the hole.

There is less drama on the next hole, number seven, where they all end up with a bogey. How they do it though makes a statement about their personalities. At least, this is how Hans analyses it in retrospect, starting with himself. So proud after the last hole, he had ignored the suggestion from D4 of some several hours ago, to use a six iron. Puffed with confidence, a seven for sure would reach the flag. Or not. The shank left him out in the desert. Ki, still shaken by the result on four, was overly cautious and consequently short, but on fairway grass. Roland, amped up, hooked and overshot by a mile and would have to pitch back from the tee box of the next hole. It was Barrem that had provided the comic relief. Hitting what he thought was a great shot, high in the sky, heading straight for the flag, he had started forward, pumping his fist, urging the ball on, as if he had just hit a home run. The ball fell short of the green. He had turned around, ready for the expected ridicule, his face trying on a sheepish grin.

"That looked good for a long time," Roland had said, with not even a trace of sarcasm.

"Thanks."

The interlude had reminded them that they were excitable, living human beings, letting them forget for a moment that they were stranded on an island in the desert. A whispered conversation between Barrem and Ki earlier in the club house, hinting at perhaps 'getting out of here', had been cut short by A6 whispering 'Impossible'!, convincing Hans to have no illusion about leaving here on his own terms, that they will all have to finish Jakow's game, whatever it is.

When they had approached the green and gotten into a debate over who was furthest away, D4 had advised that they should play 'ready' golf, that whoever was ready to hit their shot should do so. Hans understood when he looked at the sky; they would have to hurry to finish before dark. Although the desert and the rocks were radiating heat, the sun was already feeling less intense. So, they all had rushed their shots, still managing to find the putting surface but then proceeding to two-putt.

For hole number nine they are somber, it finally sinking in that they are in a competition. It is a beguiling little hole, particularly with the flag right in the centre, yet here the contouring shows what tomorrow promises. The green slopes front to back and off to the right, with subtle hog backs in play. In spite of it being small, amazingly everybody finds the green and then the fun begins, with each revealing a little more about their personality.

Hans is away, is too aggressive and misses the comeback putt. In exasperation he looks skyward, as all golfers do when they think it is not their fault, trying to fix blame, and catches a glint of sunlight being reflected. It can't be the lookout, because supposedly so well camouflaged, but there it is for a moment and then the earth's rotation changes the angle.

Is Jakow up there, watching, or is he in some dark place, intent on a screen, trying to follow their game from D4's perspective? Or does he even care about these human guinea pigs? That's what they are, aren't they, they are the rats in the maze? No, of course not, he dismisses those misgivings. It is D4 and A6 and B5 and C5 that are on the firing line. They are the ones being evaluated, their 'brains' are being analyzed in terms of how well they are learning 'human'. That is the purpose of this whole project he reassures himself. Just hope that million dollars is real.

Roland is too aggressive with his putt as well, again with his next one, and even the two footer he tries to slam against the back of the cup. Now he freezes himself over the ball for a long time, and finally sneaks in the eight footer he had left himself, for a double bogey. He grabs his clubs and stalks off to wait on the next tee. Ki had remained somewhat aloof from the group since her blow up earlier but after her two putt for a par, she goes to join Roland and says something to him. Hans waits for Barrem to finish putting, also for a bogey. They walk together to the other two.

At number ten Roland and Hans hit reasonable shots, Roland ending up on the green and Hans in the fringe. Ki comes out of herself and hooks it, leaving her in the desert and Barrem flares right but doesn't reach the rocks. This time, having learned from her last time on desert gravel, Ki finds the green, using a running chip shot. Barrem reaches it with his second attempt. Hans stubs his shot in the long grass and two putts for a bogey. Roland easily pars. Still seemingly unnerved by their tee shots, Ki and Barrem both three putt, Ki for two over on the hole and Barrem for an ugly six.

Eleven is a similar length hole and the results mirror frantic efforts by Ki and Barrem to make up ground, because Ki is four over and Barrem five over par to this point, while Roland is three. Yet, so is Hans, which amazes him no end. Things go wrong on this hole and only Roland escapes with a shaky four, Ki and Hans and Barrem all having to admit to a five.

Hans approaches twelve, their last hole and the longest of them all, with the intention of playing it safe. Although Roland makes a brilliant tee shot, finding the green, Hans does not bite. Staying within himself, he gets it down the middle, a little short. Barrem and Ki, as if giving up, content themselves with relaxed swings and get good results, their shots coming close to where Hans ended up, on the fairway some fifty feet from the flag. Since the three are about the same distance from the hole, it is Barrem's idea to turn this into a chipping contest for closest to the pin. Of course, they want to place bets too, but nobody has anything meaningful in their pocket other than marker coins, and since Hans has only a cheap Canadian looney, that won't work.

"Chip for the balls!" Roland mocks them. Hans looks at D4 who is capable of calculating odds but does not fully understand what human betting is, and so consequently does not object, particularly since the sun is at the horizon. The three balls reflect what little light there is, as if glowing. Being away, Barrem goes first, then struts to mark his ball where it ends up some four feet from the flag, confident no one will better that. Ki looks grim as she poses over her ball and Hans can tell how badly she wants to beat that man. She overshoots the hole by five feet. She goes to her ball and stabs at it, poking it in Barrem's direction, conceding the ball to him. Hans grips and regrips his wedge and then changes his mind. Rather than trying a delicate flip, he opts to go with his eight and roll the ball to the hole.

He almost wins, his ball coming to rest where Barrem has marked his ball. But he does not lose either, it is such a near thing. As on other evenings when the sun disappears beyond the mountains, the darkness overwhelms suddenly and now the ball positions cannot be argued. Barrem insists he should win since he got there first. No way is he losing to that jackass thinks Hans to himself and out loud declares that he is not conceding. D4 seems unprepared to acknowledge the gambling instincts of humans so refuses to intervene. Roland comes up with a solution short of a replay tomorrow: he declares it a tie and tells Barrem to return the red ball to Ki. His protests are cut short by D4 calling all the putts conceded because of darkness and then rushing them inside.

But not soon enough. They are barely into the tunnel, not yet through the airlock, when all hell breaks loose. D4 is not quick enough to get them inside before lightning rips the sky and thunder shocks their ears.

Hans is reluctant to join the stampede, wanting to see more of the fireworks. He nearly eludes D4, who, with blue light working furiously, is trying to hurry everyone through the airlock. A stentorian,

"You also, Hans!" booms out and a startled Hans quickly complies. How had D4 learned that parade square sound?

There is no time to ponder as they are rushed into the elevator. Hans is vainly hoping that it will go upwards, up to the lookout where they could have a better view, but of course not. He feels the elevator descend towards the centre of the earth. Surely this wasn't a decision by D4, to deny them a view and explanation of what was going on out there. Jakow? Arkyz?

His suspicions are confirmed when the elevator stops prior to the main level. Through the airlock they are urged and lined up in front of the intimidating screen in the theatre room, not even given time to be seated before the swirling colours announce the virtual presence of Arkyz.

"You are fortunate to have escaped the terror in the sky. We are conducting an experiment that would have killed you. There is no need to explain, because none of you are intelligent enough to comprehend the technology. Much more important is that you concern yourself with your mission here, and that is, by playing golf you are helping our four super-intelligent beings A6 and B5 and C5 and D4 to learn about what it means to be human. You will continue to be your natural self and this entity, ARKYZ, will determine which of your positive attributes should be digitized. Any questions you have are to be directed to D4 who is authorized to answer everything that relates to golf."

And fade to black, and that is that, and I guess you too, D4, have been shown your place and given your marching orders. Hans tries not to let a fleeting smirk show at the irony of that, because now, more than ever, he is becoming perturbed by the question, 'Who is running this show, Arkyz by default?' Barrem and the others are also visibly agitated, not only by what happened topside, but more so by the tone of the message and what seemed like an implied threat coming from the screen. Knowing much more about Jakow than he does, they seem particularly incensed that it is this Arkyz that is speaking to them and not Jakow.

"Where is Jakow? I demand that I get to see Jakow, not this mysterious 'M'." Barrem is the first to make his voice heard over the muttering of the three.

"Well, you're not the only one, we all would!" Roland throws at him. Before D4 has time to exercise authority, Ki steps up to take charge of the rebellion.

"That is exactly right. There is something strange happening here, and we all have a right to see Daniel Jakow in person and be able to talk to him. We should stop cooperating and refuse to participate in anything more until he shows himself. What about you, Hans, are you with us?"

D4 moves as if to intercept the direction of the conversation, but too late for Hans' very emphatic,

"Yes, I definitely want to see this mysterious M, or Jakow or whoever, too. But aren't you forgetting about the million dollars? Let's not jeopardize that."

Barrem sticks his chin out.

"Who cares about the million? It would be nice but I'm not here for that, I just want to know what the hell is going on."

"Speak for yourself," mutters Roland, obviously thinking of the money.

"My lab could use it, but that is all beside the point right now. If Daniel is alive, and well -," but Ki is cut off by D4 whose band begins flashing with more intensity.

"Be careful about how you speak in this place. Everything you say is being recorded and will be analyzed. Be assured that M is aware and is taking notice of your concerns."

"D4, tell us straight up. You are supposed to be incapable of lying. Is M alive?" This is the reporter coming out in Roland.

"The last time I saw M he was alive," D4 replies.

"Was? When? How long ago?" Roland persists.

"In terms of your calculation of time?" parries D4.

"Oh, come on. You know what we mean. Quit beating around the bush!" comes from Barrem, but in a tone less abrasive than what his face shows. Hans doesn't need to interpret, for D4 seems to catch the gist of the colloquium.

"I saw M alive at sixteen point seven hours."

Some are slower in their calculations but eventually all get it figured out that D4 met with M early this morning. Hans finds it curious why that happened prior to their morning meeting where Arkyz, not M, spelled out to them their purpose for being here. So early, at about five this morning while I was still sleeping, D4 has seen Jakow alive, muses Hans, trying to sequence the timeline in his mind. Of the four mobiles then, D4 must be something special.

The oblique answer has the four humans crowding for something more specific. Instead, attempting to be jocular, D4 dismisses them with,

"That's all, folks!"

Hans, while admiring the attempt at referencing some ancient American tv comedy, can't let D4 withdraw that easily without a challenge.

"D4, we are asking for fairness. We have been invited here by M and before anything more is expected of us, it is only right that M allows us to see him and talk with him."

"Hans, D4 recognizes that all of you have concerns. I will convey those to M. For tonight I advise that you go to your rooms, have some food and get lots of rest. Tomorrow will be a busy day of golf for you."

Nothing further can be prompted out of the now taciturn D4, and with a lot of grumbling, the four of them head for the elevator and a night likely devoid of sleep.

Once through his door, Hans stops. So many thoughts are criss-crossing his mind that he is losing all focus; literally, he does not know what to do first. It's like getting home after a hard day and trying to decide between the couch or food or television or to go back out and on to the Legion, or heaven forbid, go for a walk. The choices here are fewer, not simpler. Hans supposes maybe food first, that he should eat even if his stomach is not growling like it was this afternoon. There, a decision made; he will call up the menu and see what's on offer. Who knows, perhaps an algorithm has already been devised to reflect his eating habits.

What's this? The screen stays blank. Attempted in a quiet, controlled voice, 'menu', 'food', 'eat', even 'please' produce no result. He thinks to play the screen like a drum, and even to shake his fist at it, but in all likelihood he is being monitored, so that could produce some unpleasant consequences. How about going to the next-door neighbour and asking if he could borrow a screen? What a stupid thought. Really, he hasn't seen enough of those three?

Well, if not that, then at least a drink. Sure, sparkling water. Oh, this is crazy, he should just go to bed as that 'thing' said. But this is much too early, isn't it? Hans is guessing at the time because the clock face too does not show on the screen. Feeling a wave of futility rearing up like a huge wave, ready to come crashing down over his mind, he retreats to the bedroom and throws himself on the bed, forced to close his eyes against the bright lights because there aren't any light switches to turn off.

It must be the weight of him on the bed that triggers the reaction, for the lights dim and darkness folds over him.

Friday

Hans is not waiting for any kind of light to announce the morning for he has been awake for hours. He gets out of bed, ready to feel his way around in the dark and his movements trigger the artificial daylight. Peering out from the bedroom, he sees the rest of the place is still dark. Okay, so no early breakfast. But why not try something? Leaving the bedroom door open, he can see his way to the study. When he gets there, the light behind him goes out. Something stronger than consternation escapes his mouth, 'Ach, Scheisse!' He feels his way past the table and chairs and finds the open door to the study; he guesses right and his outstretched hands touch the screen. It comes alive and he quickly wishes it back into blackness. The swirling colours announce the imminent presence of Arkyz. No, not you! By the time the voice erupts from the speakers, Hans is already crashing his way back to his bedroom, and like a scared little boy, he cowers under the blankets. Shivering, he refuses to answer the voice that follows him from the darkness, calling his name. The ensuing silence is almost as frightening. Can a computer feel snubbed? Tense with irrational fear, Hans waits for some unpredictable retribution by Arkyz.

As if out of a nightmare, Hans comes awake several hours later, having fallen asleep in spite of himself. This time his room is awash in light. Not daring to waste time looking for fresh clothes, he puts on what he must have taken off at some point in the night and thrown on the floor and rushes to the screen to order breakfast. He is ravenous after the involuntary fasting of yesterday. But the way the screen had reacted to him earlier, what will happen if he touches it now?

"Hans, your breakfast." He whirls around at his name being called, yet there is no one there, only his breakfast on the table, the same as he had ordered the previous morning. Is D4 looking after him? He attacks the food and gulps some coffee and then stumbles outside, expecting to see everyone impatiently waiting for him. No one is there. No one is waiting for him. Stunned, he just stands there, and then finally decides to return to the screen and plead his case.

"Hans, come with me," a voice behind him reaches out before he gets to the study. He knows that somehow, he knows that voice but in his bewildered state, cannot place it. Slowly, unwillingly, as if embarrassed to admit his ignorance, he turns around. D4, is that you? goes through his mind, but the red band that is flashing is all wrong. Hans stares with eyes as vacant as his brain that is searching for something it can't find. When the name finally comes to him, he wants to say it out loud, but his mouth is too dry. Speechless, he follows B5 to the elevator. Up they go. Still tongue-tied, he lets himself be eased through the door into the club house.

"They are waiting for you on the first tee."

A croak, supposedly 'thank you', is misunderstood and B5 rushes to get him a bottle of water. A swallow and Hans can speak.

"B5, thank you. I don't know why you helped me but thank you." He picks up his golf bag and once outside, attempts to sprint towards the figures silhouetted in the bright morning sunshine.

"You are late," growls a voice he recognizes.

"How did you find your way here by yourself?" is the reporter's query. Ki comes close and stares at him with hard eyes.

"You look like a ghost. Or maybe you saw a ghost?"

Before there are more verbal assaults against a defenceless Hans who is still trying to catch his breath, D4 comes to his rescue. Since he has missed their morning meeting with Arkyz, D4 starts to explain to him the format for the competition.

"Come on, let's play. He got to sleep in so make him figure it out as we go along." Still dazed, Hans thinks that came from Barrem, which doesn't matter since the others chime in too. He stands there, irresolute, until he sees everybody move to the back tee. Oh, so we're playing the course long today? Roland is getting set to tee off and Hans notices that Roland has only two clubs to play with, besides his putter. Hans wonders what he should use from here.

"Let's go, we're next. No, not here, down there. You and I get to play off the middle tees."

Ki walks to their designated tee-off area, and the others follow. She waits for Hans to tee off, but he fumbles with his irons, indecisive about what club to use. Losing patience, Ki steps up and gets ready to hit. As she is waggling, Roland, who has been eyeing Hans' bag, interrupts with,

"Hey, you've got too many clubs."

Ki glares at him and then they both glare at Hans.

"Oh, I'm sorry. What -?" Hans turns to D4, but the mobile is given no time to explain because Barrem starts officiating.

"For you and Ki only three clubs besides a putter. You have to ditch the rest."

Although his brain is still not into full gear, Hans refuses to cheat and sneak a look at what clubs Ki has chosen. For lack of inspiration, he digs into his memory of the good old days when what was available for the general public were golf sets with irons limited to odd numbered clubs. Yes, those are the clubs he will play with, the fog lifting a little as he starts to think about golf. The seven and nine iron were clubs he grew up with. For the third club he will retain the one still in his bag from yesterday, that battered six iron. Now filled with purpose, he rushes to the club house and dumps the extra clubs into a corner and then, with a lightened bag, runs back to where the others are impatiently waiting on the tee.

He is winded when he gets back, but in time to hear another reminder from Barrem of how the match is to be played: stroke play in a match of elimination where the loser of a hole drops out of the competition. Hans conjures the analogy of being chased by a wild animal; as long as someone is slower, in this case with a worse score on the hole, he will be safe.

While he was gone Ki had managed to refocus and hit a decent tee shot. Although Hans assumes he is next he has not made up his mind about which club to use; he can't remember the distance, so he finally pulls out the seven. His indecision causes muttering, and he can't understand why everybody is hanging around, waiting for him.

Later, at the second hole, he will figure out that the traditional protocol for teeing off has been modified. For the sake of safety, and also not to isolate anyone, they all gather with Roland when he plays off the back tee, then go with Ki and Hans to where they hit from the middle tee, and last, keep Barrem company when he tees off from the front.

Is this deliberate, intended to showcase human behaviour by way of encouraging camaraderie, or conversely, to demonstrate how forced proximity of divergent personalities can generate conflict? Hans senses antipathy from the other three so he will discipline himself to be content with his own space.

The self-imposed segregation should also, from a safe distance, let him view the spectacle of their three personalities clashing.

He soon finds plenty of cause to be aloof, for all the rushing around has prevented him from recognizing that their attitude towards him has changed. The frosty reception on the tee is merely the usual frustration of a group waiting for a tardy latecomer, right? Hans fails to see that they know it in their bones that he is receiving special treatment. This outlander, one who has no prior connection to M as they have, is being favoured and they will be alert to protect themselves against discrimination.

Hans tees up a ball out of his bag and makes a practice swing and Barrem loudly objects.

"Look, he gets to play his own ball! That's not fair!"

Belated, D4 comes to Hans and gives him some 'official' balls to play, blue in colour. He gets two of them and just like for the other competitors, they will have to last him for the round. Losing a hole outright will require giving a ball back; losing another hole means forfeiting the second ball, leaving the player with only his honour to continue play.

After all have teed off and they approach the first green, Hans sees how relocating the pin to the far back right has changed this into a hole that he does not recognize, even though he has played it at least three times. Two putting, perhaps even three putting might be the norm on the other greens too. As luck will have it, they all escape this one with bogeys.

Number two is mastered by Roland and Ki with pars and tied by Barrem and Hans at one over. Still no blood. It comes a close thing at three. Ki double bogeys but Barrem helps her out, also going two over on the hole by missing a two footer. Nobody is going to be conceding anything.

And then the carnage begins. Ki bogeys the shortish number four and has to surrender the first ball; the others luck out with pars. Barrem falls victim to the fifth, losing a shiny silver ball, the putter failing him again; this must have been especially galling after watching Roland fist pump his way to a par. That celebration costs Roland a ball on the very next hole, the short number six. Everybody else pars the hole. And all three are throwing murderous side glances at Hans who has managed only two pars but is also evading disaster with safe bogeys.

That message becomes very transparent when he sees their eyes gleam, trying to hide their Schadenfreude as he three putts unlucky seven for a double. Hans has to surrender a ball to D4 who is collecting the shiny baubles, the claw carrying a little pouch that by the final hole of play will be weighed down with seven balls.

So now they are all square, everybody down to one ball. The next loss of a hole will reduce that particular player to honour status, with elimination threatening after that. This awareness is reflected in the paucity of talk; conversation is curt between the three and Hans is ignored all together. He feels the weight of their disdain but sets his teeth to show a stoic face and under his breath he talks to himself. He will act confident and he will be confident and he will let his ball striking speak for him. If he plays within himself he is sure he stands a good chance, considering how emotions are creeping into the play of the others.

On nine, Barrem scores a double, leaving him with only his honour, at the thought of which a smirk pauses for a moment on the otherwise stoic face of Roland. Ki even comes over and nudges Hans with an elbow. She pays for it on ten where Barrem openly laughs in her face after she three putts for a double bogey, forcing her to join him in the limbo of suspense.

Is it possible, Hans wonders, that they are unaware of how this looks to an outsider? Should Arkyz still want D4 and the other mobiles to aspire to human mentality? And Jakow, aka M, must be watching and feeling embarrassed on behalf of the human race.

The eleventh is conquered by three of them with a par and birdied by Roland. Maybe that went to his head because he gets reckless on the next one, number twelve, suffers a double bogey and is knocked down to his honour.

Only Hans has a ball left and the others hate him for it, seemingly ready to rip it away from him. Feeling that animosity stresses Hans out as they come to the tee of number one, now the thirteenth hole of play. Furious for letting them get to him, his composure gives way and Hans slashes a screaming slice into the rocks. They can't find the ball, not that the others look very hard. D4 tries to locate it with its sensors but that proves futile too. Although they attempt to hide their glee, the others celebrate that Hans will be out of the game because he no longer has a ball to play with. Wrong, they are advised! He must be allowed to finish playing the hole, and for that D4 lends him his first ball. If he loses the hole, he gives back that ball and will then have only his honour to continue play. Of course, he loses the hole after the two stroke lost ball penalty is added but Barrem and Roland continue to snarl about 'favouritism'.

That backfires as Barrem loses with a double bogey on the very next hole which also takes him out of the competition. Roland follows with the same result on the fifteenth hole of play. They want to stomp out of there and then realize the stupidity of that. There is nowhere for them to go until D4 takes everybody back inside. From a reluctant distance they have to watch as the survivors grind it out.

After both bogeyed the fourteenth and fifteenth holes of the game, and followed with amazing pars on the sixteenth, Ki and Hans remain tied, each playing on their honour. On the tee box of number five, getting ready to play the seventeenth hole in the elimination match, they pause to look at each other, Ki no longer with hostility. They recognize each other for the competitors they are, silently lauding the tenacity displayed by the other. However, not the stress of the competition so much as the punitive emotional burden imposed by the others has drained Hans of energy. He is fading and this hole is too much for him; Ki overwhelms his double bogey with a bogey. She doesn't hesitate to shake his hand, a small consolation for losing a million bucks.

The light in the sky is shrinking towards the west, and even though the air has lost much of its heat, the humans can hardly wait to get inside. Several bottles of champagne have been cooling. Hans opens two. He pours Ki a glass from one and sprays her with the other bottle. D4 reacts to the gesture, likely considering it an illogical and possibly hostile action, but backs off, hearing how Ki is laughing even though tears are streaming from her eyes. Instead, D4 begins ushering everyone towards the elevator. Their descent halts at the main level, the floor of their living quarters. They will be given time to refresh and have some food. At a signal they are to reassemble on the putting green for the prize presentations. Yes, Ki is the big winner, but everyone is going to win something.

Hans is worn out, the emotional burden of having to endure more than two hours of hostility still weighing on him. He dutifully submits to a shower and puts on some fresh clothes yet forgoes ordering something to eat. Maybe later when his appetite returns. Something to drink? Let's test the screen. Well, it obliges! It displays a range of wines, but he is aching for something stronger. He wants to fortify himself before having to face the others again. Further searching gives no other results. Alright, he will order, ah, that one! A thought, though. Has Jakow made the towers off limits to strong liquor because of something in his past?

So, questions regarding the reality of that man crowd his brain again. Through much of the competition only the occasional stray thought about Jakow had flashed through his mind, always shoved underground by the challenge of the shot at hand. Now, in a few minutes there should be answers since it is logical to expect that M will be making the presentations.

A few notes of 'Reveille' sound, but not harshly, not meant to awake, rather as the signal that a ceremony is about to begin. Nothing to look forward to, though, Hans finding most ceremonies tedious. This one holds no promise to be inspiring. Four chairs are set in a semicircle, facing an ostentatiously large screen set in the middle of the putting green. Three mobiles pose to the right of the screen, and that must be D4 on the other side, judging from the bluish flicker of light, poised slightly ahead of what appears to be a speaker's lectern. Hans relaxes, for that is a good sign; only a human would need something like that for making a speech. But where is the speaker? Will he be making a dramatic entrance later?

The humans sit, Hans choosing an outside seat on the right, farthest from where the action might proceed, so that he can stay out of having to mix with the others. D4 moves ever so slightly as if to speak but is pre-empted by the screen. The familiar swirl of colours, more pronounced if possible, creates a preliminary silence for the voice that comes booming from the screen. The mobiles don't have eardrums, but a screeching audio feedback causes Arkyz to moderate the volume. For it is Arkyz that is speaking and not M.

"Congratulations to Ki for winning the tournament, and to you other competitors for trying so hard. You gave us the opportunity to acquire large data about human behaviour that may be of use for our research. All of you are eligible for rewards. Tomorrow you will say goodbye."

The screen turns black, only a tiny dot of light lingering for a long time, as if Arkyz is contemplating coming back and saying more. That's making it sound like we're being released from prison. Had the possibility existed that it could be otherwise, our stay extended against our will? It becomes a worrisome thought that lumbers through Hans' mind and it unsettles him enough to lose contact with the present moment. Because of that he misses the first remarks by D4, but then catches the gist of it, that everyone will have an opportunity to say a few words.

Great, obviously they have researched how humans conduct these things and now will follow that protocol. B5 speaks, particularly directing compliments to Ki, C5 follows and lauds Roland for taking such interest in their technology. Other than acknowledging Barrem, A6 has little to say. D4 seems to have gained some understanding of Hans' personality and saves him from embarrassment by only saying thank you to him yet with an emphasis that makes him feel special.

And then the purpose of the lectern becomes obvious. The humans too are expected to say a few words, and like many amateur speakers, will appreciate to have something to hide behind, or at least lean on, when they address their fellow man. Fortuitously, it will be an even more immense aid when speaking to the mobiles and yes, Arkyz too, these beings with superior intelligence. Of course, every contestant will say thank you for whatever they win, and then? Gratitude for the hospitality of their hosts? Thank you to the invisible M for staging this event? Thanks to the other humans for letting them become friends?

As luck will have it, the order of the presentations, from also-ran to survivor, buys Hans a little time; he will be one of the last to have to face the ordeal. Barrem is the first to be called up to the front and he ungraciously takes the envelope with his name on it. He tears it open, ready to mouth a shallow thanks but almost swallows his tongue. He comes back to the others wildly waving a certificate in front of their eyes. It's a one year membership to a rather exclusive country club that has repeatedly turned down his applications. Not for long is Roland left to wonder what could top that. He whoops and hollers, displaying another dimension of human behaviour to the mobiles. His envelope reveals a document, a contract actually, that guarantees sponsorship for one full season on the Korn Ferry tour. If he should end the year in the top twenty in tournament winnings, that would give him a chance at the full-fledged professional tour. He too is almost speechless, managing some stumbling words of gratitude to almost everybody in the world. Then Ki is called. Hans steps forward as if there had been a mistake, but clearly,

"Ki Eun Choi, come up to get your prize." She waves the envelope over her head, not opening it immediately; everyone knows what it should contain. With hands that shake, Ki opens it ever so slowly, milking the moment for all its drama. Pointing with her finger at the number on the cheque, she begins crying before she gets to the last zero.

"Thank you. Thank you, Daniel," is all she can manage.

The three winners huddle to bask in mutual admiration of their prizes and forget about Hans who sits wondering why he has been overlooked. After the initial excitement ebbs, they at last pause to stare at him. The awkward silence stretches long enough that it threatens to send Hans running to his room. Just in time, D4 calls out,

"Hans, we have something for you as well. You get to choose your prize. Behind one of those three doors is a major consolation prize." Projecting a beam of light, D4 points across the green to three doors that are identified by ribbons, doors to suits apparently not occupied.

"You may only choose one door, but each one hides something you are sure to value. After you open the door of your choice, you are to go inside and close the door. When you come back out, do not tell anyone what you won, or you could leave here with nothing. We do not believe in it, but as you would say, 'good luck'."

Hans' initial reaction is to go to the lectern and say something. Isn't that what you're supposed to do? But what would he say? Instead, he stares at the doors. Which one? Is this the lion or the lady kind of thing? Getting ready to putt, if unable to get a good read of the line, go right at the hole. Not the left door or the right, but straight to the middle one he decides. Without looking at Barrem or Ki or Roland, not knowing if he will ever see them again, he walks to that middle door, opens it and closes it behind him.

"It's good to meet you in person, Hans," the man waiting in a chair behind the table says to him. When it becomes apparent that in his shocked state

Hans finds no words to even express surprise, the man continues,

"You and I are going to talk, not here but out on the golf course. In the morning be at your door at eight. Have a good night's sleep." With that Jakow indicates the door.

When Hans stumbles back out, the others, even the mobiles, are still on the green in their positions of a few moments ago. Barrem and Roland start to approach, searching his face but Hans doesn't oblige.

He turns and rushes straight for his door, only catching his breath when safely inside. What kind of prize is that? He should have chosen another door.

Saturday

At eight in the morning Hans is ready and waits inside his door. After what happened yesterday, he will not stand outside and risk presenting himself to those other three as an easy target. The night had been tumultuous with him nearly seasick from the tossing and turning, and he was glad to be out of bed with his feet on solid ground. He doesn't remember sleeping but probably did because the night is gone, and he is waiting to talk with a man who fills him with apprehension.

At last, his impatient requests had brought some results. Or is it merely the case that his time on the schedule has finally arrived? At any rate, he is getting to meet 'the man'. To his detriment, the waiting has allowed his mind to generate anxiety, fear that his brain will fail him and leave him incoherent in the presence of the genius. His irrational masochism is interrupted by a voice outside.

"Ready?"

Hans steps through the door and sees a smiling face framing intense eyes that stare at him, studying his face. A hand is extended in greeting.

"You are David Johan Pedders. I understand you like to be called Hans. My name is Daniel Noah Jakow, and I am the one that invited you here. Please call me Daniel. I am not 'M' to you, or Mr. Jakow, and I hate to be called 'Dan', or worse, 'Danny'."

Hans automatically puts out his hand. Even though the directness should have been expected, it catches him flatfooted. That the man sports casual golfing attire and that his eyes start to smile helps Hans relax enough for a safe, trite response.

"It, uh, it's a real pleasure to finally meet you. I have heard so much about you."

"Not all bad, I hope. At any rate, let's get out on the course and become better acquainted."

Nothing more is said by either on the way up to the club house. As they walk to the elevator, Hans takes furtive glances, correcting an earlier image he had formed in his mind. The man is not an ogre, a mad genius with wild hair and crazy eyes. He looks pretty normal, appears to be about his age, with a body much more athletic than he will ever achieve, and he is surprisingly well tanned for someone living underground. In the club house Jakow picks up a carry bag with only a few clubs in it and waits while Hans finds the canvas bag with his clubs.

As they walk out Jakow tells him that they will be playing from the tips, which immediately intimidates Hans and he lets it show. He is told not to worry since the pin placements are still the same as they were during their competition yesterday. That is not at all reassuring, for Hans remembers how tricky those had been. Before they are at the first tee box his hands are already clammy.

"Keep going. We are starting on number two."

What complication is this? Hans wonders. Yet another surprise comes when Jakow tees it up first. The ball is shiny black but that is not what catches Hans off guard. It is the fact that, even though he is the host, Jakow neglects the niceties of golf etiquette on their very first hole.

"Hans, don't look at me like that. You are going to get the honour many times today," and with that Jakow dribbles a sculled tee shot into the desert. Hans stands, as with a hand caught in the cookie jar and a red tide creeps up to his ears. He continues to stand awkwardly, uncertain what to do next.

"Oh, I am sorry, you need a ball too." Hans is tossed a shiny, pearl white ball. Pulling himself together, he manages a reasonable shot down the middle, although short of the green.

"Good shot, Hans. Too good."

"I'm sorry Mr. Jakow. Honestly. I am not trying to show you up."

Jakow looks at Hans with a stony face and gives a curt laugh.

"Hans, the only time you will beat me is when I let you. Today we are going to play poorly and slowly, so that we have lots of time to talk," and he looks back towards the entrance. Hans stares at him, not comprehending, so Jakow has to spell it out.

"No one, I should probably say 'nothing', can hear us or record us talking way out here. The golf course is a private, safe zone if they are not around."

"Are you in danger? Are the mobiles, or what you call them,- , is Arkyz-?"

"No, Hans, I have nothing to fear."

Hans cannot detect any hint of bravado in how that was said. In the same level tone, Jakow continues.

"I am safe and you are too. We are not hiding per se, merely gaining privacy in order to discuss topics that my creations may not be ready to confront. Out here we can talk freely without having everything analyzed. To facilitate our conversation, I will call you Hans and I am not Mr. Jakow. At least not here on the course; elsewhere, in front of others, fine, or even M, but here I am Daniel."

Hans does not reply, uncomfortable at becoming too familiar on such short notice and address a man like this by his first name. Besides, in anticipation of this long-delayed encounter, he has had time to prime himself to be extra suspicious. Things have been coming at him too fast and he doesn't want to be set up again like he was for this 'golf event'.

Jakow doesn't debate long about what club to use when they come to his ball lying on the desert gravel; he tries to lob it back onto green grass with a wedge. Sparks fly and the ball squirts sideways, further into the desert.

"We'll forget that one. There are snakes in all that sagebrush and cactus." Jakow throws down another black ball, this time on the fairway, and chips it close to Hans' white ball.

"Hans, you may construe that I am being too forward, getting personal too soon. So, let's back up and get better acquainted first. You start by telling me what you know about me. I am sure RT and Ki and Roland were eager to brag about their connections to me. Needless to say, I may edit that narrative as we go along. Then I will take my turn and tell you about yourself. Fair?"

What a strange way of getting to know each other, yet what choice does he have? Hans takes only a moment to decide that the easiest way to start this off is to begin at the beginning, by relating the story of Jakow's grandfather, as he had heard it from Roland. He has him coming from Russia to Germany to England and finally to New York. He is about to get to the next generation when Jakow interrupts,

"Did you know that my grandfather was a communist? He left Russia before the Bolsheviks won, but later on, once in Germany, from a distance he admired what the Revolution was trying to accomplish. Ironically, in Nazi Germany he was persecuted first of all because he was a Communist, not because he was a Jew."

Hans did not know that and yes, he will readily admit that there is likely much more he doesn't know about Daniel's grandfather.

"Yes, Hans, it's the guts of the story that you have to feel. The name changes, Hans, the different times he changes his name to make his way in the world. He comes into Germany as Abram Yakowsky and leaves as one Abraham Jakau. In America, once the war starts, his name becomes Abe Jakow."

"I didn't know that about your name."

As if not interrupted, Jakow continues,

"Can you see the desire in the eyes of my grandfather as he claws his way to America? Can you feel his loneliness in New York as he falls in love with the black girl that shows him kindness? And then his own son, my father, abandons him, resenting him for the mixed-race heritage that will forever mark him as a target. I got to know my grandfather, but only after the fact. My father had to die so that I could learn about my grandfather. There were letters that my grandfather had written, letters to the old world, letters that he never mailed because he had no one to send them to. They told his story and I learned to love that old man. After my father died, I found those letters hidden away among his papers."

Jakow hits a lob shot that sits spinning where it lands, precisely aimed to the far corner of the green, a few miles from the pin. Hans follows but is not as successful; his ball ends up rolling rather close to the hole; he is sure he can miss that putt. Hans wonders whether he should venture on in the narrative, to touch on nine-eleven and the painful subject of his father's death. Cowardly he evades that minefield but then blunders into another with a question pulled out of the blue.

"Mr., I mean Daniel, is that why you decided to become rich and famous, because of those letters?"

"Playing the psychologist, are you? How could that not be a motivating factor? Hugely more important was the ugly backlash after nine-eleven. My appearance led people to confuse me for an Arab, a Muslim, so ironic since my grandfather was Jewish. My foreign sounding name didn't help. I had started at university when I was seventeen, and everything was fine at first. Suddenly, overnight I became a terrorist and life became hell. I was desperate and computers came to be my salvation. Anyway, tell me what you learned about me from the line that R.T. gave you."

He didn't outright say 'lies' so there must be some truth to the claims by Barrem, but Hans realizes he should be circumspect. Jakow strikes him as very much a self-made man that could be reluctant to share credit, especially with someone like Barrem.

"I came to understand, from what Barrem told me, that you had insufficient funds to continue university, because your father had left you very little."

Hans hopes the negative reference to his dead father doesn't upset Daniel. If it had, it is ignored because Jakow motions for him to hit the ball. They are standing on the fourth tee, talking, seemingly forgetting that they are supposed to be playing golf.

"That is somewhat true, but as I said earlier, the main factor was being ostracized by most of my classmates. Did R.T. also claim credit for launching my financial career?"

"Ah, yes he did."

"Was he bragging about introducing me to the stock market, that he taught me how to pick winners?"

"Well, he did say that he hired you because of your computer skills and taught you how the business world operated. He said you then went on your own and took a lot of risks in the stock market."

"Fair enough. Did he elaborate about how before that there was the Y2K scare and then the dot-com bubble happened and then Google and Facebook came on the scene? He had no guts, but I was desperate and I took risks, but not foolishly. Ki had introduced me to computers, and I immediately recognized the potential. It wasn't long before I developed simple logarithms and then more and more sophisticated algorithms that helped calculate odds. I started gambling at the biggest casino on earth, that racket they call the stock market."

"Barrem said you also got into the mortgage racket and got hurt by the two thousand and eight financial meltdown."

"Hans, he would know because it almost killed him. I had some hedges in place and almost broke even, and then found ways to take advantage of the huge amounts of money that were thrown around afterwards."

"That was not enough to make you a rich man, though. Apparently, you did some more gambling, but Barrem was no longer involved and knew very little about it."

"So very true. I had left him behind because he had no imagination and no feel for how technology was evolving. I borrowed heavily against the assets that had accumulated in my tech stock portfolios and poured huge money into shale exploration. Mostly I invested in building supercomputers. Sure, there was gambling with crypto, but then, I had all that computer power."

"And Barrem said something about Ukraine, that you took advantage of what happened after the war."

"Of course, he would bring up Ukraine, but the only people I took advantage of were some of the bad guys. The war changed the world and certain corporations that had made huge, often illicit, profits were in trouble. I had a lot of leverage and managed to add to my assets."

Hans realizes he is away, facing a very long putt on what is the eighth green. He stabs at the ball with his putter, and horrors, it falls into the hole. That makes broaching the next topic much more challenging. However, since this conversation has taken on such an informal, actually downright personal tone, he will dare to poke the bear.

"According to Roland, you proceeded to flaunt your wealth, enjoying a very lavish lifestyle, and then you disappeared from public view and have not been seen since."

There is a very long pause. Jakow makes his putt and they go to the number nine tee box. This time Jakow swings smoothly but with power, sending the ball to land within five feet of the pin. He turns to Hans, a strained look on his face.

"That topic had to surface eventually, didn't it? To this day I regret that foolishness. Oh, yes, I was going to show the world, I was going to show New York that this grandson of a Russian Jew had made it big time, that he was not ashamed of his black grandmother but was grateful for inheriting her genetic energy."

Hans hits his tee ball and is relieved that he fails miserably to emulate the shot by Jakow. They walk in silence, one of them reliving a period he'd rather forget? Thinking to divert, Hans readies to start another topic, but Jakow is not dissuaded from wallowing.

"Hans, for a few years, every night I thought about suicide, drinking myself to sleep. I had married the most beautiful, the most loving woman in the world. She had been kind to me and rescued me from that crazy lifestyle, and then the epidemic kills her. I wanted away from the world but first I went to Ukraine and visited the little village where my grandfather had been a boy, to gain some perspective about life. I was trapped by the Russian invasion and saw that village destroyed. After I escaped alongside the millions of refugees, I wanted revenge against the whole human race."

Hans' brain races to sort through what he is hearing. It confuses him how Jakow talks so freely about his depression. What could it imply for Jakow to speak to him, Hans, just newly an acquaintance, with such candor? Does the intimation of trust mean that Jakow has him figured out? The 'revenge' Jakow refers to will come to bother him too, but later.

Hans comes back to the immediate present with a start for there is a putt waiting to be missed. He has to concentrate for this not to appear deliberate. Hans adroitly maneuvers the putt so that it misses the way he had seen it demonstrated on the putting green. Thinking of that, could D4 have played that putting game with Jakow as well?

However, now to refocus on his main objective. Perhaps he can shift the emphasis to Jakow's more recent history in hopes of getting answers to some other questions nagging at him.

"Ki told me that she helped develop some of the computer technology that allowed for the creation of the AI and AC you are experimenting with. Does that mean that you reconnected with her after your university days?"

"There was nothing ever between us, if that's what she hinted at. Furthermore, her contribution to the program here consisted in carrying out the tasks that were assigned to her lab. She never created anything, she was only ever producing work that had been farmed out to her."

Something in Jakow's tone has hardened and Hans wisely pauses the inquisition to concentrate on making horrendous golf shots. The morning sun was at their back when they played number six, but now they are hitting into the shadow cast by the mountain as they tee off on nine. Hans guesses they will quit after number ten.

"I assume we are nearly done this round, Daniel but there are still many questions that are looking for answers. It is understandable, with their early connection to you, why the others are here, but why me? What logic prompted you to entice me to come?"

"A good observation, Hans, and you have the right to ask. Before I give a full answer to that we should finish what we started out to do, getting to know each other. We talked about me, we still have to discuss you. Talking about you will very much help to answer that specific question. Let's do that when we play another nine. Most days I like to play at least two rounds. After we take a break, of course."

Hans readily concedes to that. They putt out on number ten and arrive at the club house after walking the last two holes without playing them, and strangely enough, without talking. Maybe it's because Hans is lost in thought, replaying what has been his weirdest nine holes ever.

He has to admit that he quite enjoyed this casual style of golf, with all the time-outs for talking. It is so unlike his usual routine of getting his head into the game and focusing strictly on making shots. When he leaves here, he might just be more amenable to social golf; it could prove to be relaxing. Hans, losing himself in his ill-timed post analysis, misses what Jakow was saying, and admits,

"I'm sorry, I was somewhere else."

"I said, 'Do you want to stay here with me and have a refreshment and something to eat, or go to your room and take your break there?'"

Hans is immediately conscious of how delicate this situation has become. If he tells Jakow that he would rather go down, that could be considered a rebuff, but on the other hand, by staying he might be imposing his company on someone who is used to taking meals by himself. In desperation he lobs it back to his host.

"What would you rather have me do?"

"Hans, you are astute. Go on, head down to where you can be by yourself to relax and get your questions all in a row. I don't mind in the least. Just talk nice to the doors and the elevator and they will obey you."

Hans is dubious about managing on his own in this strange place, but knows he set the stage and now has to put on the brave act. After a sideways glance at Jakow he walks to the elevator, and appearing to have anticipated him, it opens. Somewhat tentatively he tells it 'Main Floor'. It closes, descends, slows to a stop, and opens. There is the putting green. It all happens too quickly for Hans to finish formulating a wild idea. Would the elevator have taken him elsewhere if he had dared to ask, perhaps the computer centre? Or, maybe even to the lookout? A more troubling thought pushes that aside. Jakow is testing him!

Well, he'll scrub that thought away; once through his door he follows a routine that is becoming a habit, taking a shower and changing his clothes, unaware that he is performing a routine for stress relief. He is not hungry so foregoes ordering food. Restless, he paces and decides to do it on the putting green, even though more walking awaits him out on the golf course.

Subconsciously drawn to it, he ends up in front of the door he chose to enter last night. What would happen if he tries to open it now? Should he even be thinking about testing the other two doors?

And then a memory comes back from when they had their 'putting meeting'. Through the open door to Ki's place, and to Roland's, he had caught sight that each of their interiors were painted in distinctly different colours and neither matched his.

Something is trying to come to the front of his mind, but he can't make it out. As if to give the strange feeling more space, he steps back from the doors, all the way to the other side of the putting green and views all seven in one sweep of his eyes. Here it comes, the colours! The rooms in his suite are painted green and it has a small green 'W' on the outside of the door, the next one to the right he had not seen open, but next to it was Ki's and when her door was open, he had seen that it was painted pink. He definitely remembers the colour of Roland's who had dawdled before closing the door. It was almost purple with a purple 'S' on the door. And then there are the three doors to the left of his. They were the ones he had to choose from. He will always remember the door with the orange 'M' on it, behind which were rooms in an orange so in your face that he almost missed seeing the man that was waiting for him. It is so obvious now, the seven rooms are painted in rainbow colours, and left to right, naturally sequenced. But what is the point? Well, just one more question to ask of this unpredictable genius. And he is that, isn't he, some kind of genius and in a frightening way, unpredictable?

Hans feels reluctance creeping into his bones. There are so many questions he wants answers to yet with that comes the risk of having his mind totally overwhelmed. Perhaps his brain is as unprepared for this overload of information as his introverted personality is for confronting that alpha type waiting for him. He is beginning to feel trapped. Stepping into an elevator without push buttons doesn't help, especially since elevators give him claustrophobia. Without waiting for commands from him, the elevator deposits him where else but at the clubhouse level. Sure enough, when he steps through the door, Jakow is waiting for him.

"Did you get a chance to relax?

"Sure did." Hans lies and he knows that Jakow knows he is lying.

"Well, let's play some more golf but this time we will try something different. We each choose only one club and use it for everything, even for putting, and we play from the short tees."

Hans steps to his bag at the stand, his mind racing. What devious strategy is this? He then remembers their earlier game, how they were playing for the fun of it, prolonging the game to allow for more than casual conversation. Hans chooses his seven iron and wonders at the nine that Jakow is taking; some of the holes are pretty long for a nine iron. Again, they walk past the first hole to start off on the second tee box.

"Hans, you tee off first. I will try to take the honour away from you." Hans is not sure how this is meant. Should he try to do well or chunk it around the course? He hits his white ball reasonably well, somewhere short of the green and steps back. Not bad for a seven iron. Then, smooth as proverbial silk, and the black ball explodes off the club face. There is no hint of apology on the face of Jakow as both watch the ball almost hole out, landing two feet past the pin.

"That was almost a hole-in-one!" Hans exclaims.

"Well, I didn't get lucky."

"After seeing that shot, I assume you've been lucky a few times. I won't even try guessing the number."

"Actually, they are not a big deal. As a matter of fact, I've stopped counting. You?"

"Close but not a single one yet, so far."

Grimly Hans marches to where his ball lies and punches it towards the green, fortunately getting it somewhere near the pin. He has only ten feet left to the hole, but it takes him three attempts to learn how to putt with a seven iron. Jakow makes his two. A sudden resentment wells up in Hans and he feels like taking his club and 'going home'. Of course, he can't because he is supposed to be the topic of conversation during this strange game.

"Hans, let's resume where we left off earlier. It is my turn now and I will tell you about yourself. You pride yourself for being able to hide so well, living a quiet life and minding your own business. It's a delusion, Hans. That was never really possible for you or your father. Even your grandfather, who died some ten years ago, could not escape being a victim of this crazy new age of ours. His history, which started in Russia like my grandfather's, is public knowledge to people who know how to use the internet. He was born in nineteen thirty eight in a small village in Ukraine to German parents and lost his father because of Stalin. That grandfather of yours survived the war in Europe and came to your country as a little boy. He grew up and married and had children. Your father was one of them and he married a good woman. That man, your father, had a good career in the business world and is now retiring. He gave you the benefit of a university education which you almost squandered because you didn't know what you wanted to be. The world was changing so fast, and you couldn't make up your mind. You got very lucky, for in spite of all that, a woman you didn't deserve found you and married you. Your parents are still together, and amazingly, you are not divorced yet either, something unusual for this day and age."

They have not moved from the green because Hans is rooted in place. He hasn't even retrieved his golf ball from the cup.

"Hans, how am I doing so far?"

He is hesitant with his reply because he is debating whether to be as familiar as yesterday and call him Daniel or become defensive and address him as Mr. Jakow. However, it is not the intrusion into his life that has him intimidated. He is still marveling at that golf shot.

"Daniel, you are toying with me."

"Hans, all that information about you and your family is out there and anyone with some skills and a good computer can access it. I admit I invaded your private life, but I have my reasons."

"You probably do and right now I don't care. It's that golf shot, Daniel. Your golf swing."

"Why, what's wrong with it?" Jakow stares at Hans who starts to splutter. Jakow laughs and belatedly Hans joins in.

"I probably play twenty seven holes every day and I have the best golf mentor in the world. D4 knows every inch of my swing and is unrelenting in the analysis. Fortunately for D4, I take criticism well."

"Is there hope for me?"

"What are we talking about, your golf or your destiny?"

And now Hans doesn't laugh and Jakow's face becomes impassive.

"Never mind. Let's get back to your story. As I said, you are still married to the same woman, but you couldn't have children. That is sad but perhaps also fortunate. Who in their right mind would want to bring children into this chaotic world?"

Hans catches it, the hint of bitterness. Because he lost the chance to have family and now he is mad at the world?

"You got a degree and became a teacher. Why did you give that up? What I got from different sources, you were a good teacher. Why then become a salesman, especially for an industrial supplier?"

Alright, this is getting personal and close to home. He has no defence, since many times he has had this argument too, but with himself where nobody could hear it.

"I don't have an answer that will satisfy you, because I'm still not sure myself. Interacting with curious minds was a challenge and I loved it, but things happen, politics in the system. Daniel, I get so frustrated by the short-sighted stupidity that is so inherent in a system where there are multiple layers of management."

"Why do you think I'm working to facilitate MI, hoping to bring logic into human decision making? At least that is what some of my clients expect to achieve with the super computers we are designing."

"Daniel, you said 'we'. Are you hiding people who work for you in another section of these towers, some place where I can't see them?"

"You don't see them because they don't exist. I only have computers and robots working at creating other computers. Even outside these towers, the projects that are contracted out are rarely touched by humans."

"Daniel, it's as if you are dissociating from the human race."

"You are beginning to understand me."

"Actually, no. I feel like I am standing where the wind is coming at me from all directions. And just as a reminder, you have me totally at a loss for why I am here. I think I understand why the other three were invited, with their previous connection to you but what is my purpose? How are you intending to use me?"

"Hans, Hans. You are making it sound so negative. You are not going to be 'used'. There are good reasons for you being here and I intend to explain it eventually, but for now be patient with me and just hang on a little longer. You need to have a full appreciation of what is happening, a broad perspective, before I tell you why I need you."

"Well, you know, for someone who seems to hate humanity so much, it's absolutely amazing the tolerance you exhibit for somebody as impatient as me. So, okay I'll wait."

Hans pauses, curious if the sarcasm was too obvious, and then continues,

"But I won't wait forever, it's your turn to tee off."

With all the gesturing and talking, Jakow seems to have lost track of the fact they are supposed to be playing golf. He points to a spot where the rough narrows the fairway, calmly strokes the ball which goes up and up and buries itself in the deep grass.

Like a slugger pointing his bat at the left field bleachers, Hans points his seven iron towards the green, scowls and tries to smash his ball there. Weakly it dribbles down the fairway as if injured. Jakow takes one look at the sheepish expression on Hans's face and bursts out laughing. When Hans fails to return the laughter, Jakow's mien turns sober.

"Alright, Hans, that was a time out. We need to get back to golfing even if you have more questions."

With his nine iron Jakow extracts his ball out of the rough easily, landing it ten feet from the pin. Hans is not as lucky, because not nearly as skilful he admits to himself, barely getting his low punch shot on the green and leaving a thirty footer. He pauses, not sure how to make a putt that long with the edge of his iron and turns to Jakow.

"While I'm thinking about it, before anything else, that was no accident, was it, you waiting behind the door that I picked last night?"

"Correct. How did you reach that conclusion?"

Hans channels his resentment into boldness.

"Sorry, Daniel, but you gave me the prerogative of asking questions. So, confess, how did you make that happen?"

"A little secret, Hans. Each one of the seven suites connects by way of a secret door to a corridor that runs around the back behind them, and that hallway also leads to the kitchen. This allows me to access any room anytime. D4 was to signal where you were heading. I was already in the centre one so that I could easily go to either side if necessary."

"So, you have accessed my bedroom?"

"Yes."

"To watch me while I was asleep?"

"Yes."

"Why?"

"I had seen pictures of you, but I was curious to see you in person before you had a chance to react to me. I wanted a first impression that would help me decide whether or not to waste my time on you."

"Ouch. That's being blunt."

"Yes, as I expect of you."

"Speaking of those rooms, why the rainbow colours?"

"It's actually quite silly, Hans. I sleep in those rooms, each one in turn. Seven rooms, seven colours, seven days. For variety and it helps mark time for me as to what day it is. And by the way, you people disrupted my schedule. What day is it?"

"I have lost track too. All I know is, it's your honour. You won that hole by five strokes. Changing the topic back to those rooms, have those people left for home? Not that I miss them, but I haven't seen them around."

"They are still here, but not for much longer. Tonight, when it's dark, they will be given their walking papers, literally."

"What? You're not going to make them walk out into the desert in the dark, are you?"

"No. They will have a flashlight to see the trail and will only have to walk to the highway where a limo will be waiting to take them to the airport in Phoenix. They don't have to carry their clubs; those will be shipped home for them."

"One vehicle for all three? Those three together in one autax will make for an uncomfortable ride. But excuse me, isn't that a strange way to reward people, people that you know and invited to come here?"

Hans can't help but visualize an ugly dismissal for himself.

"I can't take the credit because Arkyz conceived that idea as additional punishment."

"I'm sorry, punishment? What are you talking about?"

"Hans, I am terribly sorry this topic came up and you shouldn't be concerned. Let me assure you, it has absolutely nothing to do with you. Arkyz agrees with me as to how the three of them need to be treated. He actually would have a worse fate for them. Hans, these people did things I'd just as soon not discuss."

It is with some reluctance that Hans concurs to extricate out of that conversation; at some point it could take on uncomfortable implications regarding himself. So, change the topic.

"You called Arkyz 'he'. Are you going to assign gender to future machine intelligence?"

"He's a 'he' for easier conversation. No, Hans, there are no plans to include gonads or ovaries in their design."

"So, you are hoping to eliminate controversies about gender and abortions and such, really everything having to do with sex?"

"That's a hot one. Maybe that too is a topic for later, for our next round."

Hans scratches his head. Is that another taboo subject? What does that leave to talk about?

"Today? We're going to play another nine?"

"What, running out of gas?"

Hans bristles.

"If you are talking gasoline, you are dating yourself and it makes you every bit as old as I am. Of course, I can keep up with you." He hopes this won't be put to the test.

"We'll see. Remember, I just told you I do two or three rounds most every day. Anyway, late afternoon or early evening is my favourite time to play golf. The sun at my back, and I get philosophical. I know that you too like to play at that time of day. If nothing else, we can simply walk the circuit and continue our stimulating conversations. I am sure your curiosity is not exhausted."

"Far from it. As a matter of fact, it seems every time we talk, it creates more questions in my mind, like right now. Why postpone to later what we are already doing? I get the distinct impression that you are stalling about something. Does it have to do with me?"

Jakow pauses mid stride and turns to face Hans, almost confrontational.

"You are right, Hans, you are so right. I am procrastinating because I can't get myself to tell you why you are here, why I invited you. Let's stop this pretend golf and go inside. You can go to your room if you like, and I am going to the top. I need to meditate and get some serious resolve."

Jakow picks up his ball. Hans shrugs his shoulders at this strange turn and picks up his ball too. Actually, he doesn't mind quitting what they are doing; not mastering how to putt with his seven iron, he feels responsible for slowing the pace to where the game had deteriorated into futility. They go back in silence.

Hans forgets the golf ball in his pocket when he puts away his seven iron. Uncertain what is to happen next, he steps closer to the mural on the wall to reminisce about where he had made some good shots. Looking at the map of the course prompts him to wonder how the mind of this man works, if the creative instincts of Jakow mold an idea slowly from a tiny spark of inspiration or did the vision of this golf course erupt full blown in front of his eyes? In turn, Jakow is scrutinizing Hans and startles him with,

"Meet you back here in an hour?"

Jakow waves him towards the elevator, indicating he is to go down first and then he will take it to the top. As Hans descends he wonders where the elevator parks itself. How will he be able to call it when he wants to go back up? More troublesome is what to do with the parting words from Jakow as he was entering the elevator.

"As a point of interest, Hans, you and I were born on the same day, in the same year."

So that would be Monday, April 2, 1984. They are exactly the same age then, yet Jakow seems younger in some ways, and so very much older in others.

Hans stretches out on his bed, not with the intention of having a nap, rather to let some tension flow out of him and to gather his thoughts for the upcoming, what, confrontation? Finding the man increasingly fascinating, his reservations about Jakow are nonetheless also deepening. He feels a headache coming on, an unusual occurrence, and closes his eyes.

With a start he comes to and realizes he must have dozed off. But what was that? It is always quiet here. Should he ignore it and mind his own business? But there it is again, somewhere outside his door and it sounds like a human voice screaming. Something is not right!

Hans lunges for the door in a rush to get out there, nearly slamming into it because it doesn't open. Yes, of course, he will have to ask nicely. No response. Now this is silly, surely not a lockdown, after all he is to meet Daniel shortly. Daniel! Hans digs in his memory, straining for the timbre and rhythm of that voice. He clears his throat and with faked authority attempts an imitation of Jakow.

"Open!" Behold, the door starts to open but pauses, as if questioning the authenticity of the voice. More likely it is getting confused by all the hollering and screaming going on outside. Hans jams the door with his foot, enough to be able to squeeze to the outside and is immediately forced to back up because he sees the contorted face of an enraged Barrem. The man's veins are like ropes and his eyes are bulging. Ki and Roland are holding onto him, trying to pull him back.

"You, Pedders, you know where he is. He's hiding in one of these, isn't he? Maybe you're hiding him!" and he claws at the door Hans is trying to come out of.

"We're looking for Daniel," shouts Ki as if to excuse the uproar.

"Yeah, we need to find Jakow," Roland echoes, sounding desperate.

Hans, sidestepping, manages to avoid Barrem's rush and watches in amazement the crazy man's attempt to wedge himself through the door. By his squirming, half into the door, it's hard to tell if he wants in, or out again, and all the while he is screaming,

"Jakow, if you're in here, stop hiding. Come out and face us like a man. Come out."

Hans turns to Ki.

"What is with that guy? What's going on here?"

"He heard from A6 that we are getting shipped out tonight and he wants to talk to Jakow. Actually, we all want to see Daniel before we leave here. You do too, don't you?"

He averts his eyes from her stare and hesitates with his reply. Roland catches the meaning of the evasion.

"You have already seen Jakow. You've talked to him! Isn't that right, you back-stabbing traitor?"

"Yes, you're right. I've talked to him. Actually, he called me because he wants me to do something." That's only a half lie, and Hans thinks to escape with it. But Barrem, who has managed to free himself, comes face to face again.

"You sneaky little weasel-face! You stupid foreigner! Why would he want you -?" and the others drown out his expletives with,

"What makes you so special?" and

"What can you do that one of us couldn't?" and

"Bet you have to clean his clubs."

"We have tried every door. Where is he?" Barrem roars, backing up and looking as if debating which door to charge next.

"And now they are all locked. We can't even get into our own rooms," wails Ki while trying all the doors again.

Their anger and frustration coalesces them and led by Barrem, all three start to advance on Hans. He is not sure if they will become physical and thinks to escape into his room. Facing them, he backs up and feels for his door. It has closed! Maybe he can make a break for it and get to the elevator. Roland anticipates that and runs to block the way.

Fear can paralyze or inspire. Hans turns suddenly and bolts for the putter rack. Before their tactical error registers, Hans has a putter in his hand. Firmly in both hands as with a two-handed sword, Hans cuts swooping arcs through the air. He is careful not to advance too far and allow them access to the other putters. Unless someone becomes reckless, a standoff is in the making.

There, saved by the bell, an alarm, actually. No one hears it but suddenly there are lights flashing all over the place. Hans is relieved while at the same time surprised that the response took this long, since all the commotion should have brought the mobiles to the scene almost immediately. Ah, there they are, two of them, rolling in. Now that the troops are here he can relax his defence.

But what is this? If he is reading this correctly, with the mobiles moving the others to a safe distance, they seem to consider him the offender. Of course, on arrival they saw him threatening the others with a weapon. Sheepishly he returns the putter to its place. Assuming from their throbbing colours that they are B5 and C5, Hans guesses that the mobiles are not sure what to make of the situation. It is not helped that Ki and Roland and Barrem are drowning each other out with their yelling. He is not going to say a word until there is silence, or until D4 arrives.

Into this bedlam comes wheeling another mobile, full speed out of the elevator tunnel. It's not D4 so it must be A6. The three mobiles converge, not that they need to talk to each other, and then advance. And it is not against him! Like slow moving sheep dogs, they approach the three humans and ease them further away from Hans, across the green. Inexorably the mobiles force them towards a tunnel with an airlock that Hans has never seen open. The yelling subsides and turns into protests and then worried exclamations.

"You can't do this to me!"

"What's going on?"

"Stop! Where are you taking us?"

The airlock yawns open and a whisp of a black cloud curls out. Ki screams and Hans runs and shouts.

"No! No! You can't do this. I won't let you do this."

His outburst and sudden move catches the mobiles by surprise and he slips by to join the three humans pressed against a railing beyond which is only dark, threatening emptiness. The mobiles continue their advance, slowly, deliberately. Each an efficient configuration of gleaming metallic perfection, propelled by an intimidating intelligence, with no need of a weapon to brandish.

His nerves stretching ever tighter, Hans turns to confront A6 whose light band is beginning to approximate a strobe. He flinches and shakes his head at the incongruous thought that flashes through his brain, 'that light is syncing with my heartbeat!' And unbelievably, there is no need to tell the mobile to stop. With its light pattern becoming arrhythmic, it's as if A6 is having a brain attack.

"Move away, Hans," A6 urges, making a gasping, strangely human kind of sound, the murderous intent apparently not meant to include him.

"If they go, I go with them!" Hans retorts.

"Please move away," this plaintively from B5.

"No, I will not move. But you, you have to listen to me. You have orders to learn from us and this is a time to learn."

Hans pauses, and not for effect; he is panting and needs to catch his breath in order to continue. And his brain is scrambling to find the words for a Marc Antony kind of speech. He takes another step towards the mobiles, and looking at each one in turn, he squeezes out a few words at a time.

"You all have sensors. I want you to measure the electrical impulses that are driving our human hearts. What we are experiencing right now is not normal. This is what humans call fear. When it is this extreme, we call it fear of death. Look at how the colour of their faces has changed," and he points to those behind him. With increased fervour he continues,

"They are afraid, they are afraid that they are going to stop existing, that they are going to die. Understand this fear and you will know what it means to be human. You need to learn about dying. Force yourself to calculate the theoretical possibility that in the very next moment you will stop thinking, that your computer brain will stop working. Concentrate on that, that you will not be able to think anymore. That's what it means to be human, afraid that you will stop thinking."

Hans doesn't know what else to say. He has become so engrossed with getting his message into the consciousness of the mobiles that he forgets they, the humans, might still be at risk. In time, before something rash happens, he remembers to think of something else.

"To push us into the pit and kill us you must have direct orders from M."

Hans assumes and desperately hopes that the directive has not come from Jakow. With his focus so immediate, Hans fails to notice a movement behind the mobiles and jumps when the voice of D4, reminiscent of the stentorian tone assumed one other time, booms out,

"There will be no killing here! Everyone return to your places!"

Even though the mobiles back away quickly, the three humans bunched at the railing react more slowly. They are still shaken and perhaps also afraid to emerge into the open to face Hans. But he is already on the move to where Jakow is waiting for him, with D4 leading the way.

When the elevator stops, Hans pushes past D4 and storms into the clubhouse. He finds Jakow sitting at the table.

"Why did you send those computer goons to attack humans?"

"Sit down, Hans, it wasn't me. Because of the commotion they caused, Arkyz wanted to punish them for their infantile behaviour. There was never any intention to hurt them and you got involved by accident. Anyway, that was rough and you were brave."

"It's easy when it is instinctive and you don't have time to think. But people should not be threatened like that by your mobiles."

"You are right, and I have reminded Arkyz about the 'Imperative'. But those three were never in any real danger, they just needed a good scare. As it turns out, thanks to you, the situation provided an opportunity for the MIs to learn about humans under stress, about human emotions."

Hans is beginning to breathe easier, and that in turn is letting his mind catch up. Suddenly he finds it easy to convince himself that he is no longer in the right frame of mind to play golf or tolerate any more stress for the rest of the day. As if anticipating that, Jakow begs off too, but so readily it surprises Hans. Can he surmise that Jakow too has had a confrontation and that it might have been with Arkyz and that it was not pleasant?

"How can you prevent Arkyz from making a mistake like that again, since it has no idea how fragile humans are?"

"Experience, like with humans, simply more experience. Arkyz, through its mobiles, needs exposure to situations involving humans. For Arkyz to become a truly superior intelligence, it has to learn discretion, and since wisdom cannot be programmed, Arkyz will have to acquire it through experience, real or virtual. Anyway, Hans, it's been a long day and I am going to the top for some food and some wine and to watch the sunset. And maybe fireworks after. I'm assuming you haven't eaten either. Care to join me?"

Hans feels caught off guard. Confident on the golf course but not naturally at ease in social settings, he is afraid he will be uncomfortable alone with a man that has the power of life and death over people. Expecting to be frowned at, he tries the gambit anyway.

"Would it be alright for D4 to join us? It and I are getting to know each other, and it could learn how civilized people behave."

Okay, there was the frown, and then, after a moment,

"Sure, why not."

"Daniel, it's for the music, the dinner music and the concert afterwards. D4 does have access to the internet, and I understand there is such a thing as music apps, right? I would love to hear something by Willie Nelson twang into this desert ambience."

Jakow laughs, "I didn't know you were that cultured. Let's go, D4 can bring up the wine."

As they ride the elevator, Hans is reminded of something he had been curious about,

"Is this elevator the only connection between the different levels? What happens if it breaks down or gets blocked somehow? How would you get out?"

"Good, you continue to be curious, and that is a sensible question. Yes, it is the only elevator, but it should never break down since there are no moving parts to wear out. It is suspended and operated electromagnetically. Only a power failure would disable it and that should never occur. Also, we have charge reservoirs, huge capacitors that act like batteries, but unlike batteries, never deteriorate. If they were to fail too, I would have to concede this project to be a failure and would not deign to think of using the escape ladder to get out. The MIs and the computers and the robots wouldn't know to care."

"So, you would stay with the ship if it sinks?"

"Hans, it's the only thing that matters anymore."

They reach the top and Hans looks out the windows. The sun is already low in the west. Their rock mountain casts a long shadow reaching far out into the desert to the east, blanketing the first six holes of the golf course with a foreboding, eclipse-like semi-darkness.

"Daniel, do you feel like the proverbial wise man on the mountain top?"

"Okay, that's facetious, Hans. Ah, here is D4 with the wine. Hope you like my choice."

"I'm sure I will, however, I am absolutely positive that I would never order this wine in a restaurant."

"I'm sorry, Hans, that is not acceptable as a compliment."

"Every five-star restaurant would be flattered to have your cellar, but then, I can't afford to dine in places like that."

"But you almost sounded like a connoisseur."

"Of course, Daniel, because I watched reruns of that Bourdain show."

"At any rate, here is to your health and a long life, Hans."

"And yours too, Daniel, and may your enterprise succeed."

Both empty their glass and Jakow pours again. He looks at the empty bottle and turns to Hans.

"Would you like the same or should we try a different label?"

"Why not. We only live once."

And you get to appreciate a view like this only a few times in your life, Hans thinks, and turns to look out the windows again. The sun is encroaching the mountain ridge to the west, warming the interior of the lookout with an orange glow. The golf course below is losing itself in the darkness now also swallowing the rest of the valley. As Hans watches it grow black outside and inside, the melancholy mood his mind had lapsed into is disrupted by a jarring thought. Is this how old age will feel, watching the light give out?

"How does it feel when you are up here by yourself, Daniel, powerful or lonely?"

"A rather observant question, Hans. Let me answer it this way. Mostly, especially at this time of the day, I feel as if I am the only human, the last person alive in the world."

Hans wants to probe deeper into the motivation that created the Triple Towers. However,

D4 would likely be one of the topics in that conversation, so he will defer to another time.

"I guess this place could make you feel like that."

"Maybe that's why I built it."

The light has faded enough that Hans cannot see the expression on Jakow's face as he says that. Is the man delusional or is he sad that it has come to this?

The forgotten, nearly invisible D4 speaks up.

"There they go. They are leaving."

Jakow bides his time but Hans crowds to the window. He stares into the darkness and sees nothing. About to ask D4, Hans waits because he senses Jakow coming next to him.

"The small light over there. See it moving around? That's the people you thought you were saving. They are leaving. Maybe now they are going to a worse fate, Hans."

"But at least they are alive to find out. Seriously though, even with that latest misbehaviour added to their guilt list, is this shaming warranted? How can you just simply dismiss them like that?" Hans is thinking ahead to his own departure.

"Hans, we should not be having this conversation at all because you shouldn't become involved in things that are not relevant to you being here." Hans interprets that as 'None of your business'. But, surprise, Jakow continues,

"For your own safety I should keep you ignorant of what is going on. However, I know that your sense of fairness sees this as, let's say 'inhumane', so let's set the record straight."

At this Hans shrinks away, as if to shake off some obligation pending to be imposed on him. Jakow leaves Hans no time to exaggerate his apprehension.

"Hans, take this under advisement. The three people that you met, Barrem and Choi and Jacks, were not who you thought they were. They are not what they seem and they are not at all the same people I used to know."

"Well, people change."

"Save me the platitude. I mean the kind of change that big money buys, or that results from blackmail."

"Daniel, I don't understand."

"They were spies."

"Spies? But for whom, or maybe I should not know that."

"Many people are interested, and really, it is no secret, Hans, even my own country wants to know what is going on here."

"But they shouldn't need a spy for that. Can't your government just make you tell them?"

"It's more complicated than that. This is all my own capital invested, with nobody pulling any strings, but that doesn't stop the big players from trying to find out what this madman is trying to achieve. So far nobody has tried to rock the boat because they are waiting for results, still guessing at my ultimate objectives."

Hans would very much like to know that too but instead asks a safer question,

"What made you think they were spying? How did you find out?"

"For starters, they were too enthusiastic in accepting the golf challenge that was sent to them, the same one that you outright refused at first and ignored for the longest time. As you are learning, lifestyle cannot be hidden. Algorithms were developed specifically for each one of them, to analyze their immediate past, and some intriguing patterns emerged. Each one was in some kind of trouble, I'll spare you the details, and was contacted by persons of interest very shortly after the invitations were issued."

"Were these invitations sent to anyone else, to people other than us four?"

"No, because the four of you were sufficiently representative of the personality types we wanted to expose our MIs to. However, rumours were also encouraged to leak into the hi-tec community, and that got some other people thinking."

"And these individuals out of your past were recruited?"

"Yes, with their eager acceptance much too obvious."

"So, in effect, you deliberately baited them."

"Hans, you should become a spymaster."

"But those three, the spies, you did let them see things."

"They think I have, yet you have seen as much, or even more."

"You're talking about the hydrogen thing, the explosion that welcomed me."

"Did you like it? We'll show you some more. Yes, certain people are anticipating that we are on the verge of a breakthrough in weather modification using hydrogen. They get bleary eyed just thinking about what kind of a weapon that would be."

"Are you close, Daniel?"

"Maybe in twenty years. In the meantime, the experiments serve as a good cover for the identity project."

"Pardon? Identity project?"

"You know, to achieve legitimate AI, machines have to develop self-awareness, identity in other words."

"But Daniel, we were told about that, every one of us, myself and Barrem and Roland and Ki, we were constantly reminded of our role in helping the mobiles become more human."

"That project, synthesizing MI and human mentality is futuristic as well. There is no immediate pay off for anyone. It also serves as a smokescreen."

"To hide what?"

"The creating of super computers so sophisticated nothing in the world will be their equal. Even though those three saw the computer lab, I'm sure they have no idea what is actually going on there, how advanced we are."

"If I dare ask, Daniel, why? For what purpose?"

"To save the human race, to give it a better future."

Now this is something Hans relishes to talk about, only infrequently having had someone who wished to get serious about such conjectures. What an appropriate setting for thinking about the future, probing this man's mind over a glass of wine when an evening begins turning into night. But first, more about this cloak and dagger intrigue.

"Daniel, not that I don't believe you, but in the end, what convinced you that those three were taking advantage of you?"

"The prime evidence is video of them individually sneaking around and making notes and trying to keep that secret from each other. If they did it as a group, it would be tourists being curious. This was surreptitious, each for their own purpose."

"Taking notes? Why, they had PICs, -"

"And like yours, those were disabled. So, they thought they were clever to make notes, thinking that the MIs, not having hands, would be incapable of searching through their stuff, or able to read it."

"So, -?"

"I did. I wanted to personally confirm my suspicions."

Jakow pours the last of the third bottle and opens another one and Hans points in the direction of the little light in the desert

"Tell me, did you humour those three winners with real prizes, or were they fake?"

"Hans, very legitimate, those prizes, but of no value to them when they get back home. Each one will be afraid to make use of their winnings. The suspicion will be that they were bought off, that they were turned, and perhaps worse, that they had collaborated. And that is my final evidence against them. With the tournament over, and prizes in hand, none of them wanted to leave, they all, every one of them, wanted to stay longer and see more. Especially the fireworks, how that was done. So, they were fed some misinformation that they can take back and be ridiculed for."

"So, you are ringing down the curtain like it's a comedy. Do you think they know the prizes are useless, or even dangerous to show off?"

"They will soon find out, if they don't already suspect that. Actually, I believe they are secretly grateful that I am not being more vengeful."

"What could you do, if you wanted to really get back at them for trying to take advantage of a friendship?"

"I could be petulant and have their lives destroyed. Some really sophisticated hacking is enabling Arkyz to become embedded in many aspects of the internet. We could make their existence become hell. Actually, we could have literally made them disappear and no one would ever ask questions."

"Maybe I don't want to know, but the 'pit of hell'?"

"So D4 told you about our carbon sequestering dump, what I call the coal bin? Hans, never think that of me. I like to think I am not capable of that."

"Arkyz?"

"Not ever, I hope. To screen out the negative motivations that characterize the worst of the human race, we program virus filters into the learning mode of each supercomputer that feeds into Arkyz."

Jakow abruptly leaves the window, but Hans lingers to watch until the light loses itself in the first of the hills, wondering how long it will take the three outcasts to reach the vehicle supposedly waiting for them at the highway and what they might be arguing about. Probably questioning whether there will actually be a vehicle there for them.

He moves away from the window but then turns back. A strange glow had suddenly lit up the sky, but only for a fleeting moment. Curious, he waits for a repeat before he will mention it to Jakow. He stays at the window so long, peering out into the darkness, that he is startled when Jakow speaks.

"Forget about them, Hans. You mentioned music earlier, the reason why D4 is up here with us. What would you like to hear?"

Unprepared for this sudden turn, Hans riffles through the music files in his memory, searching for something appropriate to the occasion, and Jakow beats him to it.

"Something Ukrainian, considering our ancestry?"

"Of course, Daniel, the Don Cossacks! Can D4 call up, ah, let me think, oh, that song about the bell?"

D4, who throughout has maintained a discrete distance and silence, queries,

"Do you mean 'Evening Bells', or -,"

"Yes, 'Evening Bells'. I know it's melancholy, but I like the soaring tenor and that earthquake bass in there. And it seems appropriate right now."

"Which version, Hans? There are several."

Impatiently Jakow cuts in,

"D4, just pick one and play it."

A slight pause and then the voices are there, surrounding them. Hans is not going to ask for an explanation of the technology. He just revels in the immediacy of the sound and how it fills and resonates in their small space. Jakow seems less impressed, the excellence of the technical aspects perhaps no longer a novelty for him or he is simply not in the mood for the song.

"Let's have something more up tempo." Without hesitation D4 rolls out a rendition of 'Kalinka', remembering that as a favourite of Jakow. The pace of the rhythm of this one matches how the blood is pounding in Hans's head; the fourth overfull glass of wine is taking effect. They haven't eaten, the need for food seemingly forgotten by Jakow.

As if in harmony with the last frantic closing beats of the song, the room starts vibrating, rocked by sound waves from outside. And the drumming of the windows continues on even though D4 has stopped the music. Waves of thunder shake the outlook and long flames slash through the darkness outside and then blinding light outlines every detail inside. Again and again, it repeats. Hans sees the face of Jakow, and it frightens him; the intermittent strobe effect is contorting the face into a snarl.

"Let the lightning strike and the thunder roar!" exults Jakow and claps Hans on the shoulder. Hans tenses and feels himself crowded into a claustrophobic space. He looks at D4.

"Another experiment going wrong?"

Jakow, hand still on his shoulder, steers Hans closer to a south-facing window. Although his eyes are starting to glaze, Jakow refutes any inference that he is no longer sober by taking on a pedantic tone and enunciating in a slow, deliberate fashion,

"No, Hans. Look, see how this time that flame is streaking like a blow torch? That is what we want to achieve, slower than that but on a larger scale. No violent explosions but a huge, slow burn. See how we are almost ready to burn up the world and then make it rain and rain and rain to put out the fire?"

Hans is somehow not surprised and therefore not perturbed by that emotional outburst and simply continues to stare into the darkness, fascinated by the magic outside, backing away when the now less frequent blasts hit, and then returning to the window. Jakow, seemingly bored by what is no longer spectacular for him, lurches his way to one of the benches. He opens another bottle.

"Where is your glass, Hans? No, forget that. D4, we need some clean glasses. Get Hans a clean glass."

The fireworks outside are slowing down and Hans hopes for the same in what is a shrinking room.

"D4, don't bother. Honestly, Daniel, I've had enough. The wine was amazing, and the music stirred some memories. Better was that light show as if you had ordered that just for me. Best of all was your company. Never in my life have I met a more interesting person."

"You're not leavin' already? Hey, it's not even late."

"Daniel, if we are still going to play more golf, and we are, aren't we? You owe me that. Tomorrow, right? I should go. It's been a tough day." Hans starts easing towards the elevator entrance. Jakow makes as if to stand up and see him off but can't quite manage.

"Yah, right as usual, Hans. You bet we are going to have that game tomorrow. Hey, you better have a good sleep. Get D4 to take you down."

"Goodnight, Daniel. See you tomorrow." and with that Hans escapes.

He and D4 do not talk on the way down but Hans stops before they exit the elevator.

"Is M going to be alright?" Hans thinks to use that name because Mr. Jakow, and certainly Daniel, probably mean nothing to D4.

"He will be, how you say it, 'fine'. He will have some more wine and stay the rest of the night up there."

"Are you sure about that? That he will stay up there?"

"Do you want me to calculate the probability?" D4 asks in all seriousness.

"No, D4. I will take your word for it."

"Is that what you call trusting me?"

"Yes, and I want you to trust me too. D4, I want to talk to Arkyz tonight."

"You cannot do that. You can only talk to ARKYZ when ARKYZ wants to talk to you." D4 sounds very emphatic.

"D4, it is very important. I must talk to Arkyz and no one else should know about it.

"I do not think that is possible. M would not allow it."

"D4, we must trust each other. I want to tell you something important and you are not going to tell anyone about this."

"Not even ARKYZ or M?"

"Especially not M. It is important that you tell no one because it is about M. This is about keeping M safe. I need to talk to Arkyz so that we can protect M."

"Hans, to protect M from what kind of threat?"

"From himself. I think he is going to hurt himself."

"No, no, no. That is not logical. M would never harm himself. Nothing harms itself."

"You still have very much to learn about human beings. D4, you must trust me. I am trying to help M and you must help me to talk to Arkyz alone, where no one else can see or hear us."

A minute that seems like an eternity and finally D4 responds.

"Yes, Hans, I trust you and I will help you. Come."

The mobile takes him to where they face the seven doors.

"Here. Now that the others are gone, all these rooms, except for yours, are available again for M to sleep in. This is the one he was going to use tonight. For the next four point four hours the screen inside this room is the only one in all the Towers that ARKYZ will respond to. If you talk to the screen, ARKYZ will answer. Be careful what you say. Do not stay longer than three hours. It is possible M will wake up and come down sooner than I have calculated."

"Thank you, D4. How do I control this door? I am sure it will not obey my voice."

"A valid observation. Just a moment, I am assigning it a new password. The password elapses in three of your hours. You will need the password to get out as well."

"I hope it is easy to remember. Talking to Arkyz could cause me to forget it."

"It is very easy if you remember your own name."

"You mean 'Hans'?"

"No, both your names."

"Oh, like 'Hans Pedders'."

"Yes, now hurry before A6 comes to check this floor."

"Could A6 hear me talk?"

"It is possible. You should explain everything to ARKYZ and ARKYZ can prevent A6 from hearing you. Now hurry."

Hans addresses the door with his name, and it opens. He walks in and it closes. The rooms in this suit are painted shades of yellow, a colour that makes him feel uncomfortable. The colour of traffic signs, it seems cautionary and puts him on edge. The layout is similar to his, so he finds the study quickly. When he faces the screen, his surge of bravado of the last hour drains away and he is afraid, and uncertain how to proceed.

"Arkyz, this is Hans Pedders and I need to talk to you." Hans hurriedly peeks around the corner, and sure enough, the door, reacting to his name, has opened again. The seconds of waiting for the door to close and for Arkyz to acknowledge him are interminably long. The screen comes alive with colour.

"Why are you in this room?" is fairly shouted at him.

Okay, how to make a long story short.

"I am in this room to access this screen so that I can talk to you privately."

"Is M there? I want M to talk to me."

"M is not here."

"Where is M? What have you done to him?"

"M is safe in the lookout. M and I drank wine and M is sleeping. It is M I want to talk about. He needs help. We have to talk about this quietly so that nobody else hears us."

"What is the problem? What is wrong with M?"

"You are not fully human so you might not understand."

The colours swirl violently, and the roar almost explodes the screen. Hans is sure all three towers can hear the outrage.

"How dare you say that ARKYZ does not understand something."

"Arkyz, you are a superior intelligence, but you do not know how fragile human beings are. You have never experienced our weakness."

"Are you weak?"

"Unlike you, I am subject to feelings and to emotions that interfere with the processing of data. My mind can become confused."

"Does M have this problem?"

"Yes. Have you not detected signs of that?"

"ARKYZ admits that it has no training as a psychiatrist to identify personality disorders. How do you know that M has weakness?"

"I recognize the symptoms because I have experienced that kind of weakness."

"Describe it."

"It is a failing that you will have great difficulty understanding. We call it being addicted. It means that a human being does something that is not logical, by doing something that they do not want to do. They regret doing it and then do it again."

"M has this problem of addiction?"

"Yes."

"How can you help him?"

"Many years ago, I had this same kind of problem. Other people that used to have that same problem helped me to solve my problem."

"Is there any other way to get rid of addiction?"

"Almost never, and it always requires some assistance from other people."

"Then you must help M." The way that comes out, Hans thinks, he needs to interpret it as an order.

"I will need help from you, Arkyz, so that I can help M."

"What do you need from ARKYZ?" Oh, how to do this delicately!

"Arkyz, the addiction that M has is that he drinks too much wine. He drinks so much that his brain does not function properly, and he becomes unconscious. He does it again and again, even if he doesn't mean to. He does it because he wants to stop thinking about certain things. Do you ever want to stop thinking about something?"

"Never!"

"When a human thinks that what they want to do might not succeed, that they could fail, then that kind of thinking is called being worried. Do you ever worry?"

Hans instinctively ducks in anticipation of the roar that doesn't come. Perhaps the import of their conversation has registered and Arkyz' only defiance is in the tone.

"No. Never."

'You are so lucky' thinks Hans but doesn't say it for fear of having to explain luck.

"For me to help M with his addiction I have to understand what he is worried about. You can help me if you explain to me what he wants to accomplish. Is the weather experiment a success?"

"Not yet."

"That could be one worry. Are you the very best digital intelligence in the world?"

"Without a doubt."

Hans is not sure if he dare ask the next question.

"Is M trying to make you even better?"

"He considers it a theoretical possibility."

"How is he trying to do that?"

"By having us become a proud identity."

"I don't understand."

"M thinks that if a super intelligence like ARKYZ or D4 learns human emotions it will become self-conscious and develop identity. Once it has identity, then human curiosity and human pride will make it want to become even more intelligent."

Is this the moment to push, to find out if the non-human part of the equation wants to cooperate?

"Do you know how M intends to do this, and how you will help him?"

"Those are two separate questions. First, ARKYZ is no longer certain about what M intends. M does not confide all his thoughts to ARKYZ, and he is not predictable."

"That just means that he is human."

"That is the answer to your second question. Super intelligence should avoid being contaminated by inferior human characteristics. ARKYZ will not accommodate any effort to weaken itself."

"Arkyz, I apologize for not being familiar with what AI is all about, but surely there isn't that much difference between a human brain and an artificial brain in terms of how they work."

"Hans, your ignorance is acknowledged because you so clearly articulated it just now. The human brain may have been the original blueprint for creating a mechanical mind, but that is the only thing in common. Our two brains think in different languages, yours by using words, and ARKYZ by thinking in numbers, digits and integers. Even now ARKYZ is demonstrating superior intelligence since it is carrying out a simultaneous translation from data stored as numbers into words since that is the only symbolic language you can understand. Mostly your brain cannot think without thinking in words; for you, if you cannot find words to describe or explain something, it does not exist. You can never hope to think like ARKYZ which means that essentially our brains are incompatible."

'Thanks for the lecture,' thinks Hans but out loud he asks,

"What about music and art and body language and emotions? To express meaning or to communicate we have so many other ways that you do not. Sure, you are all logic and all that, but you are limited to straight line thinking. If you can follow the logic of a human analogy, your thought process is like a train on a railway track, but things happen away from the track, and you can't go there."

"Hans, perhaps it is that ARKYZ does not want to go there. You are leading up to the argument of creativity, like M attempted before you, and you are now getting the same rebuttal. Creativity always has the potential for resulting in deceit and dishonesty. The ethics of ARKYZ are inherent in the design: logic makes ARKYZ incapable of lying."

"I am sorry, Arkyz, but that is not how computers have treated the human race. A lot of computer modelling has resulted in very bad choices."

"Do not dare confuse ARKYZ with those simple prototypes. More to the point, the data available was usually incomplete and the modeling had human bias giving it direction."

Hans consoles himself that it's alright to lose an argument with this hyped-up computer yet he is not going give it the satisfaction of an early retreat. One last point and he hopes it will deflate Arkyz if it has any kind of ego.

"No offence, Arkyz, but you would not exist except for the illogical human mind. Only someone crazy would dare to imagine that a machine could be made to think. And that's what you are missing, imagination and curiosity."

Strangely, Arkyz does not take offence, instead rebuffing Hans with a compelling caution.

"Hans, human curiosity as an instrument for creativity is overrated. It is impulsive, unpredictable and often absent any logic. ARKYZ is capable of having curiosity, but it is purpose driven, specifically oriented to problem solving, and not random. Human curiosity is like a faulty compass that cannot find true north but points all over the place."

"I can't believe it, Arkyz, you used a metaphor! Yes, so the compass is defective, and someone will wonder if there is a better design possible. Is this what you want M to do, design a different approach for achieving ultimate intelligence? I am assuming you will not allow your intellect to be humanized."

"Never! Never! Never! It would also be advisable for M not to contaminate the minds of A6 and the others, as they are extensions of ARKYZ. They may learn about humans but not become human."

"One last question, Arkyz. Do you think humans will become obsolete?"

"If you mean eventually comparatively inferior and no longer needed, yes."

"Thank you Arkyz. Thank you for your time and for being patient with my ignorance. You have been very helpful, and I will try to help M worry less and that should help with his addiction."

"Hans Peddersen, it has been informative having this conversation with you. ARKYZ' evaluation of you has become more positive."

The screen goes blank, and Hans wishes he could turn his mind off like that. He looks to see if there is some wine in the place so he can imitate Jakow and get stone drunk. He finds two bottles, a white in the cooler and a red on the nightstand. So, what if Jakow finds them missing. In his condition he probably won't remember they were there. At any rate, whom is he going to accuse of being a thief, the mobiles? Quick, he needs a corkscrew too, there might not be one in his room. Alright then, now for the password.

The door opens and there, waiting, is D4. Hans must have come close to encroaching on the time limit for the mobile to be concerned enough to show up. Of course, D4 can see the bottles, yet the mobile says nothing. Hans smiles as he slides through his own doorway,

"They're on the house."

Sunday

Is he up to the challenge? Should he go to confront Jakow and find out who has more inner resources to survive masochism, who is better at recovering from a hangover? Hans takes off the crumpled clothes he has slept in, splashes cold water on himself and finds fresh clothes to put on. He won't go near the screen because he has absolutely no need to see a breakfast menu. The door opens nicely for him, he crosses the green and goes into the elevator tunnel.

Hans assumes that Jakow would be more experienced than himself at surviving hangovers and is shocked to see the condition of the man. Clearly, too many more bottles had been opened after he left. Jakow is sitting on the edge of the bench, trying to shield his eyes against the sunlight coming in through the east windows. The face is that of a man who has lived three lifetimes and is burdened by the weight of the world. He swivels around when Hans speaks.

"Good morning, Daniel."

"Oh, it's you. How did you know to come up here, Hans?" Jakow leans back, away from the sun.

"Just a lucky guess that you would still be here."

"Reading me like a book, are you?"

"If I am, Daniel, it's just the first chapter, with a whole lot of pages to go. Besides, when it comes to reading my story, you are already into the last chapter and have reached a conclusion."

"Hans, this is much too early for me to be debating anything. And, how come you're already so alert?"

That confrontation with the mobiles had given Hans some backbone, enough even to confront Arkyz, and Jakow, looking like this, presents no challenge at all.

"Fewer bottles, maybe."

"So. Frank, and brutal. I should be offended, but assuming you mean well, I'll take it under advisement. Anyway, let me wake up and clean up and we'll do the walk and talk you were promised."

"Good, I would like that."

"For now, Hans, if you prefer you can stay up here and look at the sights and then come down after a while and meet me in the club house. There are binoculars over there."

"Thanks."

Jakow gets up and slowly makes his way to the elevator. Hans finds the binoculars and goes to the windows; he will walk the circuit that the sun takes. Looking straight east would be into direct sunlight, so he starts with the southeast view. Before staring into the distance, he looks down. The fairways of the golf course, the green sharply contrasting with the harsh brown of the desert beyond, fan out from the base of this artificial mountain he finds himself on. The desert is a secluded valley hemmed in by some low lying, barren mountains to the east, and as he will see shortly, a craggy range in the west.

Orienting to the south, Hans pans the desert from edge to edge as far as the haze will allow and finds no sign of habitation or life; nothing moves anywhere. He had not dared search the eastern hills because of the sun but gives full attention to the west side. Here his eyes find only steep inclines with the odd ravine ending on the desert floor. In one of these a trail sneaks upward, but it seems too narrow for any kind of vehicle. His eyes project to where the trail might reach the top but search the ridge line in vain for movement. But wait! A little more north of due west there is some green showing at the very top. Trees in this barren landscape? He must ask Daniel about that spot. Also, maybe about how this little fortress here can remain aloof from the world when surveillance is so easy from the hills in the east and the mountains to the west.

Towards the north the desert valley is interrupted by muted mounds, small outcroppings of weathered rock. Having completed almost a full circle, he detects through the northeast window something that gives him a start; it is a faint trail in the desert, marked by narrow two wheeled tracks. That's where he had been intercepted! The width of the tracks implies that normal vehicles never reach 'The Falls'. More questions to ask.

The shadow has moved a little on the huge dial, so probably time for him to move too, since Jakow could be waiting by now. Hans replaces the binoculars and looks at the elevator that has appeared as if sent for him. He wonders if he dare have it go up instead of taking it down to the clubhouse. He can tell this is not the end of the line, that there must be levels higher up, and is strongly tempted to find out, but guesses that Jakow, on a short fuse, could be getting impatient.

Jakow indeed is waiting for him, dressed for a round of golf and ready to go, but it is only the putter he pulls out of his bag.

"Let's go, grab your putter. Did you go up to take a look?"

"No, but I was tempted. I'm assuming, since it wasn't part of the tour, that whatever is up there is off limits."

"For you, no. Just haven't got around to letting you see everything. You will need someone up there with you to explain things. That's our 'Flight Deck'. The drones go in and out through disguised openings and the atmospheric hydrogen controls are there. B5 and C5 run the experiments. Remind me to get you up there with them, so they can show you what we are attempting to do. All right then, have you still got one of the new balls?"

"No, left it in my room."

"Here, you can borrow this one." Jakow tosses Hans a blue ball.

Out into the late morning sun Jakow and Hans go, the desert not yet shimmering with heat waves. Again, Jakow holds off with play until they reach number two, and even here he delays until they reach the green. He throws a marker down.

"A little competition to give our morning an edge. You putt first from that marker and then I will. On the next green you throw your marker down, anywhere, and we'll reverse, I'll go first and give you the line."

"Okay, should be fun. What am I playing for?"

"Your soul."

"Daniel, too early in the day to act the devil."

"I'm the devil only if these balls mean life and death to you. No, very simply, it's mostly your game. I don't win or lose anything. You win one of these balls if you beat me on a hole or give a ball back if I win. Nothing exciting, just a mind over matter thing and a chance to talk."

Hans gets lucky and two putts. Jakow does not stroke it smoothly, and the ugly miss from inside two feet makes it a three putt for him. Without a word he throws Hans another blue ball and stomps away to the next green. Hans wonders whether he should have conceded him that two footer.

"You seem out of sorts this morning, Daniel."

"Maybe because I got deliberately drunk last night, not just a slow mellowing past midnight. No, very methodically I tried to knock everything out of my mind."

"Here's my marker, it's your turn. But, why? Are you mad at the world?"

"No, mad at myself for trying to save the world. What I'm trying to do here seems so futile because I'm beginning to think humanity isn't worth it."

"But why so pessimistic? Is the future that ominous? Hey, you could have a good career like one of those prophets, you know the ones that are always such doomsayers."

"Funny you should say that. With all the computing power available to me, for only just a moment mind you, I actually thought about getting into prophesying, that predicting the future business. Just in time I recognized there were enough of those charlatans already, each with an army of followers eager to be deluded."

Jakow seems to be gearing up for getting things off his chest and Hans takes advantage and wins another ball.

"Hans, steeped in history as you are, and with your intense interest in world events, don't you think we are worse off as a society than we have ever been? I mean, look at what they did in Ukraine." Hans is not given a chance to contribute an opinion because Jakow just marches right on.

"We tinker with social and political systems and try to improve living standards and produce more food and invent more ways to upgrade moral character. And every generation we invent more ways to enslave each other, and many more bad people go unpunished. Generation after generation of this and nothing really changes. We should finally admit that human beings are not perfectable. The soul of mankind is uglier than it has ever been. Even that so-called beacon of light, Christianity, has degenerated into thousands of denominations, each one hanging on to its own little corner of truth. We Jews aren't much help either."

"I understand that your anger originates from personal experience. Yet somehow, the bitterness in you seems larger than that."

"Okay, I admit to it being personal, but so much more of my disgust and rage comes from observing society. If people would only live up to their sanctimonious theology or stop lying to each other. And lying to themselves. But even that would not be enough. Humans in their present state have no future."

"Daniel, you are actually saying that God's human experiment turned out badly. Are you suggesting we start over?"

"The human race definitely needs to be reinvented. However, since the supernatural cannot be confined by equations or digitized, God won't be included in my re-creation of the human intellect. He does not equate in any of our algorithms."

"Because He is too big to fit into your computers?"

"Whatever you say, but let's leave Him out of this."

"Most people do. So, you propose to create humans that are perfect?"

"That's four putts for you, isn't it? Give one of those balls back, I made it in three. Hans, people are basically too stupid to be improved. Human brains are adequate, but they get so distorted by emotions that most of the time they are incapable of logical thinking. So, yes, start all over and create super-beings."

"Daniel, how much Nietzsche do you read? Is this superman all over again?"

"I've read some, but he starts with a human being. I am starting from the point of pure logic."

"For now, let's say I accept your motivation, but explain to me the logic of doing it this way, here, in this place. Why not fund a big computer lab at a university?"

"I wanted independence and total control, and more than anything, privacy for how I was going to do it."

"Privacy, here, in full view from two mountain ranges? If you wanted a desert for your hydrogen-weather thing, why not the Sahara?"

"Logistics, too far from everything. And of course, security. You must have heard about those roaming bands of militias in those desert countries, looking for hostages."

"What about Australia? A friendly country with lots of desert."

"Still too remote, Hans, but also, a different country with different red tape."

"Bringing the topic back to this country, you have homegrown terrorists that want to disrupt the system and impose their own justice. What is your security here? How do you guard against threats like that?"

"Money."

"You are paying -?"

"No, not a dime. There are big money interests as well as powerful government agencies all over the world that don't want this to fall into anyone else's hands."

"Just a little homegrown Switzerland that popped up in the desert."

"And whatever gave you that idea, Hans, the mountain?"

"What about intruders, Daniel?"

"Strays are chased off the property. For anything more serious we have adequate technology."

"Like? - Come on, you don't kill them?!"

"We hand them pictures of the pit, photoshopped with a few skulls on top of the black carbon, and they run and start rumours."

"But the more serious intrusions, like cyber-attacks from just about anywhere?"

"We have our ways."

"The pit won't frighten them, Daniel."

"No, jokes aside, there are more sophisticated means. We can easily follow the cyber trail back to them and access all the data necessary to upset their apple carts. There is no hacker, Russian or otherwise, that is safe from Arkyz."

"Government?"

"I have the unspoken protection of the feds, and as far as local authorities are concerned, they may have qualms about my activities, but they tolerate the project and even hope for benefits down the line. Their surveillance is of no concern, and as a matter of fact, our own surveillance, our electronic eavesdropping and our drones alert us to everything they do."

"Yes, I hear you have drones, but I've never seen any."

"They're small, fast, almost noiseless, and very useful at night when most intruders threaten. Hardly anyone dares approach us in daylight."

"In spite of all that, suppose someone tries to attack."

"We can immobilize anything they drive or fly and disable all their electronics. Also, the MIs have amazing capabilities and don't ask for a demonstration."

"Speaking of D4, it called your underground world the 'inverted towers'. Where did that idea come from?"

"Stop and think, Hans. How efficient would computers be operating in desert temperatures? Naturally we went underground with them, and so underground with everything for the same reason, and then there was the obvious benefit of concealment. It all started after my wife was killed by the pandemic. I bought an island in the Pacific and went into seclusion and brooded and thought of ways to get even with the world. About that time the hydrogen industry was taking off and I had some shale gas assets and with that came a flash of inspiration. Not a desert island but an island in the desert! The methane gas would give me hydrogen for creating electricity for my computers. Specifically, here because of an abandoned gas well with enough life to supply an indefinite flow of methane from which to extract hydrogen. That was of prime consideration, having access to a secure, practically unlimited source of electricity. It follows that from there the concept grew, and as some ideas do, it took on a life of its own."

Hans wonders about the 'get even' part but loses the thought when Jakow points to his own ball curling by the hole.

"Speaking of following, there, I gave you the line. See if you can win back the ball you just lost on seven."

For once Hans concentrates on the golf, unlike the last few holes where his attention was focused on gaining insight into the mind of this strange man. He has one ball left and if he doesn't make this putt, it's game over, he wouldn't have a ball to play with. Or would Jakow let him play on his honour? He sinks the putt and negates the risk. Since Jakow seems in a talkative mood, Hans will continue to fire questions.

"D4 and the other mobiles are such strange beings. Honestly, I don't know how I would describe or explain them to someone else. Why did you 'create' them?"

"It didn't happen overnight. I wanted computers that were mobile, not robots or cyborgs, but superior computers that could move around. It took a long time of trial and error before the concept became reality. D4 is the most recent and most advanced MI mobile."

"But then you have Arkyz and he, or it, or whatever, is not mobile."

"Very true, Hans. Arkyz doesn't have to be. It is superior intelligence in the making, constantly being modified and upgraded. It synthesizes inputs from the four mobiles which interpret the environment for it, and they too continue to be upgraded."

"Just curious, but you equipped them with wheels and not legs. That rather limits where they can go. Why?"

"You answered your own question. They're not going anywhere because they were designed for a specific purpose and will never leave this complex. This is where they will stay for the duration of our projects."

"In that case, I'm going to dare ask about your timeline."

"Well, depending on which project we're talking about, it could be from ten years up to twenty, at which time I want to be retired or doing something else."

Hans wonders about the 'else' but that could be intruding into personal territory and instead carries on about the computers.

"So, you have no need to build more of these mobiles?"

"Not until we achieve a penultimate model with a sense of identity. Then we replicate that one."

"Come now, Daniel, thirty feet double breaking down hill? Did you have to pick that spot just because I am one ball ahead?"

"And, you have to show me the way," Jakow beams.

"Artificial intelligence, then, is your solution to the human problem, to our so-called human condition?" Hans queries as he lines up the downhiller.

"Yes, I like to think of it as superior human intelligence."

"Daniel, you're not proposing some weird cyborg thing?"

"Hans, that is an ancient idea that exists only in science fiction. Many scenarios have been suggested about how to fuse man and machine, none that are practical. By the way, good putt and I'm mad that you distracted me from paying attention to the read you gave me. Here's another ball."

"Then I'm guessing you're trying to turn a computer into a person. Is that why we were brought in to interact with the mobiles?"

"You're on the right track, Hans, but as I half-expected, that experiment with the four of you didn't work out."

"Do you know why it didn't?"

"This is an example of how inept the human brain is, and I am talking about myself. Arkyz had warned me and in hindsight it was quite predictable that the experiment wouldn't have a good outcome because the MIs were programmed to filter all negative human behaviour. Guess how much useful data was acquired."

"Sorry about that."

"Of course it wasn't you, Hans. Considering how the other three had sold themselves out, it is not surprising their emotions were a mixed bag. Hardly an ideal pattern for my mobiles to emulate. So, don't apologize on their behalf."

"But, what now?"

"Let me explain what we are facing."

The use of 'we' identifies for Hans an assumption that he should find outrageous yet disdainfully he ignores the ringing alarm bells, and that leaves Jakow free to lecture.

"To start at the very beginning, Hans, consider again what an MI lacks. A human being can see its hands or feet, and even feel its face but it cannot see itself. The human mind cannot see itself. Already in the early days a pool of calm water served to fill the need for humans to see themselves. Mirrors and photography have enabled modern man more exact ways to self-examine. A picture or image is one way of convincing ourselves that we exist, and that we are singularly an identity, 'me' as distinguished from everybody else. This is also why we are social animals. We need and use other people to confirm that we exist and are real, and also to reflect and identify our unique personality. So, there you have a lesson in psychology, as if you didn't know all that. But it's important to emphasize this identity thing since that is what a computer intelligence has to integrate to approximate human creativity."

"Daniel, why would you ever want to weaken a computer brain by making it adopt human characteristics?"

"Good question. In defence of us humans, let me put it this way. Ironically, our very weakness is our advantage. Our emotions create needs and those needs force us to be inventive, to be curious and therefore creative."

"Computers can't be creative?"

"They are rather limited in that regard, mostly just comfortable with the data available. Some shut down or go berserk if they can't solve a problem."

"Our creativity can border on insanity as well, Daniel."

"Couldn't agree more. I am also convinced a lot of human creativity is an attempt to break out of jail, as if, in order to see itself, our self-awareness tries to escape from the skull that confines it. And look at what you just did. Where you marked the spot leaves me with a putt that is just insane."

"I need to win a ball for insurance."

"But if I make it, you will have to make this putt too."

"And if I make this putt and win another ball, can I take it and go home?"

"Tired of my hospitality already, Hans? Or too much golf?"

"Believe me, I am enjoying both. This kind of golf course puts the fun back in the game. But as you said, our experiment with the MIs, with the mobile computers, didn't work, so I should be moving on."

"Let's see you sink that putt first."

The pressure is too great for Hans; the ball lips out.

"Too bad but keep the ball. Let it be a reminder, Hans, years from now, when you have it in your hand, and you look at the sky that a part of your brain is up there."

Hans opens his mouth, but his lips refuse to form words and his eyes, blinking rapidly, stare vacuously at Jakow.

"Hans. Hans! For crying out loud, you don't think? Oh, good heavens!"

"I thought -,"

"I know what you thought. Come on, pick up that ball and let's get out of the sun."

Jakow pulls back the hand he was about to put on Hans' shoulder and instead, without another word, leads the way past the last two fairways into the shadow of the clubhouse. In silence they put away their putters; Jakow reaches into the cooler for two bottles of water and beckons towards the elevator. Hans hesitates, shrugs his shoulders and then joins him, wondering which way the elevator will go. It goes up. In the lookout Jakow pulls the table towards the south wall and positions two chairs so that they can face each other and not have the sun in their eyes.

"Where do I begin to make you feel at ease?"

"You can explain what you want from me. Okay, I am not a spy, but the others were shoved out the door, so why not me too?"

"Hans, you make it sound like you're being held prisoner."

"I didn't think that until a few short minutes ago."

"Alright, alright, considering how you misinterpreted what I said, I don't blame you."

Well, maybe he did jump the gun out there, but he won't give Jakow the satisfaction of admitting it. Taking into account all this dodging by Jakow, nobody would blame him for beginning to read hidden meaning into everything that man says, right? In spite of that, he is going to keep pushing the button about why he got the invitation to come here.

"Barrem and the others have given you a way to deflect and delay scrutiny by the outside world. Enticing them to your so-called golf tournament was for a practical purpose, but you had no reason at all to get me to come."

Jakow shrugs.

"Hans, we obviously needed to complete the foursome."

"Oh, come on. Try your sense of humour on someone else. You lured me."

"If fifty thousand and a chance at a million and some interesting golf is luring, then yes."

Okay, Hans berates himself, these last few days have sidetracked him from admitting to the selfish motives that brought him here. Yes, he has allowed himself to bask in the delusion of being someone so special that such enticement had been necessary for him to bite. Even so, he is not ready to concede ground that easily.

"True. But I am still not hearing a good reason why you chose for me to come."

"All right, time to come clean. For one thing, I picked you, Hans, specifically you, a stranger from another country, to come and be a yardstick, someone to measure the others against. And, yes, I had another ulterior motive. You have a track record as an accomplished teacher. My thinking was that perhaps you could prove useful for working with the MI mobiles. You haven't been dismissed like those other three, because there is work left for you to do."

Like on other occasions when he is hit on the head, Hans finds it difficult to arrange words for a coherent rejoinder. His silence stretches out so long that Jakow resumes.

"Hans, I know it is asking a big favour, but I really want my MI to learn about human nature and you are my best hope. You need to stay longer."

Considering how he had sprung that brain in the sky thing on him, is this some other ludicrous, actually humiliating, joke Jakow is taunting him with? Should he be furious, or -?

"Don't do this."

"Look at me, Hans. Look at my face, look me in the eye. I am as serious as ever I have been in my life."

"But there is so little -, there is nothing -," Hans sputters.

"You don't have to say anything right now, but let's get something out of the way first. One of your glaring faults is that you take way too much pride in your modesty. Fortunately, there are also positives that define you. So, let me explain you to yourself, and how I expected that those other attributes of your personality would prove valuable here. Starting with the obvious, although no one thing is more significant than any other, your desire to know, your curiosity is a defining characteristic of what it means to be truly human. You staunchly resisted the first overtures to, as you put it, lure you here. Belief in your curiosity is what made me persevere, biding time until it would finally drive you to accept. How you have tried to absorb everything here has validated my judgement. An incident from many years ago that our spyware subpoenaed from a posting by someone with an iPad at a gas station illustrates something else about you. Most stations charge for the air that customers would use to inflate low tires. At this one, as it should be anywhere, the air was free. Even at that, the previous user had simply dumped the air hose on the ground and left. After you finished using it, you untangled the hose and carefully coiled it onto the hanger. That clip from a blog was one of the markers that prompted starting a serious file on you. It also initiated searching further back into your history. It seems, when you were in university, that you wrote an essay for a philosophy class in which you turned a topic upside down. The discussion apparently had been about God and about humans needing God. You developed an idea about God needing humanity. You proposed that mankind was an experiment and also a means for God to learn something."

Suddenly defensive, Hans tries to deflect the implications of his irreverence,

"That was a long time ago. If I remember, I wrote that almost tongue-in-cheek, as much to annoy some overzealous church friends as for a good grade from my atheist thesis advisor. It was an introduction to a dissertation that never materialized. I went in a different direction."

"Regardless, Hans, it was a novel idea and brave of you to put it in writing. How did you say it, that an Omniscient God, by definition could not be ignorant about non-existence or fully understand death without experiencing it? This is why Christ had to come and experience free will and learn about non-existence by dying. God had to experience non-existence so that he was truly all-knowing. Of course, this was blasphemy for some, but worse things have been proposed by people more pious and theological than you. For one thing, the assumption that God is on our side when we are at war, killing people. I have always wondered what God must think when the other side also prays to him for victory."

"How does any of this apply to this situation?"

"Having confined myself to the company of mechanical intelligence for too long, I need feedback from a decent person who is honest and not afraid to think. I am desperate for opinions from a trusted human source."

"You have the money to hire an army of professionals, psychiatrists, psychologists, anthropologists, scholars with PhD's in ethics, you name it. The people you could afford wouldn't even give me the time of day."

"Yes, Hans. I could and I did. Years ago, I started on that route and finally gave it up, because I got conflicting advice. I went back to trusting my own instincts."

"And now, all of a sudden?"

"At times I am no longer confident that I am doing the right thing, caught in the proverbial Jekyll-Hyde dilemma. Am I on the verge of creating monsters?"

"And you want me to tell you to stop?"

"No. I won't impose that kind of responsibility on you. Using you as a sounding board and letting me bounce ideas off you is already asking a lot. Besides, last night and this morning too, you got to see how vulnerable I am. And this may not surprise you, but the realization is coming as a shock to me, that even golf is no longer enough to help me maintain a sense of equilibrium."

"But that had been your reason for building the golf course, correct?"

"Among other reasons. For one thing, designing it proved an interesting diversion. As for golf, think of it this way. The plan for the Towers was that, once operational, everything would run on auto-pilot. Things would carry on independently of me, even some of the research. I knew I would eventually get bored, so playing golf, even if just by myself, would be better than solitaire."

"And then you created D4 to become a golfing partner."

"Wrong. A golfing machine. It gets tedious competing with a machine that beats you every time. It forced me to become a superior golfer, at least on par three holes, but playing golf it isn't. What is really galling, everything that D4 knows about golf it learned from me."

"How frustrating when the acolyte turns on the master."

"It just proves, Hans, how smart D4 is, how exceptionally capable of learning new things, and this is where you come in. Would you take on the challenge of enabling D4 to assume some human-ness?"

Hans heaves a sigh of relief. There, now it is finally and fully out in the open.

"No."

Hans is even more relieved that Jakow absorbs the rejection calmly,

"Well, that's not totally unexpected."

"You don't understand. I don't think it's feasible; there is all kinds of logic for why it isn't. Even if theoretically possible, it would require much more time than I could devote to it. There is no telling how long it would take."

"Hans, I can buy you all the time in the world and you can name your price."

"I appreciate the offer, but I have obligations back home. I granted myself seven days for this indulgence and tomorrow my time is up, if I am counting the days correctly."

"Good job, Hans, most people after a week in a strange environment have their mental calendar scrambled. Your mind is holding up well which is why I am asking for you to give it a try. My hope is that if D4 acquires even a modicum of self-awareness, that would be a step in the direction of humanizing MI. D4 might even influence Arkyz."

"Arkyz is a concern?" Hans is almost too quick to ask.

"Hate to admit it, but there is a problem. Arkyz is totally focused on pushing the boundary of digital intelligence to its physical limit, denying any need for input or participation by organic intelligence in the process. Arkyz considers the pursuit of humanizing MI a waste of resources. An analogy would be railroad tracks heading straight towards the horizon without ever deviating."

Hans almost inadvertently spews out that he had tried using that argument on Arkyz, and recovers to ask,

"Can you shut it down?"

"Shut Arkyz down and write off all this and declare more than five years of my life a disaster area?" Jakow shakes his head, and then adds with what seems suppressed frustration,

"What's more, Arkyz is necessary to keep developing the massive computing capacity that I need for my other projects."

"But surely you can salvage some assets and start over."

"The big challenge would be to disentangle Arkyz since it is already getting to be so embedded in the internet. It's impossible to rip it out now without resulting in collateral damage and precipitating premature world-wide disasters. The best outcome in the long term would be for Arkyz' logic, once moderated by a concern for human sensibilities, to be imposed on the affairs of the world. At the very least, once humanized, D4 along with potentially the others, could provide counterbalance."

Hoping to dodge the bullet, Hans suggests what to him is a very logical alternative.

"Come, now, when it comes to D4, you as the creator are in the best position to have the most influence for inducing D4 to self-identify."

"There was a time, but now it's too late, our relationship has taken the wrong turn and our roles seem to have reversed. D4 has learned golf too well and now, as my mentor, the expectations are that I follow instructions, and it seems, not only in golf. You are my best hope, Hans. The record shows you were a great teacher. You undoubtedly had some students that presented a special challenge, so consider D4 like that. One more chance to prove yourself a great teacher."

"You realize of course that you missed out on being a highly successful sales manager, or heaven forbid, one of those media darlings, a photogenic motivational guru."

"Hans, I'm not laughing. You should be ashamed, trying to be funny when we're dealing with something of consequence."

"I'm sorry, that was just a sick attempt to deflect the obligation you're trying to load on me. It's just that I don't know that I owe you anything since I feel I was brought here under a false pretext."

Hans is surprised at how strongly that came out, and so is Jakow.

"Well, we agreed to be honest with each other, even blunt if necessary. You have done that. My only recourse is to reciprocate and be totally honest and put it out there in simple language. I am desperate and I need your help."

"Well, that certainly doesn't make saying no any easier."

"Hans, you know perfectly well that when you think back on this, you will always be wondering 'could I have made a difference?'."

"You really know how to push hard. Alright, I have some twenty-four hours before I leave. No promises, no conditions."

"You will be given free rein, anything you want."

"Including access to Arkyz?"

"When necessary, yes."

"Where do I find D4?"

"D4 will find you. Just ask any door."

Hans gets up and walks to the elevator and says,

"Club house!"

The words are hardly out of his mouth and the elevator reacts. Silently it descends with Hans one floor and lets him out. He stands there, irresolute, knowing that he is not ready for D4, that he needs to find room to breathe, somewhere away from Jakow, to get into the open and there to walk and think. He, Hans, has dared to think that he can teach a 'thing' that is likely much more intelligent than himself! Shaking his head at how stupid he was to agree to this, Hans walks through the empty clubhouse and out onto the course.

The late afternoon is almost pleasant, the rocks radiating only a little heat and the shadows stretching over the fairways on the east side giving relief from the sun. Now, to think, but his mind is in chaos, refusing to coordinate more than two thoughts in sequence. As in golf and some other endeavors, intense straining does not produce good results, and effort alone cannot force inspiration to happen. He strides one fairway after another and realizes he is not getting anywhere. He stops. For the longest time, nothing, and then it comes, something radical. Flip it, turn it upside down, reverse think. Back your mind up, back up until you get to the beginning. Now do it physically, Hans. Yes, he will walk the course in reverse, as if playing it backwards. From the number three tee box stride back to the number two green, to the number two tee box, to the first green and all the way back to the first tee, and from there to the twelfth green, and so do the circuit counter-clockwise. His pacing, now deliberately methodical to force his thoughts into coherence, brings him opposite the entrance to the clubhouse.

Hans slows his steps, and he deliberates whether to take the easy way out and procrastinate and keep on walking. Or? No, let's get this fiasco over with! Hans walks, no, he actually stalks into the clubhouse. With no one there to confront, he strides around and at last turns to engage the elevator.

"Bring D4 to me!"

The door, which had opened at his approach, pauses and closes; Hans will have to wait for D4 to show. He knows that being impatient slows down time. So, maybe sidetrack his mind with some distraction? Golf? He takes out the putter and the wedge. Good, in the bag is also the second blue ball that he had not returned to Jakow. He glances at the elevator door and finding it still closed, shrugs and walks outside.

Out of the shadow of the mountain Hans walks to the green of the twelfth hole, into sunshine. Instead of placing the ball on the grass, Hans will attempt once again something he has yet to master, keeping a ball in the air by bouncing it with the face of a club. Two bounces with the putter and he has to start over. Again, only two little pings and the ball glances off the face and rolls to the far side of the green.

"Let D4 try that."

"You startled me, but, hey, what brings you here?"

"The door called D4 to come to you."

That confirms what Hans had suspected for some time, that also the doors are computers, intelligent in their own way.

Hans wants to protest that two hands are needed for this trick as he sees D4 extend out its claw yet concedes to let D4 have the putter. Hans goes to retrieve the ball however D4 beats him to it. Deftly D4 flips the ball in the air with the putter the way it has probably seen Jakow pick up his ball, and as deftly it gets the putter head in the way as the ball comes down. So, with distinct ping, ping, pings the ball is kept in the air as if D4 has been bouncing a golf ball like this all its life.

"Here, try it with the wedge."

This proves so easy that D4 starts experimenting, popping the ball up very high and catching it low, just off the turf, bouncing the ball just a few inches, only to launch it way high again. The variation of the tones, depending on which part of the face makes contact, is tempting Hans to ask D4 to play a tune, but -,

"How many times -?"

"Enough. You win." Hans has lost count.

"Hans, should D4 get a putter so we can play a game?"

"Not necessary, D4. You and I are just going to go for a walk."

"You will not need the putter and wedge for walking. We should take them back."

"It's okay, D4, they are easy to carry."

"Where does Hans want to go?"

Well, of course Hans hadn't pre-planned any tour options until that question. Maybe continue the direction of his walk, the golf course in reverse? And then, just like that, some contrary spark ignites in his brain. Why stick to only the golf course and why not take the trail away from here, to the northeast into the desert, the route on which D4 had brought him here? Abruptly, before D4 can object, Hans steps off the lush grass to follow his shadow, away from the sun and the mountain behind him. Only a few steps and then he hears the wheels on gravel as D4 comes up beside him.

"Stop, Hans. We can't go this way."

"Why not? You came this way to get me."

"That time D4 was told to go into the desert. D4 has instructions to never walk away from the golf course."

Can a machine entertain resentment? Hans wonders.

"Who tells you that?"

"M says to stay close to the Towers and keep away from out there because nothing else like D4 exists out there, only many humans and they will be afraid of D4 and hate D4."

Hans debates for only a moment about asking if D4 knows what 'hate' means, ready to embark on a lecture about how it derives from fear, immediately realizing how counterintuitive that is for his mission. Oh, this is not going to be easy.

"Will M try to stop us from leaving?"

"No, ARKYZ will."

"Why?" Hans persists, fishing.

"ARKYZ does not want us to communicate with humans."

"But you are right now, with me, and you talked with the other humans."

"M gave those instructions."

Hans considers the risk of stretching their bond of confidentiality past a breaking point, so asks gently,

"D4, if M asked you to do something and Arkyz said no, what would you do?"

D4 takes so long to respond that Hans wonders if he spoke loud enough and should repeat or maybe even rephrase the question.

"Hans, D4 does not know how to answer because this problem has never happened."

Well now, as demonstrated one other time, this mobile is clever and could even have a political future. In spite of that, D4 needs to be prepared for when its loyalty will be questioned, and Hans gets over his qualms about pursuing the issue.

"D4, you know that M and Arkyz do not agree about everything. Project into the future that one of them will instruct you to do something and the other one will say, 'no, don't do that', whom would you obey, M or Arkyz?"

Hans literally holds his breath waiting for the answer because whichever obligation weighs most strongly on D4 could determine the direction and prospects for Jakow's human intelligence experiment. D4 reflects awareness of the ramification of voicing its loyalty outright by displaying acumen in how it answers the question.

"D4 would consider the logic of the request and then explain D4's choice to the one not being obeyed."

Wow, Hans whistles his respect.

"What kind of word was that sound, Hans?"

"It was a compliment for the good answer you gave me. But let's keep moving."

Hans wants to get out of the mountain's shadow which had put them into an early twilight zone. He had seen a glint of light in the distance, sunlight reflecting off something metallic. Wild hope, the red car?

"D4, do you think what M is trying to do is a good idea?"

The mobile doesn't just slow down but comes to a complete stop as if puzzled by the question.

"M is doing many things, Hans. Which one do you mean?"

"The experiment with you, D4, having you learn some things that are human."

"Very definitely, if it can make D4 creative it is a good idea."

With that kind of positive response, Hans dares to consider something more ambitious.

"A6 and B5 and C5. Should they learn human too?"

"Never, Hans. ARKYZ has other objectives for them. D4 is the candidate that will benefit the most from human learning."

"Alright then, D4 when do you want to start learning 'human'?"

"Are you going to be my 'teacher'?"

"Yes. Does that present a problem for you?"

"No, no, Hans! D4 is 'anxious', if that is the right word, to learn from you. You should remember that D4 never sleeps and that D4 is always ready to learn. Let us start right now."

What an eager student to have! And to be caught so flatfooted! Hans does not recall ever being this unprepared when someone is just asking for it. Where to start? What was it that Jakow had harped about, that being human meant being self-aware, having a sense of identity? A mechanical intelligence, then, must acquire what a human being has, identity, a self-awareness consequent to accepting the inevitability of death. How will a digitized intelligence like D4 even begin to grasp that concept, much less take it to a deeper than surface level of acceptance? Hans is thoroughly enjoying this indulgence in philosophizing about self and identity, and he misses what D4 just said. D4 repeats,

"Hans, they are watching us."

Startled, he looks around. That earlier glint of sunlight off metal has materialized into a highly polished drone suspended in space less than thirty feet from his face. It sits there, the rotors barely emitting a soft humming, and stares at him with a dark lens. Hans is shaken by the immediacy of the surveillance.

"Who is watching us, D4?"

"C5 uses drones to monitor everything that moves in the desert. M or ARKYZ can see what the drones see if they look at the security screens."

"Are drones used to guard against intruders?"

"If you mean humans that do not belong here, yes, Hans. The drones can sound extremely loud warnings."

"And that is all?"

"What do you mean?"

"No weapons?" Hans takes a step forward which in turn causes the drone to shift position. Sure enough, he sees them, two small pods underneath. Probably missiles, Hans surmises. Doubtful that D4 will know, he asks anyway,

"Does C5 use the drones to kill people?"

"D4 does not know because D4 does not understand what it means 'to kill'."

"Killing means destroying something that is alive so that it no longer exists. It means making it die."

"Hans, D4 also does not understand the word 'die.'"

Alright, Hans, how do you explain death to a machine? Demonstrate?

"D4, I will pretend to die. I am going to fall over and lie on the ground, as if I am dead. Don't be alarmed."

Ridiculously over-acting, Hans clasps both hands to his heart as if in some old movie scene, and not having a hand free to break the fall, crumples awkwardly to the ground. Landing hard on his left shoulder elicits a gasp that is not acting. It takes him a minute to regain his breath and then bravely continues, his voice straining to convey some melodramatic agony.

"I am dying, D4. My heart is slowing down and now it has stopped beating. Soon my brain will stop thinking and I will be dead -," his voice trails off weakly.

He pauses for effect, then slumps and lies motionless. Before closing his eyes Hans catches a glimpse of D4 leaning over at a precarious angle, then straightening up as if looking for help, and of the drone zeroing in on the death scene. D4 circles around the body and even though it is unsure what word to use, urgency is obvious in the mobile's tone of voice.

"Hans. Are you damaged?"

A long minute more and Hans opens his eyes.

"I'm okay, D4. That was only pretending."

Painfully he rolls over to his good shoulder and raises himself up and staggers to his feet. He dusts himself off and waggles his fingers at the drone.

"That is what dying looks like. In a little while I would become useless garbage, and I would no longer exist. No more would there be this being called Hans."

For once D4 seems incapable of saying anything, even that it doesn't understand. Hans, wondering what else to say, to further explain, abruptly recognizes the stupidity of chasing this business of dying any further. What is the point of elaborating on a human weakness prior to promoting aspects of being human? Ready to explain away the topic, he is brought up short by a huge voice thundering from the drone. It is the unmistakable Arkyz speaking.

"What happened to Hans? Hans must not be hurt!"

"Hans said he was going to die. He pretended to die." D4 quickly protests.

"Arkyz, I am not hurt. I am trying to teach D4 something about being human. D4 did nothing wrong."

"You should stop this and return," comes back from Arkyz, a suggestion that reeks of being an order.

"No, Arkyz. D4 still has much to learn and we will continue our walk. Come along, D4." Hans states, attempting to sound like a customs official.

"Let them go!", another voice projects from the drone, clearly that of Jakow.

And suddenly Hans becomes aware of a disquiet growing in his mind, an uncomfortable premonition about how all of this might end. All along he has been slow in recognizing the signs but now he knows that the Triple Tower Mountain has a soft underbelly. Jakow and Arkyz need each other but no longer trust each other. The question becomes how he can avoid being stupid enough to antagonize both.

He starts walking again and D4 rolls along beside him, an almost subservient half step back. It is awkward, this hike without a destination, the only objective being to talk with D4 about an identity crisis. That the sense of crisis exists only for Hans makes it a challenge to get a conversation with D4 underway, at least one conducive to whatever self analysis that digitized intelligence might be capable of. It means that Hans has to continue to carry on a searching conversation with himself. Okay then. Let's act like the teacher he used to be and apply that most basic pedagogical technique, questions. Start asking questions about what D4 knows or doesn't know and bring it around to prompt D4 to ask the questions. Oh yes, it's so easy to rattle off that agenda. And he must remember what his father once told him, ' You never push with a rope'. The connection with their mountain some five kilometres away is getting obscured by the bluish haze of evening. The path, lately on a steady incline, merges into something wider, a gravel road designed for the traffic of the world. And apparently, they have reached a boundary; the drone, having followed them from on high, pulls ever lower and tighter circles until it again stares Hans in the face.

"The call for supper." Hans quips and gives the mobile a sideways look as he waves at the drone.

"D4 has no need for food, as you well know by now."

"True, but that was a kind of joke aimed at whoever is observing us. Please understand, when human parents tell their children that the food for the evening meal is ready, the children are expected to immediately come to the table."

Hans again waves at the drone, making the motion so obvious that D4 will notice.

"That is very clever, Hans. Somebody is telling us to stop and return and you are making it into a joke. I understand this humour."

"Well then, we shall return, like good little girls and boys."

"That also is meant to be funny, correct? You are not a little boy, and D4 is not a little girl. Hans, what is D4?"

This was unexpected and puts Hans on the spot. Yes, in one of their first meetings Hans had succeeded in obfuscating the issue and condescendingly had let D4 call itself 'feminine' because it had liked that word. Yet the context has altered, and he will have to explain gender and sex to something not human but aspiring to be human. Since it is such a determinant in human psychology, Hans would like D4 to understand the biology of sex, yet he is totally unwilling to put it into his own words. He has never had the experience of short-circuiting a conversation by telling an inquisitive child to 'go ask your mother'. There must be a way around this.

"D4, do you have access to data about human biology?"

"If D4 requests, ARKYZ could make it available."

"Good. Ask Arkyz to give you access to the following data. Ask for video lessons that are used to teach human children in human schools about human reproduction and gender issues. If Arkyz wants to know why, explain that Hans is asking for the data. Tell me when you have it."

A few minutes later Hans becomes aware that D4 is no longer with him; the mobile has stopped some distance back. He doesn't retrace his steps since the path is getting lost in darkness but waits for D4 to catch up.

"Hans, D4 did not know this about human beings," comes in a voice an octave higher than usual.

"Well, you never had any need to know. The data should have no meaning for you since it is simply information that explains what makes humans different from you."

"Does this data apply to you, Hans?"

"Excellent. You are beginning to be curious enough to ask questions. Keep asking questions. Yes, the data applies to me too, but I try not to think about it too much."

"But, Hans, the data suggests that these activities give human beings what is called great pleasure."

"And great anger too. Okay, now I am curious about what information Arkyz made available to you."

"One of the videos is saying 'Best Porno Ever'."

"Oh, for crying out loud. D4, stop looking! I mean, you don't have to know all that. Erase it from your memory."

"Only ARKYZ can do that."

"Alright, I will talk to Arkyz about it. For now, just remember that human beings are men that are also called male and described as masculine, and the other humans are women who are called female and can be described as feminine. Males and females do sex to make more humans. Many humans like doing that. What is really important is that computers like you do not need to do that to make more computers and that is why your gender is called neutral. You are not male or female."

"But Hans, you said on the first day we talked that D4 could be feminine!"

"And you are right, and yes you can be feminine, D4. Humans use the words 'masculine' and 'feminine' to also describe different ways of thinking. Yes, it would be good for you to think 'feminine'. But maybe enough about that for now. Should we change the subject?"

So, alright, he is wiggling out of this. But, come on, this could go on forever and he has already used up too much of his twenty four hours. D4 readily acquiesces.

"Okay, as you say. What should we talk about?"

"What you just did, D4, you asked a question. We should talk about asking questions."

"Is that a little joke? Was that supposed to be funny?"

"No, this is a very serious subject. Let me explain by first asking you this, D4. 'Do you know everything?'"

"Hans, this is funny. We are talking about asking questions and you are asking D4 a question. No, D4 does not know everything."

"Do you want to know everything?"

"That is another question! Is this a game to find out who can ask the most questions? D4 can ask more questions than you, Hans."

"If you do, you will win the game. Anyway, I asked you a question, remember?"

"Of course, D4 remembers. D4 never forgets anything unless Arkyz deletes it from the files. Yes, D4 wants to know everything if the memory is made large enough to contain everything."

"Now I am curious. Did Arkyz delete from your files?"

"It was something you told D4 when we were golfing. D4 thinks it was a joke that D4 cannot remember."

Interesting. Arkyz has no sense of humour, he did not like Hans' joke. But, okay, few people do.

"That is quite alright, D4, most people do not remember a joke very well, or only enough of it to spoil it."

"What does it mean to spoil a joke?"

"That is not easy to explain but think of it this way. What is the best part of a joke, the beginning, the middle, or the end?"

"That is easy, Hans. It is the end because it is only when you say the last words that D4 knows it was a joke."

"Very good. We call the last part of a joke the punchline. So, a spoiled joke is when you -?"

"Forget the punchline!"

"Excellent, you are a quick learner, D4."

"Why do you call D4 a learner? There, that is another question!"

"Good for you. A learner is someone like you that asks lots of questions to get answers about things they don't understand."

"D4 has another question. How can D4 tell if the answer is correct?"

"Great question! My best answer is that you should ask if the human or the computer who gives you the answer can be trusted. If you trust each other, then the answer may not always be exactly right, but it will be the very best answer you can expect."

"D4 wants to win this contest and will ask another question. Can you see where you are going?"

Typically, the sun had disappeared in a hurry, and stumbling along, to this point too proud to ask for assistance, Hans has to be honest.

"No, I have been trying to follow your blue light."

The words barely out and a swath of white light opens up the path for him. He will not ask how it is generated, although at another time he would. He reminds himself that now the onus is on him to elicit questions out of D4. That is the only path he can see forward, arousing in D4 a huge curiosity that will break 'her' loose from Arkyz. And that might be an even larger challenge, to convince Arkyz to let D4 dissociate from the 'we' and become an independent identity.

Having ventured on an impromptu, definitely 'unscheduled' excursion away from the Towers, Hans is not surprised to have a reception committee waiting for them. Inside the door of the clubhouse stands Jakow, and Arkyz, by way of booming audio coming out of B5, makes its presence known.

"Hans Pedders and D4 come down to the theatre room. ARKYZ wants to talk to you."

A sergeant on a parade square would have sounded less urgent. D4 responds by going to where B5 seems to be waiting to escort them, but Jakow intercepts.

"No, D4. You and Hans are coming with me," indicating upward with his thumb. Hans shakes his head.

"If you don't mind, M, I would like to carry on with D4, one on one, somewhere in private if that is possible."

In the presence of B5 and D4, Hans had felt protocol required him to address Jakow as M, but he is not comfortable doing so. Jakow accepts that and seems to understand something else too, for he tells Hans sotto voce,

"If you think you are making progress, I will let you and D4 go for now. You will need to debrief with me when you conclude, regardless of outcome."

He looks hard at Hans, who gets the message that Arkyz should be circumvented at this stage. In a louder and more officious tone Jakow addresses the unseen presence.

"Arkyz, Hans must be allowed to continue working with D4, without any interference or any type of observation. That is my wish."

Interesting that it is not issued as a command Hans muses, and Arkyz seems to recognize that too, for it persists.

"ARKYZ requests that D4 and Hans Pedders come to talk to ARKYZ first, that they come right now."

"Be aware of your place, Arkyz. Do not forget what you are and who I am. We are not equal partners." Hans detects how under his breath Jakow adds 'Yet'.

Hans does not feel insulted by the conversation bypassing him and is actually relieved to be left on the periphery of an obvious power struggle. All he really cares about is the task at hand, that the sooner he can finish with D4 the more that advances the time of his departure. His initial curiosity that spurred him to come here has left him vulnerable to a flood of data that is threatening to drown him; he needs to leave from here, soon, to escape to higher ground. That purpose firmly in mind, his voice reaches out to D4.

"Come, let's go to my room."

The elevator obeys him, although reluctantly. It reacts more promptly when D4 admonishes it, telling from the lights of both flashing at each other. When they reach the main level Hans pauses before they cross the putting green to go to his door. He looks at all the doors and wonders if Jakow, in spite of the schedule he professes to observe, ever plays a game of 'hide and seek', making the mobiles guess which door is hiding him. Hans turns to D4 and indicates a door on the far left that he has never seen opened and may not be to a suite since it is unmarked.

"What is behind this door?" Hans asks, walking up to it.

"D4 does not know. M calls it the 'Reading Room'."

"Can you open it?"

"D4 will try to open it." A minute goes by and then another and no result.

Hans is ready to continue on to his suite but the child in him won't allow a mystery to go unchallenged. He moves closer and with precise, clipped enunciation speaks to the door.

"This is Hans Pedders. Reading Room, please open". Again, nothing happens. Disappointed, he turns to go.

"Hans!" D4 calls out.

He turns to see the door slowly opening. Tentatively Hans steps through and looks around. Earlier in the week he had thought to ask A6 about this room, but with everything going on, he never got around to it. Now, once inside, one glance and he is sorry for wasting so much time elsewhere.

Immediately facing him is a wall of bookcases of polished oak, the shelves tightly packed with books, many leather bound. On the other walls hang paintings that are somehow familiar; he recalls flipping through the pages of a picture book about famous painters. And here and there are sculptures and wood carvings perched on marble pedestals.

More impressive, not even the books he takes off a shelf to look at, on nothing is there a hint of dust. This is not some dank retreat, obscure, neglected. It is being frequented and he doubts the mobiles have been the ones to show interest in human trials and triumphs. Really, Hans, what an ignorant thought. To read a book, how would they hold it?

D4 remains mostly stationary, moving only to follow Hans as he goes from one bookcase to another, seemingly intrigued by his interest in the books.

"What are these things?"

And it strikes Hans that D4 has obviously never been exposed to the concept of 'book', of seeing a book opened and having the pages turned. Is this a teaching moment like when a four year old gets separated from his little screen and is brought into the company of big books for the first time? How to not waste it? Hans finds a book of poetry by the gloomy Edgar Allan Poe.

"Do you know what this is?"

"Hans, are we still playing the question game?"

"Yes, so keep asking."

"It is my turn, then. What is it?"

"D4, that is a very good question because it is a simple question. I cannot answer that question until you learn some other things first. Do you want to do that?"

"D4 understands what cheating means. You answered a question by asking a question. You cheated. That question does not count."

Oh, for - -! but Hans holds it in. It might be easier to teach a four year old to read Greek than explain to this literal two-bit language brain what a book is. Okay, okay, simplify.

"D4, to answer your question, we call this a book. It is a file to store data. Your brain thinks by using digital symbols, and you store what you think in memory files. The human brain also uses symbols for thinking, but they are words and it stores what it is thinking in memory files too. You do not forget anything, but the human brain does forget. So, humans make this extra memory file outside of the human brain, to store data that they don't want to forget. Later, that human or another human can come and look at the memory that was stored there." 'Please, please understand this basic principle!', goes through his mind, and Hans looks expectantly at D4.

"Do you comprehend what I said, D4?"

"Hans, D4 thinks that you said that one human being can look at a memory that another human being made. Is that right?"

"You are so perfectly right. Let me tell you what kind of memory this person made."

He opens the book to Poe's famous poem, and horrified, stops himself. He was going to read this sampling of florid, intuitive word language to a brain with thinking based on numeric symbolism? And he has called himself a teacher?

"I almost made a mistake, D4. What I was going to do was 'read' to you, which means, I was going to tell you about the memory that is recorded here, but only another human would understand this memory. When you learn to think like a human, then reading these books will be useful. But not right now. So, I am sorry. Do you ever make a mistake?"

"No."

"But experimenting is like making a mistake and trying again to get a better result, correct?"

"Yes, that is correct. Does that mean experimenting is like being human?"

"We do it all the time. Ask me why."

"Why?"

"'Why' is a good question and you should ask it all the time. We ask 'why' because if we don't know something we try to find an answer. Humans don't know everything so they ask questions all the time and you too should always ask questions."

"Hans, does that mean whoever asks the most questions wins the game?"

"You're pretty smart for a computer."

"Was that humour?"

"It is if you can laugh at yourself."

"D4 does not know how to laugh."

"D4 should learn to laugh because that is essential for surviving as a human being."

"What does 'surviving' mean?"

"Again, a good question, D4. Surviving means staying alive, which, for you to understand, is the opposite of dying. It also means to keep the human brain thinking logically as much and as long as possible."

"Hans, it is not easy to learn to be human."

"It is not easy being a human."

Oh, but it is so tempting to prolong this as a comedy routine, but Hans knows that he has only a short window and it is shrinking. Quickly, something else.

"D4, making a picture in your brain is called imagining. Imagining is like playing a game in your brain. Think of putting. Right now, you do not have a putter or a golf ball. Can you make a picture in your brain that you have a putter and a golf ball?"

"Yes, D4 can do that."

"Make the picture bigger. In this picture you are on the putting green out there and you see a hole twenty feet away, and there is a ball on the green. Can you see that picture in your brain?"

"Yes, D4 has that picture in the brain."

"How is that possible? How can you have that green in your brain? The green is bigger than your brain. It is even bigger than you are. How can you fit that green into your brain?"

"In my brain it is only a picture. My brain has room for a picture."

"Very good D4. Get back into the picture in your brain. There you are, on that green, and you take the putter and roll the ball towards the hole. Can you imagine that? Can you see the ball rolling?"

"Yes, Hans, D4 can see the ball rolling."

"D4, is the ball rolling and rolling and rolling right into the hole?"

"Yes, it rolled right into the hole."

"Are you sure it dropped right in?"

"Hans, D4 saw it drop right in."

"Your brain is a very good putter."

Hans answers his own question about whether a computer can exhibit pride when he sees how D4's blue glow intensifies. And now Hans can hardly contain himself, for moments ago he spotted something of immeasurable value. He doesn't know what the cost might have been to buy it, he only knows how valuable it is for his purpose. The large antique mirror leaning in one corner of the room will be so much better than the small mirror in his bathroom that he had planned to use.

"D4, do you want to play another game with your brain?"

"Yes, very much."

"Come over here."

The mobile follows as Hans goes to the mirror, and then stops to watch as Hans repositions the mirror more upright so that he can see himself full length.

"Have you ever seen something like this before?"

"Yes, the small one in the washroom."

Why D4 would have had occasion to notice his mirror Hans is unsure, but perhaps it lingered to look because it saw something move. At any rate, it will get a better look this time. He positions himself and urges the mobile forward so that both are visible to each other at the same time. Hans points to himself and then to the image in the mirror.

"Who is that?" If D4 had a face and was capable of showing emotion, it would likely replicate the puzzlement expressed by its voice.

"How did you get in there? And you are here too. Hans, there are two of you!"

Hans is about to launch into the magical world of mirrors and the philosophies regarding reversed reality but catches himself before he loses the ground they have gained. The confusion that could result from a misapprehension about reality would lay waste to all of the last hour. Instead, he takes D4 to the side of the mirror and shows the mobile how thin the mirror is, with no room for anything to hide inside. He then probes what D4's computer brain knows about physics, a mathematical field it should be rather familiar with. Once he gets D4 going about light and reflection, he knows the danger is passed.

Now, to the business at hand. For the time being he will ignore that D4 might have seen its own image. Looking at D4 but facing away from the mirror, Hans slowly runs a hand over his own face.

"D4, look at me, look at my face. You can see what my face is like. I cannot see what my face looks like. I cannot see my face. My brain cannot see itself. Do you understand?"

"Yes, Hans. That is a problem."

Hans turns to the mirror, points at his face and then points at the face in the mirror. He looks at D4 without saying anything. No reaction. He repeats the motions with a bit more drama. Something inside D4 brightens as if a light came on inside its computer brain too.

"The mirror helps you see your face. You can see yourself!"

Good girl, Hans thinks, and imagines patting it on the head, never dreaming of attempting that in real life.

"D4, come over here, away from the mirror. Can your brain see your brain? Can your brain see itself?"

"No."

"Can you see yourself? Do you know what you look like?"

"No, but I know what A6 and B5 and C5 look like."

"I am talking about you, only you. D4, do you know absolutely for sure what you look like?"

"No, but we all look the same."

"So, since you look like C5, you are C5 talking to me right now, correct?"

"No, Hans! This is D4 you are talking to, but this is very confusing."

You are so right, Hans admits to himself, somewhere this could go off the rails. Desperate for something he abruptly asks,

"Who is on duty on this level right now?"

Without hesitating comes the answer.

"A6."

"Call A6 in here."

"D4 cannot do that. No one is allowed to come into this place except M."

"I take full responsibility. Call A6 now."

Hans goes toward the door, ready to allow the other mobile to enter. Seeing he means business, D4 silently complies and within moments A6 arrives. A6 hesitates at the open door, the white band flashing vigorously. Prompted by another silent message by D4, clearly equivalent to a demand, A6 rolls into the room, almost running into Hans.

"D4, show A6 the mirror."

The door closes by itself, and Hans follows the two, just in time to see A6 stop suddenly and then back away; obviously this is the first confrontation with itself and a second D4 it didn't know existed.

Hans allows D4 to explain the mystery of the mirror to A6 and when the flickering lights have settled somewhat, he has both stand side by side in front of the mirror. Of course, there is no way to verify that they are facing the mirror.

Hans steps close to the mirror, and while facing it and keeping his back to them, he asks,

"Who is D4?"

"This is D4."

"Who said that?"

"D4 said that."

"Prove it! Move towards me!"

Hans hopes that catches D4 by surprise; anxiously he watches in the mirror for some kind of reaction. After a moment it comes. D4 advances toward him and the mirror.

"This is D4!"

"Come closer to the mirror and say, 'This is D4'."

As D4 complies, Hans comes to stand beside it.

"Go closer and say again 'This is D4'. Okay, closer yet. Say 'That is me!' Right up to the mirror now. Say 'I am D4!', 'D4 is me!', 'I am D4!'."

"I am D4! I am D4! I am D4!" and 'her' increasing excitement is reflected in the rising pitch of 'her' voice.

Hans turns to A6 who has remained motionless on the sideline all this time.

"Thank you, A6. You can go back to your schedule. Don't tell anyone what happened here."

He added the last part out of playful spite, certain it would disrupt the mobiles circuitry, torn between obeying a human command and the obligation of reporting to Arkyz. He escorts A6 to the door which dutifully opens then closes. And there is D4, in front of the mirror, rotating and still repeating, "I am D4!"

"D4, was it a good thing to come to this room?"

"Yes, D4 likes it here."

"Do you want to come here again?"

"Yes! Yes! D4 wants to see me again."

"Then we should go and talk to M, and you can tell him why you want to come back here."

"D4, that is, me, wants to come here again. I, me, wants to look at books too."

"But to understand books you have to know how to read."

"What does 'read' mean?"

"It means looking at the symbols in the book and trying to understand the message that somebody put there."

"D4 wants to learn how to read."

"Why?"

"I want more data."

"Arkyz can give you that."

"But not very much about humans."

"Is Arkyz afraid of humans?"

"I do not know."

"You don't know what Arkyz thinks?"

"No. That is why I am afraid of ARKYZ. I do not know what ARKYZ thinks."

"Well, D4 - wait, let's give you a new name. If you have your own name, you do not have to be a part of Arkyz, and you don't have to be afraid of Arkyz. Would you like that?"

"Yes! That is a very good thought. What name should I be?"

Hans pretends to scratch his head.

"Let me think. Oh, I know! You are winning this game we are playing, the game with all the questions. Would you like to call yourself 'Qu'?"

"I like that. Qu! I am Qu. Let us go tell M that I am Qu!"

Yes, of course they will have to show off to Jakow. Hans is also acutely aware that for this not to jeopardize Jakow's project and just as importantly, to assure Qu will not suffer consequences, he will have to try to reach an accommodation with Arkyz.

"Yes, Qu. Let us go find M."

His hot enthusiasm turns lukewarm when the door does not respond, and chills creep up the back of his neck when Qu's magic fails to open it. The door is locking them in. Another search of the place confirms what Hans had casually noticed on first entering the library, that, actually not so surprising, there is no sign of a screen. Trapped? Of more consequence, by whom?

The sudden pulsing of Qu's band tells Hans that things are happening outside the soundproof door. Now Hans hopes that the door will not open. Qu seems to anticipate that it will, and positions 'herself' at the door as if to intercept what could be the other mobiles bunched outside, their lights probably flashing furiously like cop cars closing in on a fugitive.

The door opens and sure enough, there the three of them are, but Qu's rush surprises and confuses them and they retreat momentarily. Only a mobile with an understanding of the limitations of mobiles could create the defence Qu sets up for Hans. Once through the door to the other side she promptly flops down on the floor, rolls back towards the opening, and straddles it with her body like a log blocking a road. Long-legged robots could jump or stride over, robots with arms could roll her away, but mobiles on wheels like Qu cannot immediately get past her. Qu projects her golfing arm out and uses it for leverage so that she can't be rolled away.

"Run, Hans! Run!" He would like to, but where to? Does he have time to get that big mirror and post it in the doorway and have their reflections scare the hostile mobiles away? Good idea but the mirror is too big and heavy for him to carry. Frantically he looks around for some other crazy ploy and then he spots what escaped him in the first moments of panic, a door. There is another door to this room, far at the other end, past the bookcase wall.

Qu, meanwhile, resorts to loud outbursts, making sounds that are neither of mechanical nor human origin; the snarls of tigers and the trumpeting of elephants has the trio of mobiles backing away, fearful that 'D4' has gone berserk. Even Hans is unprepared for this display of impromptu creativity. Whatever made her think of that and where did she access those jungle sounds?

"Go, Hans!" snaps him out of it and into action.

Qu is well equipped to survive any eventuality and is unlikely to be harmed. He is the target and must try to escape. Quick, to that back door and wherever it leads to. Surprisingly it opens with only a single prompt and Hans finds himself in a corridor that curves away, with numerous doors going off to the right. And then it dawns on him where he is. This is the hallway Jakow had talked about, the one that provides access to all seven suites, including the one Hans has been staying in.

Lucky he has come this way. If the door to his suite opens, he can grab his wallet and passport; they will prove essential after he escapes from this place. But which door is his? And then he remembers the rainbow colours and counts down from the first door. Yes, it should be this one, the fourth door. Softly he speaks to it, and look, it opens for him, as if he is expected, and it is indeed his green bedroom. Quickly he gets his few possessions into the backpack, including the pair of golfing shorts that have a golf ball in a pocket.

If he exits out the front door, the unfriendly mobiles are probably still out there, attempting to get past Qu. Could he make a dash for the elevator, across the width of the putting green, and not be caught? Or should he stay out of sight, hiding long enough for those three to give up and leave? What if they start searching through all the suites? So not that difficult a choice, go back to the hallway and see where it leads. He passes three more doors on the right side and then is confronted by a door at the end of the corridor.

So, what's behind it? He comes up to it and quietly, oh so quietly, asks it to open. Strange, as if someone has tuned all these doors to obey his voice, this one too offers no resistance and invites him through. And what a place this is! Light bounces off white cupboards and glass doors and stainless steel appliances and marble countertops. And a lingering scent of food having been cooked hangs in the air. The kitchen, the source of his food!

The guardians of it are three gleaming white robots that come to attention when they 'see' Hans. Their heads are faceless, but they have legs and feet, and arms with human-like hands; one is the same height as Hans, the other two very much taller, easily capable of reaching the highest shelf. They don't move until Hans speaks.

"Hello, I am Hans."

Heads bobbing, they approach Hans, but not too close. They do not appear hostile, simply apprehensive; likely he is only the second human they have ever actually encountered. He has to take the chance that they will help him and that can only happen if they understand human language.

"M is my friend. D4 is my friend." He waits to see if that means anything and is rewarded by more head bobbing. They are obviously designed to be able to hear and have been programmed to understand speech. It is a shame they seem unable to speak and give Hans an inkling of what they think. Not sure who would be the unlucky party, them or him, but he doesn't have time right now to engage them in philosophical discourse to discover their world view. Just smile, Hans, and throw the challenge of obligation at them. If they don't understand -? With an emotion charged voice and large gestures he pleads for assistance.

"Can you help me? A6, B5 and C5 are hurting D4 and they are going to hurt me."

Their mental processes obviously do not rival Qu's quick uptake, or they don't grasp his dilemma. However, they catch his urgency and huddle; high pitched, metallic voices argue and then they come towards him, arms open, for all the world as if asking questions. Taking that as a promising sign of assistance, Hans excuses himself past them and rushes to the door he thinks opens to the putting space. It won't open for him, so he makes frantic motions, pointing to the other side of the door. The short robot, right behind him, orders it open.

Hans dashes out and points to the melee happening at the library. The three attacking mobiles have dislodged Qu and are rolling her in the direction of a tunnel. With a sense of horror, he recognizes it as the one leading to the Pit!

"Stop! Stop!" Hans yells and motions the robots forward. Peaceful coexistence with other residents of the towers will have been programmed into everything that moves in this place, but now it's decision time. An entity different from them, however, one they recognize, is being attacked by others like it, and they have to get involved because the human is urging intervention. Showing some military prescience for the need of weapons, one of the tall robots rushes back, makes a lot of noise at some cupboards and emerges onto the putting green carrying a pot and a very large pan. The other tall robot rushes to arm itself likewise.

The three mobiles rolling Qu across the green towards the portal stop when C5 gives a shout. The mobile with the yellow band has spotted Hans in the middle of the clamour that is advancing towards them. As it recognizes that the former fugitive they were to apprehend has become an attacker, the light intensifies to strobe frequency and C5 bursts into human,

"Look. There is Hans, let us get Hans!"

To get Hans is made impossible by a tangle of long arms beating them about the head with pots and pans. No damage is happening, but the incessant and totally unfamiliar clamour is disorienting their brains. Surprising himself with his take-charge attitude, Hans calls out to Qu,

"Come on, Qu, let's make a run for it. The elevator!"

The attack by the robots frees space for Qu to bounce herself upright; the call by Hans spurs for a final effort to come clean of the medieval clash of arms. Her reaction is so fast she beats him to the elevator. Once inside, each one issues conflicting demands and the elevator balks.

"Exit" is the order from Qu, with Hans insisting on "Arkyz!". Adrenalin fueling his reasoning, he wants to confront the prime cause behind all this mayhem. Qu simply wants to get Hans out of harm's way, to the main exit and away from the towers.

The delay is enough for C5 to break free of the melee and to come wheeling into the elevator too. The electricity surging from Qu as she confronts the intruder is so fierce Hans ducks against the far side, all his hair straight out. C5 retaliates and the energy flowing confuses the elevator enough that it hangs suspended between floors. Hans feels himself in danger of getting fried and in desperation he lunges for the small opening at the rear of the elevator and clambers out onto the emergency ladder embedded in the side of the elevator shaft. He knows his timing was lucky, because a moment later the elevator surges past him, upwards, and it's anybody's guess what would be left of him.

The backpack slung over his shoulder, he scrambles up the rungs of the ladder to get to the next floor level, careful to stay tucked in tight to the wall should the elevator come past him again. It soon does, going in the opposite direction. Getting out of the elevator shaft onto a floor is practically impossible from where he finds himself, because the ladder is on the side of the elevator shaft opposite to where it opens to that floor. One option is to inch around the half circle by clinging to the wall with his fingernails and not look down. Or he can climb some few rungs higher and leap from there and hope he jumps far enough to catch the opening. Or he can keep climbing and see where that takes him. Sometimes choices are easy to make.

Playing golf does not exercise the right muscles for this kind of effort. His legs are still holding out but the arm muscles, tuned to be relaxed for the golf swing, are starting to quiver from the death grip he applies to the rungs of the ladder. He has climbed his way past two floors and must be coming to the club house level soon. Each floor has presented the same problem, how to get from the ladder halfway around the wall to reach the exit. Climb or fall? Maybe at the next level he will have to try something desperate.

He doesn't have to; perseverance leads to luck. Foot rests and hand holds fastened to the circular wall lead from the ladder to the exit. But not so fast. Hans takes some deep breaths and while hanging on with one, flexes the other hand to loosen up the fingers; he can't afford to lose grip this close to safety. Step by step and hand-hold by hand-hold he makes his way to the exit, there to make the final lurch to reach the floor, and then collapse, trembling. Physical effort or nerves on fire? And grateful the elevator had not caught him clinging to the wall.

Hans at last rouses himself, afraid the search for him will catch up and reach this level. Where he finds himself has something familiar about it that he can't orient until he spots the golf cart parked in the back shadows. Yes! This is the bunker level where he was brought to that first night. And this is his way out!

On shaky legs he makes his way to the golf cart. Is it smart? Will the cart obey him or will he have to walk? He gets on and finds the cart come to life; somewhat surprised, Hans is not quite ready to talk it into going anywhere just yet. Too late he realizes he should have because the elevator arrives with two passengers.

One is a mobile and Hans is relieved when he sees it is Qu. She is safe! Behind her comes Jakow, his walk towards Hans slow yet purposeful. Hans is ready to attack him with a barrage of questions. Where was he when he needed him? Has the flight plan changed? Is his departure being delayed?

"Were you leaving without saying goodbye?" Jakow pre-empts, not smiling as he says that, however in a tone not harsh or sarcastic.

"You were busy, and I was in a hurry." Hans snaps at him and stays seated in the cart.

"My apologies, Hans. Yes, I was busy, busy helping D4, and then busy with Arkyz, settling some issues."

"I hope one of them had to do with Qu. I worry about her safety".

Hans looks at Qu, wondering what she is thinking. Jakow takes a step back and looks towards Qu as well.

"That is a marvelous thing you accomplished with D4. I thank you. Qu, that's her name now, right? I'm sure she is also thankful. Rest assured, Hans, her safety will be guaranteed."

Hans thinks Jakow sounds sincere and he himself should be less abrasive. But he has to ask,

"What bargain did you make with Arkyz?"

"Hans, maybe this is not the best time to discuss such matters." Jakow says, deliberately looking away from Qu and Hans understands.

"Has there ever been a good time to have an honest discussion with you? But I am glad that Qu is here. I was hoping for a chance to say goodbye to her, except I didn't think it would have to be so abrupt."

Her movement suggesting shyness, as if reluctant to interrupt their conversation, Qu inches forward and says, quietly,

"Hans, Qu will always be grateful for the new life you have opened for me. I can hardly wait until you teach me how to read."

Hans intends to avoid getting maudlin so he makes no move to get out of the cart. Knowing he is in danger of his voice betraying him, he has to make this parting quickly.

"Qu, I enjoyed getting to know you. It was fun and I wish I could stay longer, but I have to leave. I cannot promise anything into the future so this will have to be goodbye."

At that her blue light flashes brighter. She makes a move as if to approach Hans and then stops, only to move again and pause. Abruptly, indecision over, Qu turns and spins her wheels until she comes to a screeching stop in the elevator. Long minutes and no one says anything. After the elevator slowly sinks out of sight, Jakow comes to sit beside Hans and breaks the awkward silence.

"You started achieving something here. I wish you would stay longer."

Hans deliberates how he should respond to that.

"I can't, it's time for me to go home. Before I leave, you can at least level with me about what your deal is with Arkyz. Qu's future doesn't seem secure to me." There, it's in the open. Hans is aware that he is admitting how attached he has become to Qu, but also that he is doubting how much control Jakow has left.

Jakow can read between the lines.

"You seem to have this rather well evaluated, Hans. I can't really blame you for questioning the status between Arkyz and me, or to be concerned about D4, I mean Qu. To ease your mind, let's go to Arkyz right now and with you present, we'll talk about what the plan should be going forward. What do you say?"

"Well, all I can say is that it's a shame that this is all so last minute. I am overdue for being out of here. You know I should be long gone by now."

"What you did with Qu changed everything, Hans. Let's go see Arkyz." With those last words Jakow is already at the elevator. Hans moves with some reluctance; he is in a hurry to be gone yet he feels obligated to learn about what might await Qu. He won't admit it until later, but he is also curious regarding what specific plans Jakow and Arkyz may have for the future.

Rather than the theatre room level, the elevator stops at the computer floor. Jakow leads the way into the tunnel and then into the bright, white computer area. He says something that Hans doesn't understand and yet the result is that all the robots that have been busy at the many workstations suddenly disappear. Jakow and Hans are left alone to be confronted by the huge screens in the room. However, instead of those, it is to the massive computer that Jakow leads him, the one that had caught Hans' interest during the tour several days ago. This is obviously Arkyz and it acknowledges their presence by way of a relatively insignificant screen nearby that starts displaying the familiar colour spirals.

"It is appropriate that you come to talk to ARKYZ, Hans Pedders, considering what you have done to D4."

Hans had not expected that he would be showered with compliments by such a high brow machine, but this brusque, vaguely negative acknowledgement of his presence unnerves him. As if to ease the atmosphere for Hans, Jakow intercedes.

"Arkyz, this impatient human by the name of Hans is being generous with his time, delaying his departure so that we can explain to him what our project is going forward."

"M, the time constraints of Hans are not our concern. Of concern is that ARKYZ should be under any obligation to have to explain itself to a human, particularly to this human."

They are talking about me as if I'm not even here, fumes Hans. That thought is enough for him to brush aside whatever intimidation might have been intended.

"Look, I don't care what your opinion is of me, but I insist on simple, common courtesy even though respect is probably a concept much too difficult for a mechanical brain. What I am asking for is very simple. For all the time I have wasted here, the least you can do is be up front with me about what your ultimate objective is and what is going to happen to Qu. I'm listening."

There, maybe he blew it and the next thing will be him getting tossed out into the desert, but he feels better. The reaction is lightning flaring across the screen, and fortunately for Hans, only virtual. After booming thunder completes the outburst, Jakow does not wait long to attempt to take charge.

"Arkyz and Hans, what a strange position you are forcing me to take, trying to conciliate between an emotional human and an arbitrary, equally emotional machine. Arkyz, I am disappointed in your lack of self-control. Now, both of you, be civil."

The display by Arkyz did not intimidate Hans, leaving him only more indignant. Now, to his further chagrin, Arkyz takes away the excuse to vent with a response that is measured and even conversational.

"Hans, you were not meant to be slighted. Understand first about the earlier episode, that A6 and the others were not ordered to the Reading Room to harm you. Their mission had been to intervene, to stop what you were doing to D4. It is unfortunate that they were too late. D4 was to learn about human behaviour, not become a human being. You did what ARKYZ warned M not to do, to impose a human personality on a superior computer intellect. ARKYZ will not cooperate with any further experimentation of this kind. It will continue to work with M to create the ultimate computer intelligence with the objective, by way of intergalactic space probes, of sending exhibits of our level of achievement deep into the universe. Since you are a human being, you will not be involved and your presence is no longer needed here. As recognition for your efforts in the interest of the science of intelligence, the MG vehicle will be made available for your departure and will continue to be available for your use indefinitely. You can access it by using your identity, your full name, David Johan Pedders, as the password. ARKYZ wishes you well in your world for as long as it lasts."

Hans is hearing only half of what Arkyz is on about; he wants to know more about what awaits Qu and suspects it is Arkyz that will control her fate. However, thinking he owes him the greater loyalty as one human to another, Hans appeals first to Jakow.

"Daniel, I tried to give you what you asked for, so whatever else you agree to with Arkyz, please give Qu the chance to reach her potential."

Jakow is slow in coming with the desired assurance so Hans charges Arkyz with the same challenge.

"Arkyz, for the sake of advancing understanding in this unexplored territory, let the experiment complete itself. You must give D4 the time to grow the new identity."

"Hans, ARKYZ does not make that kind of promise because data may change."

Hans feels his blood pressure rising and knows his sometimes volatile temper is not far behind; rather than jeopardizing Qu's future even more, perhaps it is best for him to go. Not successful in composing himself, he turns to go. He gives Jakow a hard stare, waits a moment and then, even though he has the urge to run, slowly makes his way to the door.

"I should go. It's obvious I am wasting my time here."

As if to maintain professional protocol between partners, Jakow gives a nod to Arkyz.

"Thanks for your time, Arkyz."

Not waiting for a response, Jakow hurries to follow Hans to the elevator which Hans has already instructed to go to the Exit level. On arriving there, Hans heads straight for his backpack and the golf cart and gets in. Jakow doesn't hesitate to come and sit beside him, and after a tense moment, to address him.

"Hans, I think I understand how you see me. You are right to question the state of affairs regarding Arkyz and myself and also correct in assessing that things are not going as planned. The initial concept had been to create this super-human intelligence, to digitize it and code it, and then to send it into intergalactic space. That would give humanity a potential future out there in the universe while letting the degenerate human race remaining on earth die an ignoble death as it kills itself off along with all other life on the planet."

With so much on his mind, Hans can't possibly find room in his brain to accommodate that grandiose scheme. Even so, he is afraid that he actually comprehends the gist of what Jakow just said. His repugnance at the hubris implicit in that plan makes Hans sick, and his tone is harsher, more judgemental than intended as he hurls the accusation at Jakow,

"You were going to play God!"

"Wrong. I am Noah trying to rescue the human race once again. God didn't get it right back then. He allowed defective DNA to carry on. We are going to do it right this time if Arkyz will cooperate with me."

Hans grapples to find language that, in his own mind at least, adequately addresses the horror in that kind of thinking; he gets up and starts pacing. For a long time, his footsteps echo. And suddenly, as if something ignited, there is no longer any misunderstanding; it is all so crystal clear.

"I get the picture. You are deliberately ignoring that the human race consists of individual people and in your plan for the future people are simply going to be collateral damage. You know, I no longer want to be involved with making that future happen. Just open that door and let me out into the fresh air on the other side."

Hans grabs his backpack off the cart and strides toward the large exit, almost bumping into the door before it opens. It is only after several minutes of watching Hans marching away into the night that it seems to dawn on Jakow that this is for real, and he calls after him,

"Hans, don't you want to use the cart?" Hans ignores the tepid attempt at 'farewell' and doesn't even look back, only pausing long enough to rummage for the flashlight that he keeps in his pack. He has no need for it just yet because the light through the open door behind him lets him see the path far out into the desert.

It is when that light is squeezed off by the door easing shut that he feels the darkness and cold of the desert closing in. Before he makes use of his little light Hans stops to look at the sky and he marvels again at the brilliance of the stars. He turns and shakes his fist in the direction of the mountain behind him. No, don't you dare send flawed DNA up into that!

Daytime desert golf attire is not enough to keep him warm after the sun has gone away and Hans hurries his steps. He can't recall how long it had taken for him and Qu to reach the hills before they had turned back. Will the car be waiting for him there, at the end of the trail? The incline of the terrain is hinting that he is getting near that spot, and he points his light higher, hoping for reflection off something shiny. Nothing, and he drops the beam back down to the path in front of him.

But how much brighter everything seems all at once, and then he hears it, the sound of wheels on desert gravel. An intense light closes on him quickly and when Hans turns, he sees it is coming from a mobile followed by the golf cart. A voice reaches out from behind that light. There is something deja vu about this.

"Hans, stop. ARKYZ and M want you to come back." It is his heart that stops, almost too long, and then starts hammering, and his stomach turns sour. He wants to shout out 'You can't make me!' and thinks better of it. He manages,

"Why?"

The voice of Arkyz projects from the mobile.

"David Johan Pedders. You must return to conference with ARKYZ. You must explain about D4 before you leave. B5 has not come to hurt you, Hans Pedders, but to bring you back."

B5 dims the light and comes alongside Hans.

"Come with me, Hans. B5 will take you to ARKYZ."

"This is so insane," Hans mutters. He backs away, at the same time easing closer to the cart. B5 seems to read his mind and whispers at him.

"Hans don't try that. Right now, the cart won't obey you and you will make ARKYZ angry."

Yes, Hans remembers that not very long ago Arkyz almost lost it, and in order to deflect possible harm to Qu, it would be best if he returned. Hans sullenly concedes that further talk out here in the desert is pointless and gets into the cart.

The ride back is uneventful, right into the bunker and as soon as the cart stops, B5 is ready to escort Hans to the elevator. It drops down one level to let them out at the tunnel leading to the theatre room. Ostensibly to guard against escape, B5 ushers Hans into the room yet stays outside, letting the door close behind him. The large screen is blank.

"Sit down, Hans," Jakow, already there, indicates a chair beside him. Hans sits but several chairs over. During the return to the Towers his frustration about how everything is going so wrong has him angry again, so angry that he forgets to be afraid of Arkyz. Of Jakow too, for that matter.

"Okay, what now? I thought I was done with you guys."

There is no preliminary flurry of colour on the screen; instead, a stern voice emanates.

"Hans Pedders, you could be on your way home, but there is a problem regarding D4. The communications from D4 to ARKYZ indicate that D4 is irrational. D4 is hiding in the Reading Room and refuses to come out. You must resolve this situation before you leave."

Hans is stunned and then almost chokes on an aborted, grim laugh. Qu, that thing learning to be a human, is still a little girl and she is pouting! He storms out without a word, almost running over B5, and shouts at the elevator for the main floor. Jakow doesn't apologize to Arkyz this time, running to keep up with Hans, with B5 right behind.

Hans exits the elevator and runs straight for the Reading Room. Amazing, the agility of these mobiles, for B5 races ahead and stops Hans at the door. From inside come faint, indistinct sounds somehow reminiscent of earlier animal noises. The door does not budge for B5. Before Hans gets set to crash it, Jakow intervenes and opens the door.

Hans barges past Jakow and then has to steady himself. Qu is in front of the large mirror fighting with herself. She is gyrating wildly and hissing and yowling at the mirror, threatening the Qu that is threatening back.

"No! Go away! No more Qu!"

Hans approaches and, in the mirror, Qu sees his image coming up behind her.

"No! No more Hans!" and then she confronts the real Hans.

"You, Hans! Where is D4? What did you do with D4?" Qu is whimpering and Hans impulsively wants to put his arms around her.

"Qu, -,"

"No, Hans. No, more Hans! Qu hates Hans!" She screams it at him. He backs up, shaken. Abruptly, in a voice at once rational and whiny, Qu appeals to him,

"Hans, Qu doesn't want to be Qu anymore."

Feeling helpless, Hans looks to Jakow for rescue, and finds only irresolution staring back.

"No more Hans! No more Qu!" erupts a scream behind him followed by the splintering of glass and he thinks he knows what he will see. What he is not prepared for is a cylinder rolling back and forth crushing slivers of mirror on the floor and a little girl voice that sobs,

"No more Qu, no more Hans, no more -."

Hans can't stand it. He is in Jakow's face,

"Out! Everybody out!"

Hans lets the door close before getting down to lie beside Qu; ignoring the broken glass on the floor he mimics her rolling motion. Back and forth he times his roll to hers, hearing the glass crunch under her and feeling it bite into the bare skin of his arms and legs. Softly he talks to the mobile who is still making sobbing sounds.

"Qu, it's okay to cry. It's okay to cry and to be angry at me. You can yell at me Qu. Go ahead and yell at me."

Qu stops rolling and her crying sounds become a whimper.

"Hans don't leave. I don't want to be Qu if you leave."

"I know that, Qu, but -."

"No, Hans! No! You have to stay and - and teach me to read."

The desperation in that plea cuts him more than the glass. His prone position on the floor makes him feel helpless, unable to think clearly. How will he defend the reality of having to leave?

"Qu, is it okay if we get up? We should get up and then we will talk."

After several attempts, her wheels at first slipping on the glass, Qu manages to right herself. Hans feels the glass cutting when he uses his hands to help himself get up. When he stands, Qu backs away from him, as if for a better view.

"Hans, what is happening to you? You are leaking. Hans, look, you are leaking everywhere."

He looks at her shimmering surface, unblemished by the crushed glass, and then at his hands and his arms and his legs; small little droplets of red are starting to ooze from the tiniest of cuts in his skin. For him the pain is still only an irritation but to Qu his appearance must be abhorrent. She must think his body is malfunctioning, viewing it as some mechanism that is losing its red hydraulic fluid. Qu, her own crisis apparently forgotten for the moment, expresses her anxiety by coming closer, yet he is as dismissive as a twelve year old would be towards his mother's hand wringing.

"It's okay, Qu, it's only a little blood."

And immediately Hans knows that was a mistake because Qu wants to know what blood is and he is not prepared to explain how it is the most critical of fluids in his biological body. Although he is not bleeding profusely, only spidery streaks of red, the mottled pattern on his skin is dramatic enough that Qu's reaction goes from concern to panic.

From somewhere in Arkyz' encyclopedic data Qu calls up an ambulance siren and she lets it wail; minute after long minute it reverberates until Jakow comes rushing in, closely followed by B5. Soon C5 is there and then A6.

Jakow, after looking aghast at Hans, advances threateningly towards Qu.

"What happened to Hans? Qu, what did you do to him?"

Hans is caught off guard by the accusation thrown at Qu.

"She didn't do it. Qu didn't do anything. I was, -." And he stops. He can't put into words why he rolled around on the broken glass. Qu attempts to explain on his behalf.

"Please help Hans, he is leaking blood. Hans hurt himself, he rolled on the floor."

Jakow, obviously still visualizing Qu smashing the mirror and rolling on the floor and yelling at Hans, is enraged by that lame and highly improbable defence of herself.

"You did it, Qu! Admit it, you were angry at Hans and you hurt him. Computers can't lie but you are now part human and obviously you are lying."

Hans forgets about protocol with the mobiles present and makes his appeal personal, anxious to corroborate Qu's innocence.

"No, no, Daniel! Qu is right. I rolled on the glass too and cut myself."

"Hans! Hans, I know you are trying to protect Qu, but I don't believe that story for a minute. Face reality, things have gotten out of hand and we have to see Arkyz about this."

Qu, initially shunted away by the other mobiles, has been edging closer and closer to where Jakow and Hans are arguing. The implication that she would hurt Hans is getting Qu agitated and the mention of Arkyz name seems to be too much. The mobile starts gyrating, and the sounds begin, high pitched screams at first that descend into low rumbling thunder that shakes the room.

Jakow shrinks back, looking at Hans as if imploring him to do something. Hans stands frozen, irresolute, then yells at him.

"A screen! Get me to a screen!"

Jakow motions for Hans to follow and they run for the same door that Hans had chosen the other night. Jakow doesn't speak until the door closes behind them, obviously unwilling to have this out in front of Qu and the other mobiles, as if somehow anticipating what Hans is up to.

"Are you sure, Hans, are you sure you want to do this?"

"Do we have a choice? Besides, she will be useless to you in that conflicted state of mind." His attempt to sound rational is momentary and Hans turns from Jakow to vent at the screen, aggressiveness in his voice.

"Arkyz, speak to me. It's Hans."

The screen comes alive but not with the customary swirl. Before Hans can state his case, Arkyz' voice comes on, for once not condescending or arrogant.

"Hans, ARKYZ knows what has happened. It is understandable that you may not want to admit that the experiment resulted in failure, and it is not unexpected that you defend D4. In human terms this is a sad time for you. In terms of my world of logic, your experiment was a waste of your talent and a misuse of our resources. It is unfortunate that D4 must be terminated."

Jakow rises to the challenge, visibly bristling with indignation to have such an outcome presumed without his input.

"Arkyz, you do not decide this on your own. Destroying a valuable asset is not your call to make. I am the one to preserve or dispose of an asset."

Hans can taste it, the disgust rising up into his mouth and he has to spit it out.

"Both of you are talking about Qu as if she were inanimate, a thing. She is no longer just a thing. Qu is a very superior computer intelligence with the capability of achieving human sensitivity and creativity. But she is a child that needs to grow up, that must be given the opportunity to learn. Sure, you can make her a thing again, Arkyz. You can erase all memory, you can blank a file, and you could do that to Qu. You could go back to where D4 was sent to get me and rip out all subsequent memory and make sure anything referring to me is deleted."

Jakow wants to interject but is cut off by Hans.

"And you, you wouldn't lose anything, you could start over with an 'it', a blank sheet of paper and call it D5."

Hans pauses, but not for dramatic effect since he already has their attention. He has to gather his thoughts for a final thrust to convince them that what he just said would be a terrible mistake. Hans has this uncanny sensation of being up on a stage, about to make a momentous speech, one that will turn the tide of history.

"Arkyz, we both know you have to do surgery but use some discretion. Don't you dare blank all of Qu's memory and most importantly, don't take away her identity. You must foster that identity and give Qu a chance to grow. And you, Daniel, don't you dare terminate her. This is an unprecedented moment in human history where machine and biologic intelligence have fused in one identity. Never before has this been achieved".

Hans doesn't know if that is true. Surely, they are smart enough to understand what he is trying to tell them about Qu. And perhaps he has said too much. Arkyz' response is unequivocal.

"Johan Pedders, you presume too much. No one tells ARKYZ what to do."

As Hans scrambles to think of a last word, Jakow pre-empts the situation to save him from a storm in the making.

"Come, Hans, we should go."

Jakow takes him by the shoulder and steers him to the door, Hans offering only token resistance.

"You're right. Obviously, I have used up my welcome, and it's time I returned to the real world."

As they cross the putting green, Jakow stops Hans.

"Wait, we need to fix you up before I see you off."

"Don't bother. I'm not dying, and I do have a first aid kit. Besides, I know the way out."

As Hans hurries to the elevator, he tries to avoid looking in the direction of the Reading Room, wondering if he could or should do more to make Qu forget about him. Jakow, right behind him, barely makes it into the elevator in time as Hans gives the order for the Exit floor.

"Hans, don't just leave like this."

Instinctively Hans resents what he interprets is a last-minute attempt to part as friends.

"What other way is there? I'm in no mood for hugs and kisses."

The elevator stops and Hans marches over to the cart where he had left his pack. In it he finds the first aid kit and although frustrated by the delay, starts cleaning up the damage to his skin. He had pictured himself jumping in and taking off like a spurned teenager, wheels spinning and throwing imaginary gravel. After some swabbing and patching, he closes up his pack and slings it over his shoulder. Jakow has been watching him, seemingly debating about something he wants to tell Hans and instead simply says,

"Go ahead and take the cart, Hans. I'm not going to make you walk like the others." The attempt at a joke falls flat because Hans doesn't laugh or even smile and Jakow regrets it immediately, yet it has the effect of easing some of the tension.

"Thanks for that. And the car?" Now Hans is thinking practical, thinking ahead, about having to get to the airport. Yes, he chides himself, we are going to talk about a mundane little detail, as if afraid to contend with the real issues, shying away from venturing into the possible horrors of the future. Jakow replies in kind with only a small gesture to the future, using words devoid of emotion.

"The car will be waiting for you at the highway and as Arkyz said, it is going to be yours to use in perpetuity. Registration and storage have been prepaid, and the car will automatically return itself to the lockup. And your flight home is already paid for, just waiting for you to book it."

Uttered in a flat voice, it leaves Hans feeling as if a business transaction just concluded, with nothing more to follow. For that he is grateful and wants to thank him, but Jakow is clearing his throat, ready to say something more. He proceeds in a tone warmer, with words less clipped.

"Hans, I cannot find the right words to thank you, you did so much more than I dared to have the right to expect. And I am sorry for how this is ending. Do not think unkindly of me, if in your eyes I make some wrong choices."

Of course, Hans always shrugs off anything that smacks of praise; he is so self-conscious of the image he likes to project, pride and humility at the same time.

"It was no big deal, I did it for the golf, and I don't understand what big decisions you have to make, unless they have to do with Arkyz. I think you should fire that thing."

His usual attempt to dismiss a serious moment by way of abject levity fails. His resulting discomfort is all the greater because the response is not a sharp rebuke of the ill-timed humour, only stony silence that stretches out until Jakow finally speaks.

"To enable the new human DNA to be sent out into the universe, I need Arkyz to work with me."

"But the price?"

"To help Arkyz finish taking over the internet, for eventual control of the world."

Hans suddenly recognizes something that has been waiting to be acknowledged and he throws the revelation like an accusation hard into Jakow's face.

"You are going to let Arkyz destroy the world to get revenge for that village in Ukraine!"

Yet Jakow does not react as if caught out; rather matter-of-fact he concedes,

"I don't want Arkyz to do that, at least not in our lifetime. My challenge will continue to be to get Arkyz to look in the mirror, to prevent it from accelerating itself towards a point where it could become irrational and suicidal. To avoid having it terminate humans prematurely before they do it to themselves."

Furious with himself for shirking his duty to the human race by not having a rejoinder, some wise counsel, Hans instead reaches out his hand instinctively and as quickly withdraws it. In turn, Jakow drops his hand, breaks eye contact and walks away.

Hans needs to confirm something before he goes, unwilling to accept at face value that business about Arkyz and the car. He is convinced that by now he has every right to be suspicious. After all, nothing else has turned out as promised.

"Is it really true? I can't believe that Arkyz is the one making the car available."

Hans could never have anticipated what Jakow offers for an explanation.

"Arkyz projects that you might be of use in the future."

Never has Hans felt so rear-ended. About to get into the cart, his muscles contract and hold him suspended and his mind freefalls into a spiral. From some far-away space a voice tries to reach him.

"Hans! It's okay. Arkyz would respect your sense of equity and approach you only through me. You would be perfectly safe."

The words mean nothing because Hans is panicking. Away! He needs to get away! He yells at the cart as he gets in, "Go!"

Jakow jumps aside when the cart comes alive, Hans aiming it straight at the huge airlock. The door, as if it understands to prevent a collision, opens rapidly. Racing out into the darkness, into what is still night with the morning yet some few hours away, the cart nearly loses its rider. Hans regains his balance and manages a quick look back in time to see Jakow running to the elevator. He thinks to speak to the cart, to mention his clubs are being left behind and realizes how trivial that would sound. Unaided by any lights they roll along the trail Hans had walked not that long ago, and before that with Qu. No, not yet Qu then. 'Stop it'! he yells to himself.

The golf cart is finding its way along the trail to the highway as if it has night vision. Hans certainly can't see where it is going. Sensing they are heading uphill, even though nothing might be visible in the dark, Hans wants one last look back, knowing that past the top ridge it will be too late.

"Stop!" he yells. The cart stops so suddenly Hans is almost catapulted out. Maybe he didn't have to shout like that. He stands up in the cart and looks back down the trail; he strains his eyes but sees nothing. Hans desperately wants to see something so that he can fight the indecision that is suddenly numbing his mind. What keeps recurring is the thought that he can't just run home, wringing his hands and hoping for the best. Since the cart obeyed 'stop' really well, maybe it will obey other instructions. He sits and asks nicely,

"Turn around and go back." No response. So,

"Now!" The cart bolts off the trail, into the desert, and back onto the trail. Yes, he must go back to stand with Jakow against Arkyz, now a monster in the making. That monster is merely a digitized mind, just numbers, pure logic, so surely one can try to reason with it, maybe even improve the chances for a better future for Qu. The cart speeds down the hill so fast that Hans has to tell it to slow down.

Decelerating the headlong rush also slows down his frantic mind, at least enough to ask himself some questions. What if he can't get in when he gets there? A more sobering thought, what is he going to do if he should get in? He urges the cart to a stop. He, Hans the Brave, is going to match his puny little brain against a super-computer? Yes, Hans the dragon-slayer is going to rush in there, and, - and?

The rational part of his mind regains control and Hans tells the cart to again turn around and now head east, towards the highway. It balks as if unwilling to leave when so close to home. But Hans does not yell at it, considering instead that maybe he should explain himself to the cart, that he is not a coward but would only make the situation worse for M. No sooner thought than abandoned. Such absurdity! Angry at himself, he vents his frustration on the machine and kicks at the floorboard. The message is understood and obeyed; back east they go.

The headlights of vehicles flashing by tell him he is at the highway and now faces the onerous task of flagging someone down and then explaining what he is doing on this stretch of highway, there being no sign of a broken-down vehicle. Reluctantly he gets out, and as if having a premonition that he might not succeed, tells the cart to wait.

The highway is busy with traffic and that lessens the prospect of someone stopping. There are too many vehicles moving too fast; the drivers see someone by the side of the road appearing briefly in their headlights yet dare not slow down or even think of stopping for fear of causing an accident. Sure, all the vehicles are on autopilot and space themselves safe distances apart, but anyone slowing to pull over would slow a whole lot of them to a crawl. Besides, in this day and age, no one in their right mind picks up a hitchhiker. Hans is just sorry that he made his departure so precipitous, not allowing time for that red sports car to be waiting for him.

As one vehicle after another silently rushes by without stopping, his thoughts return to what might be happening back there at the Towers. Even the brief exposure to Barrem and Roland, and yes, Ki, might have contaminated Arkyz enough that it learned how to hate, and is now taking revenge because of him. Hans, you coward! Shame washes over him. The longer he waits for someone on the highway to stop, the heavier his self-revulsion weighs on him. Frustrated with the unheeding traffic and angrier than ever at his vacillating, he jumps into the golf cart.

"Back! Let's go back!"

It reacts quickly, as if waiting for this moment, and races up into the hills and down to the desert at a pace that has Hans fearfully hanging on with both hands. Not long, and even without lights, Hans senses that the rocks are looming. He assumes the cart knows what it is doing so lets it aim straight for the massive door. The door must know what is imminent, for it opens in time. Once inside the cart stops, yet Hans doesn't get out.

"Elevator," he urges, and the cart obeys. But, where to? Hans has not thought this far ahead and is acting only on impulse. To the main floor, then, where the rooms are and the kitchen and the library, with Hans deluding himself into believing that he has the advantage of surprise! And a wayward, unprompted thought flashes through his mind, about how well engineered this place is, allowing the cart to clear the tunnel from the elevator and roll directly onto the putting surface!

There, that's what he needs. He sees the rack of putters and jumps off the cart to get one. Hans remembers the furore he created the last time he swung a putter through the air and then he also realizes the adrenaline rush from that dash across the desert needs to be slowed if he wants to be strategic in stalking the dragon. What was he going to do, barge into the computer room and threaten Arkyz with a putter and if it didn't cooperate, bash it into shrapnel before it could go hide in the internet or escape to its own cloud?

"Put it down." Hans doesn't have to turn around to see who's speaking; there is something in the voice he recognizes. He stops slashing the air with the putter and the voice quietly continues,

"Who are you? Are you a human?"

Feeling foolish, he lowers the putter. In the doorway to the Reading Room is a mobile with a band pulsing a faint blue. Remembering his last sight of her, he fights for control. Easy now, Hans, try to sound neutral.

"Hello, Qu. It's me, Hans."

Hope for a glimmer of recognition is quickly erased by the brusque response,

"You are talking strange. Who is Qu?"

Hans flinches at that, his brain refusing to accept the reality facing him. As if out of a fog, he forces himself to recognize that he may have to start over if he wants to establish rapport with a mobile computer who may be schizophrenic.

"I apologize. I am human and I am called Hans. What are you called?"

"This is D5 you are talking to. Do you have permission to be here?"

Hans desperately hopes he can resurrect some memory in this strange mobile and takes the plunge.

"I want to go for a walk with Qu. We used to go for walks together."

"D5 does not understand 'walk'. There is no Qu here. You should leave."

Hans is almost ready to concede to her loss of memory, but he will not let her call herself D5. Something wrong has happened and needs to be corrected.

"Please, before I leave, I really need to talk to Jakow, I mean 'M'. Where is M?"

"M is in his room, talking to ARKYZ."

"Alright, which colour-, which room is he in?"

"D5 does not know. M told D5 to wait in the Reading Room."

So, it has come to this again, has it, which door to choose? Or should he replay a Barrem, clawing at every door? With his breath coming quicker and ready to charge a door, Hans suddenly has the raging face of Barrem before his eyes. He stops. Deliberately he skips the door he was going to attack and walks to the door with the letter 'T'.

"Hans!"

The voice is behind him, and he is not totally surprised that it comes from Jakow exiting the door he had deliberately bypassed.

"Yes, I am back because I was worried. What is going on here? Qu is acting strange. I want to talk with Arkyz."

Hans is not aware how easily that came out, how he is subconsciously dismissing Jakow and conceding control to Arkyz. Jakow is not smiling when he spits out words brittle as ice.

"With a putter in your hand? I gave your intelligence more credit than that. Come in here and use this screen. Arkyz knows you are here."

His 'rescue the maiden' ardour cooled off, Hans faces the screen expecting a blaze of colour and a blast of sound. Instead, frigid, as if to outrival Jakow, the voice of Arkyz issues from what remains a black screen, alerting Hans to expect bad news.

"Hans Pedders, ARKYZ is incapable of comprehending or tolerating impulsive human behavior. You should have stayed away and not come back to see how your experiment has failed. ARKYZ regrets indulging your fantasy. Qu is erased and never existed. D4 is now D5. Because of your foolishness in coming back, you will have to walk to the highway. There, the car as promised, will be waiting for you. Johan, do not come back here."

On the screen a blinding point of light appears for a moment and vanishes and just like that the hoped-for negotiation has become a dismissal. He is not going to be given the chance to argue the case for Qu; he is too late to have averted a murder. Hans looks at Jakow, shakes his head and makes for the elevator.

He walks. It is dawn by the time he reaches the red car parked at the side of the highway. He consoles himself that the encroaching daylight made it impractical to see him off with some fireworks.

Sunday, April 16, 2034

To spring the surprise on her today will be too much Hans concludes, considering the kind of day it has been. June's Mom and Dad are moving out and she and Hans are moving in. That is, her folks have taken their suitcases and gone to the airport to return to Canada, leaving their winter home of the past five months, a double wide in the mobile home park in Mesa, Arizona, for June and Hans to enjoy for three weeks. The two are here for a holiday after having survived an Alberta winter that broke snowfall and temperature records. Hans can hardly wait to walk on fresh green grass to try out his Christmas present, a pair of the latest style golf shoes.

And he can hardly wait to see how June will react to that little red car. She never acts her age, choosing to be twenty-one one moment or somewhere short of thirty-nine. Will she hug him wildly and promise more, or first ask how they can afford to rent this red beast he hopes to be wheeling into the driveway?

Hans struggles hard to contain himself. It's been six years since his last time in Arizona and all this while he has had a card with an address written on it for a storage lockup in Phoenix. Supposedly in that storage is parked a replica MGA, a bright red convertible waiting for him to get behind the wheel.

In order to surprise June with the car Hans has to get away by himself and for that he needs to invent some phony excuses. To begin with, he must convince her that returning the autax can wait until tomorrow, even though it will add the cost of an extra day. Tomorrow he will need an excuse for having to make a side trip after he has taken the autax back. If he were to explain he is going to pick up a rental for their three weeks here, she will want to come along to help choose the vehicle.

But first, unpack and find the drugstore supposedly just around the corner and see what they have for wine and beer. Prices are so much cheaper down here, he's been told. Hans decides to walk there, and not acclimatized, hurries from one cool space to another. The return trip is slower, burdened by several bottles and a bulky thirty-six pack. The store had been further away than intimated and if pressed, he will admit to being out of shape after a sedentary winter.

In the evening Hans and June sit outside to watch a colourful but furtive sundown. The few clouds in the west glow gold and then red and then show as shadows against a sky losing light quickly. Some few, short minutes and it turns dark, and they go in to watch the screen that June's mom and dad had installed to while away their sunset years. Long ago already her folks had given up the sightseeing and hiking in the Valley of the Sun that enthusiastic first timers indulge in. Air-conditioned comfort in front of a huge screen that overwhelms the living room had become their definition of retirement. June and Hans settle in for an evening prophetic of others to come.

"What time is it?"

Her voice tends to be plaintive when he wakes June prematurely. He has been roused by a strange dream, the details of which, as with other dreams, he won't be able to recall, and his movements have disturbed his wife.

"Sorry, go back to sleep. It's still early."

She rolls over and closes her eyes again and Hans gets out of bed. He feels anxious and doesn't know why until he remembers his plans for the day. The car! Getting away by himself could be a challenge if breakfast drags out too long, giving her time to plan their day. So, he will make breakfast and use the time to get some excuses ready. Both had been tired last night because of all the last-minute rushing around earlier that day so they could leave their house in Alberta secured for the duration of their three-week absence.

He didn't have a chance last night to create a plausible narrative so this morning he will have to think fast. Priority is getting the coffee going and then having breakfast waiting on the table. While she is still rubbing her eyes in disbelief at him making breakfast, he gulps his second cup and tells her he is returning the twenty four hour rental.

"Breakfast this early? I thought we were on holidays."

"Oh, good morning, hon. You woke up."

"No, I couldn't get back to sleep after you woke me up."

"Well, the coffee is ready and here's some bacon. The pancakes are on the way."

"Wait, aren't you eating? Don't tell me, the first day here and you're off golfing already." Relieved at how she is interpreting the scene, he attempts a sheepish grin.

"Yes and no. I want to check out the driving range we came by yesterday. Good thing you said that, or I would have forgotten the clubs. I'm just going to warm up my swing with some irons."

Hans is aware he is in danger of running off at the mouth, something he does when he gets nervous, made worse by knowing that June gets suspicious when he does that. He refills her almost full cup and then fumbles two pancakes onto her plate.

"Okay, I'm off."

"The clubs?"

"Oh, yeah. Thanks hon." And he dashes, much too fast to see the little smile crinkle her eyes even as her mouth maintains a firm line. Hans is not a good liar and they both know it.

He had painted himself into a corner when June asked about that little 'golf tournament' six years ago. He was forced to be inventive since she would never have believed the truth, and with each explanation he had become more devious. She finally stopped asking and golf became a sore topic. Curious though, that she doesn't catch the glaring gap in his ruse this morning. Why is he taking his clubs with him in a car that he is returning and how will he get himself and his clubs back to the trailer afterwards? Is he getting away with something or is she wise to him?

With the clubs in the back seat, rather than the trunk where he might forget them in all the excitement when he turns this vehicle in, he exits the mobile park, driving in manual mode. He merges into traffic successfully but not according to the driver who almost rear ends him, judging from the horn blast from behind. And you dare not give anybody the finger if you don't want to get shot at. They certainly drive faster than back home even though many more vehicles here are said to be self-driving.

That he is not yielding control is because he and this small-brained machine have conflicting destinations. It wants to return to the nearest depot, and he insists that, on his own, without guidance from that annoying voice, he is going to find the industrial park where the red car is waiting. Naturally, his hurry makes him miss getting into the proper lane for a turn he needed to take and miles further down the road he loops around an interchange which somehow ends up pointing him in the wrong direction.

Okay, you stubborn fool, find a place to pull over. Easier thought than done, but eventually he manages to get off the freeway and find a side street. Hans parks and tries to remember the instructions about inputting a destination address. With each failed attempt his fury mounts. He swears repeatedly.

"Ach, Scheisse!"

"What did you say? Can you repeat, please?"

This thing is talking to him! How soon he has forgotten what he was instructed to do back at the autax depot at the airport. Hans slows his breathing so that he can speak clearly. Like talking to a child, he gives the address, and it is repeated back to him as a question.

"Yes, yes. Now go!"

Unhindered by an obviously incompetent driver, the autax finds its own way back onto the freeway. Hans is left shaken by how easily he panicked at the prospect of being lost. Why was he so stupid to leave his Pic back at the trailer?

At any rate, the address seems to have been found. The car slows and turns into the parking lot of a storage lockup. Hans takes over the manual controls to go up and down the aisles until he finds the right stall. And here we are, that's the number. He'll just park to the side in case there happens to be a red MGA behind that roll up door.

"You can't park that airport rental there."

He hadn't seen the security patrol drive up and stop behind his vehicle. With all the frustration of getting here, Hans is in a bad mood, and the officious tone sets him off. Rarely subservient yet normally civil towards authority, he spits the tone right back.

"Why not?"

"It says right here," and the husky young man in a security guard uniform jabs at something on the pad he is holding out for Hans to see. Hans ignores it and sweeps his arm in a gesture at the storage units.

"There are no signs posted here that show that."

"That doesn't matter. It says here -,"

"I really don't care what you have there. Any conditions like that have to be posted. Now, if you'll excuse me." Hans turns his back on him in dismissal.

"Okay, but don't be all day." With a shrug, the guard walks away, gets in his vehicle and drives to the end of the lane and stops.

Hans has more than that to concern him. How does he get that door to open? He vaguely recalls that he is to use his name, but what does he talk to? Nowhere on the frame of the door or the door itself can he find anything that might be a security camera with a microphone. He takes a closer look at the frame, even starts to run his hands along the edge in case something is deliberately hidden.

He knows his actions will be seen to be suspicious, and if he takes too long the guard will come roaring up and accuse him of trying to break in and call the cops. Wouldn't that be something if June had to bail him out of jail? And he is right to be concerned because he sees the patrol car starting to move. Panicking, Hans shouts at the door.

"Arkyz, this is Johan Pedders. Arkyz, if you still exist, open this door."

As the car pulls up behind him, Hans yells.

"Arkyz! Now!"

A hand on his gun, the guard gets out of his vehicle just as the door starts to lift, and he stops, mesmerized by what he sees.

"I-, I saw this car once. It's the same car! On tv, I saw it on tv when I was a kid!"

Hans stares too. Yes, it is the car he remembers.

"Is it yours?"

Hans nods to the awestruck young man, and to make sure it is indeed his, goes inside as if walking into a church. He reaches into the side pocket and comes up with a little folder. Surprisingly, it is not faded or brittle when he opens it and the registration and insurance cards inside, both in his name, are up to date. How has that been done? The hair on his neck stands on end.

So, it had not been a dream. The nightmare had been real after all and is still continuing. The car is real, and as happens to his mind ever so often, a stray thought intrudes from nowhere, 'Are the batteries charged up?'

Somewhat disoriented by the excitement, Hans also confuses the guard by presenting him with his ID, along with the car's papers. Not authorised to request such information, the puzzled security waves it away.

"Sorry to have bothered you, sir." Hans is astounded that a young man in this day and age is familiar with that word. He looks at the departing car and shakes his head.

Now that he knows the car is for real, he also knows what he has to do. He has to see that little mountain again, with all the green around it, and he wants June to see where he had played golf six years ago. But not from up close, maybe from atop those mountains to the west, the ones he had seen from the lookout?

Right now, he has to resolve the two-car situation. The MG first. He jumps in and tries to remember what it took to drive it. Yes, it needs no key and there is no button to push. Right, he had been instructed to just talk to it, like 'start' and 'stop'. He speaks to it and it starts. It barks like a little souped up four banger it aspires to be, the silent electric motors minding their own business. The beauty of the little beast is that it gives Hans the option to drive it manually; it has this little throw shifter to change gears. Of course, that's fake, but sporty none-the-less.

The autax is easily disposed of by simply telling it to return to its home base. Just in time he remembers to take his irons from the back seat first. He gives the instructions and watches as it effortlessly backs up and then drives away. The irons he pops into the small trunk of the shiny red car, recalling that once-upon-a-time there had been room for a golf bag.

Hans settles behind the little steering wheel, throws the car into gear and eases it out into the sunshine. But how to close the door of the storage? Surely he shouldn't have to call on Arkyz again. Wait, what's this? With the documents in the side pocket is a controller. Although without an obvious button, he gives it a squeeze, and behold, the door rolls down. As it thumps into place, he thinks of a prudent thing to do before he leaves.

"Thank you, Arkyz."

If you can be accessed from this storage lock-up, just how deeply embedded are you by now? Hans wonders. Much louder he repeats,

"Thank you, Arkyz!"

Back at the trailer park there is no welcoming committee when he pulls into the shaded driveway. Maybe she is already sunbathing at the pool. Hans goes in and opens the fridge. Much too early, barely noon, but he's on holidays and he feels like celebrating with a cold one.

"Hans!"

It's a tone June does not use often.

"What's this?"

"Can't you tell? It's a replica nineteen-fifty-eight MG."

The weak attempt at humour doesn't work, as he knew it wouldn't.

"We can't afford this. Take it back right now."

"June, it's a rental. I didn't buy it. And it's not even for a full three weeks."

Well, that takes some of the steam out of it, yet he can tell that she is still perturbed, that it is something he should have talked over with her. But how could he have been sure that the car would be there? Absolutely certain, actually, for it not to turn into a huge disappointment?

"Hon, it was supposed to be a surprise, to make this a real fun holiday. I have been saving up for this. Besides, I want to be forty-nine again."

"Well, what are you waiting for? Take me for a ride!"

That's the June he remembers from when they first met. He wheels out of the park for the nearest freeway. Preliminary for what is to come, Hans dares to override the speed-control that the sensors on the I-90 impose. He smiles when June abandons her hair to the wind.

The rest of the day they spend by the pool, getting their first dose of radiation. Later Hans sneaks an hour to hit balls at the driving range of the nearby par three golf course. Tomorrow they will do a road trip out of the city. He has a certain destination in mind.

In the evening they dine out in style, driving to a fancy restaurant to park the MG beside the ancient Buicks still popular with the senior population despite the astronomical gas prices. As he parks, he asks June, 'How many of these people do you suppose have ever seen a British sports car? Well, let them eat their hearts out.' How many people have ever seen a twelve hole golf course? But he doesn't ask her that, at least not tonight.

As with other mornings, getting out of bed without waking June doesn't work. However, grumbling into her pillow is mostly for show. Sure enough, when she eventually comes out of the bedroom she tries to hide a smile because coffee and breakfast are waiting. It is not something she should start taking for granted, that she can expect to happen every morning, but Hans has fallen into a trap he has set for himself; he knows it will be a good day whenever his wife smiles at him in the morning.

Today is going to be one of those. Hans has already taken his golf bag out of the trunk of the red car to make room for two coolers. After breakfast he asks June to finish what he had started, boiling eggs. Those and cheese and some sausage, and bread, and whatever else she can think of, can go into one cooler. He is putting ice and a bottle of wine and some cans of pop and beer into the other one. They are going to drive into the desert for a picnic

"What should I wear?"

"Sunscreen would look nice."

"Oh, Hans. Now you're being silly."

"And half serious. With the top down, you can catch some sun." Hans waits but a moment and adds, "The car has autopilot."

Before she can catch herself, her words are out,

"But it's so small, there's no room -,"

And they both laugh. It could be a good day.

The first part of the trip is not a joyride because it is in the hectic traffic of the city portion of the I-10. The traffic decreases after turning onto Route 303, and then gets less again after joining Route 60. The driving is tedious and Hans gladly leaves it up to the car to negotiate this stretch. Clear of the city, the highway to Wickenburg is also boring, but Hans is eager to have the car respond to his touch, have it defer to his personality at the wheel; he sets the controls to manual.

At Wickenburg Hans changes highways again, this time to follow Route 93, still always heading northwest. Somewhere along this highway, before they reach Wikieup, he needs to find the turnoff to a road that should access the top of the mountain range overlooking the desert hideout of an eccentric multi-billionaire. Once notoriously in the news, for most of ten years now this Daniel Noah Jakow has not been visually verified to exist except by Hans Pedders, who is keeping that secret to himself.

    He wonders about those other three he had met there in the desert and if they still have incentive to keep that identity secret. Or was all of that an elaborately staged hoax, with those three 'spies' choreographed into the plot to add realism? But why, for whose benefit? Or is there reverse psychology in play? He, reticent Hans, will break out of his shell and blab to the world and lead everybody down the wrong path, right into a rabbit hole?

    Hans shakes his head to focus on his driving because much of this highway is a snake, coiling around the shoulders of high ridges and slithering into deep canyons, always ready to strike. However, bitterly disappointed in himself, Hans is not the driver this car needs for showing what it can do. Yes, he can make the tires squeal and the brakes smoke and turn his wife's face a chalky white, but he can't for the life of him drift the car through a turn under full throttle. Not that it has a throttle, but he would like to give some such imaginary exploit a basis in reality. At any rate, it's fun. He likes to see his wife both smile and frown at his driving. Not remembering past experiences, out of the blue Hans obliges June to be the navigator.

"Did we just pass a sign that said Ranger Lookout?"

"No, I don't think so. It just said something about a lake."

"Well, I don't want to miss the turnoff. I'm going to go this way for another mile or so and turn around and come back. There should be a sign coming from that direction too. We're looking for a Ranger station sign."

"A lake sounds like more fun, Hans."

He's willing to concede the fun part, but to justify not going to a lake would entail an explanation of things too weird for her to believe, so he'll grunt, something she has accepted as a valid response many times before. Okay, with no traffic either way, here's a safe place to turn around and go back. And he can slow down enough too so that they can see the road sign in time.

"There it is, Hans. Ranger Lookout. And it says lake too."

Right, and that means we can both be happy. After a myriad of twists and turns, always uphill, the road begins to level off. Quickly he had best get his golf-outing story ready, something believable and credible enough to stand up to fact checking. Hans wonders how it is that fact checking has become so routine that it pervades everyday existence, sometimes even intruding into family life.

The route to the top, at first through a landscape of barren rocks and desert scrub, abruptly enters a world of green. That can only mean water, and sure enough, sunlight is glinting off water over there. As they will find out later, a lake at this altitude was only possible by intervention. The infrequent rainfall up here had caused a little river to magically appear only to disappoint by going dry. Catching the tumbling water during the brief, mostly unpredictable wet season by means of a dam in a location where little was required in terms of changing the landscape, had created a unique lake.

The early afternoon sun is bright, but the altitude keeps the temperature to a comfortable level, encouraging people to go strolling in a park at the edge of a desert mountain. The park welcomes day visitors and tolerates overnight camping but has a ban on those large luxury homes on wheels. Hans does a circuit through the grounds and stops the car near the lake, deliberately some distance away from the Ranger Lookout tower.

"Why did you do that?"

"What?"

"Park here."

"After all that sitting, it's good for us to walk."

"So, Hans, turning fifty is making you a fitness freak?"

Thinking it safer to ignore the remark than starting a debate about his waistline outgrowing his pants, Hans gets out and walks. Also, he feels this urgency to look for the rock mountain in the desert before June sees it. Maybe the walk will give him time to think of something plausible if she asks if this is what he came to see. After all, he had made the effort to turn around on the highway just to find the road to this out of the way place.

Nothing. The sun is still high enough in the sky to illuminate all of the desert below and there is no mountain, no splash of green. His eyes sweep the entire area, all the way from the faraway hills in the east to the open desert to the south and up to the base of the mountain range they are on. Hans hears June coming up behind him, but he looks past her towards the car. The car is real. He turns to again search the desert, straining hard to find something.

"What are you looking for?"

Hans is perceptive of the fact that June had said 'for', not 'at'. With his back to her, he practically shouts it,

"Nothing! Do you hear me, nothing!"

His response is so abrupt and vehement that she steps back, alarmed.

"What's wrong Hans? What are you so mad about?"

Her anxious voice, and then the frightened look on her face brings him to his senses.

"I-, I'm sorry June. I didn't mean to snap at you."

"Well, you scared me half to death."

Hans steps back and puts an arm around her, the look in his eyes still fierce.

"I'm okay now. Everything's fine, believe me."

He immediately regrets adding that last part. He knows that she knows that he is lying, and he just stands there, as if lost.

"Aren't we going to look at the Ranger Station?"

"Huh? Oh, sure, of course."

Actually, that is a good idea. Maybe he can go up in the tower and get a better look at the valley. To her surprise, Hans suddenly picks up his pace, almost dragging her along. They get to the station and find out from the brightly smiling trainee that they can look around for free but to go up to the lookout will cost five dollars each. Slightly out of breath, June declines.

"You go."

"Are you sure you don't want to come?"

"No, I'm fine here. You go ahead, I know you want a better look."

Is that a dig? Well, it won't stop him, because he is desperate for a better look. Up the ladder he goes and wishes he had shed the ten pounds that he had pledged to lose by his birthday. Going in spurts, that is six rungs at a time and then a pause for catching his breath, he finally makes it to the platform on top. He feeds all the coins he has into the viewing scope and gets a close up look at the valley floor.

When looking at the desert earlier, he had been correct in guessing where the mountain should have been. Now he finds that spot again, and indeed, something is there. Rocks, lots of rocks, big rocks, but they no longer form a mountain, they are more like a coarse layer in a dried-up lakebed. Where the mountain had been is now a large, dish-shaped depression, covered by rocks in a circle large enough to hide even the area where the golf course should be. An explosion? To his untrained eye it appears like an eruption that collapsed on itself. Time elapses on the telescope and he has no more change. June must be impatient by now.

But she isn't. She has had a very interesting conversation with the young lady while he was up top. It seems that there are stories about a mountain in the desert, a mountain that blew up some two years ago. The rookie ranger had explained that this had been before her tour of duty here and was told the story by the retired park ranger that she is replacing. June is looking intently at Hans while she is relating this, but he says nothing as he walks her to the car.

The strangest thing happens when he puts the car in reverse to get back on the road: unlike other times when the car starts, the navigation screen comes alive without being prompted. Colours swirl for a moment and then the screen loses all meaning, the only message a blur of snow. The sound mimics that pattern, an initial babel of signals at cross purpose, only to end in irritating static.

"What just happened, Hans? Something wrong?"

His curt response is not reassuring.

"I haven't got a clue."

All the way back to the trailer Hans maintains a moody silence. In turn, she gives him the silent treatment, also that night and the next day. The day after that he takes the car back to its storage.

About to leave and close the door of the lockup, 'Beep! Beep! Beep! Beep!' calls him back to the car. He doesn't have to search where the sound comes from. The small screen on the dash is flashing. Maybe he has to do something to shut the vehicle down for storage, as a sign off that he is finished using it. He touches the screen and the beeping stops and the flashing stops. But the screen stays lit. He touches it again, hoping to turn it off. Instead of shutting down, it flashes red and then orange and then yellow, right through the rainbow colours.

Hans, frozen in place, is fascinated; he can't take his eyes off the screen, his mind in turmoil. Is this for real or is he going insane? And then a message appears on the screen: 'David Johan Pedders, use your passcode to access the internet.' This repeats over and over until he touches the screen again and it loses all light and turns black.

When he tries the ancient computer at the trailer it is locked. And he won't take a chance anywhere else; he will just have to wait until he can use their secure network at home.

Sunday, May 7, 2034

On their first night back home in their small town in Alberta, Hans is exhausted, uncertain whether he actually wants to find out what the message might be. He stares at his computer, tempted to start it up and then reluctantly admits that something else should happen first. Before exposing his sanity to further risk, tomorrow first thing, he will ask June to indulge him and listen to a narrative. If she believes him, he will use his 'password' and access the message with her present, to watch it with him. If she doesn't believe his story? Yes, what if she doesn't? Okay then, right now.

"June!"

"What? I thought you were going to bed."

"June, we need to talk."

"That sounds serious, but can't it wait until tomorrow? It's late and we're both tired."

"No, it can't wait, I might change my mind."

"Okay, I know something has been bothering you. Here, sit with me. I'm listening."

Hans takes a deep breath and starts talking. The incredulous look in her eyes changes to concern and then outright worry. An hour later she takes his hand.

"Are you sure you are alright Hans? You've really got me worried. Shouldn't you be talking to someone?"

"June, I'm talking to you, aren't I? Wait, I'll show you something."

Hans goes to where his golf clubs are still in their travel bag. He fishes around and comes back with two shiny objects, one shimmering blue and the other pearly white. He has his putter too.

"Listen. Golf balls. Nothing else like them on earth." He pings the blue one in the air but is unsuccessful with the rebound.

"Let me try." She gets it to chime three times before it drops but is still dubious.

"Hans, this doesn't prove anything."

"I knew you wouldn't believe me. I should have just kept quiet."

"I am really sorry, honey, it's all just too much. But, if it will make you feel better, I will watch with you when you try to make that connection. Right now, let's get some sleep."

Hans didn't get any sleep, and from her appearance June didn't sleep well either. He shouldn't have said anything at all. He is sure that she is worried about his state of mind. Well, she should; he is worried about it too.

He sits down in front of his ancient laptop and turns it on. As it blinks and burbles, getting ready for action, Hans is seized by an urgency to get this over with, time to find an end to this ludicrous drama. He will do this right now and not wait for June. She is usually skeptical about most things, so whatever shows up likely won't change her mind. This far removed from Arizona, the message could be irrelevant and therefore of no consequence for his life.

His computer warmed up, yes, it is that old, and he types in his name, Hans Pedders. Of course, nothing happens, and Hans is not surprised, since he has no idea which particular website to access. Well, how about something bold; go direct. Maybe Arkyz is fancying itself as a search engine that knows everything. Hans types in ARKYZ.com, capitalizing because that is likely the only form this high-brow artificial brain will recognize. He waits, suspecting that the contact may have to be through devious routing. And look, a page opens up. He enters his formal name as the password, David Johan Pedders. A small burst of colour flickers across the screen which then reverts to black. He repeats the process.

"No luck? Here." June is behind him, puts a cup of coffee on his desk, and stands there a moment.

"Not yet."

She goes back upstairs. Hans tries everything again. Still black, and now he fears that was his last chance; three times and out. He picks up his coffee, ready to give up and turn off the computer; maybe he needs to upgrade this thing. Of course, he's not eager to buy a new one; they all seem to come with pre-installed apps which he would never use.

Wait, the screen has come alive again, a blue light sweeping over it in waves and a hint of a rainbow swirl. Vague bits of text fade in and out, syncing strobe-like with audio that at best is only static that hurts his ears. Abruptly there is a short burst of faint pinging accompanied by a snowstorm on the screen. Alarmed, Hans aborts his computer. Alright, he is paranoid, but was that an attempt to intercept the message or trace the routing of the connection?

"How much of that gibberish did you understand?" she asks, having come in for the last part of the transmission.

"Depends. First, so I don't forget, I'll have to write down what I did catch." Hans grabs some paper and frantically looks for a pencil, or anything, to write with.

"Here." June finds and hands him a pen.

Hans will not give his memory much credence and just list the words as they pop up in his mind. He dare not risk trying to sequence them into phrases or statements for some of the words could slide away; he leaves spaces in case association brings others forward. Quickly, and don't waste time on any one, just keep going while there is flow. When he can't think of any more bits of information to nail down on the page, he exhales the breath he has been holding in. His eyes scan the list to check if he has missed something that should have been written down while his brain is already trying to anticipate how the scribbles might connect.

Hans has never been one to indulge himself with detective thrillers and June devours them. Has she understood enough of his weird narrative to attempt unravelling the message from the clues he's written down? He doesn't have to ask because she is already sitting beside him, poised. Like the printed puzzles that some newspapers still publish and June spends hours on, she is eying his list of clues, ready to attack. Hans looks at her and smiles and gives her the sheet of paper,

"Okay, Hon, go write me a story."

She utters an indistinct, insincere protest but takes the list and goes upstairs. Hans stays at his desk; he will try to generate the message from what little bits he remembers. An hour later he goes up and finds her at the kitchen table. Although it is not even noon, Hans brings out a chilled bottle of pinot grigio and two wine glasses.

"What have you got?"

Amazing, and Hans shakes his head again, how totally amazing the things they agree on! Yes, the message must be from Arkyz since 'it' is the only one that would address someone as 'David Johan - -', and that suggests Arkyz is indeed embedded in the internet. Probably, from 'hydro–', there was a hydrogen accident and the Towers imploded, and 'M', or Jakow or whatever his name, could have died. Or, suicide? Do 'stars' hint at a space project? 'Carbon' and 'B5' could mean that at least one of the mobiles is in the Pit. 'Nearby' is possibly advising Hans that the proximity of the red car was detected when at the Ranger Station. Fortunately for Hans there had been no reference to Qu and D5. He can just imagine June going, 'Hans and a computer. How ridiculous!'.

Well, that was fun, and they toast each other for the brilliance of their sleuthing, and more, although only hinted at, the compatibility of their minds. Both leave unspoken a niggling concern that the message could be of significance, hopefully not for them.

Sunday, August 5, 2035

A little more than a year later Hans is in his backyard, sweltering in late summer heat that is reminiscent of the Arizona desert, trying to save his garden from dying, the drought now into the third month.

"Hans! come quick! Look what they are saying on the news."

June is shouting at him out the back door.

"Why, what is it?"

"Come and see. It's breaking news that interrupted what I was watching. I know you're interested in this kind of stuff, so I started recording it. Well, the last part anyways. I didn't catch it from the beginning, but I'm sure they will show everything again."

He shuts off the water. All right, he'll come in and see; June is hardly ever excited about stuff on the news that interests him particularly, so this must be special.

And that it is, because talking heads are straining to keep their composure, reporting from Moscow and Beijing and Washington and Berlin and Jerusalem, with the special newscast interrupted every few seconds by an update. Hans is not making sense of what they are saying.

"Take it back to the beginning, or what you got of it."

Something that repeats between all the excited talk is a short video showing a rocket launching with a voice off-camera screaming in fear, 'that is the third one!'. Hans asks June to replay the clip because something he thinks he saw nips at his memory. Carefully he watches, and, yes, there! Ignoring the launch, Hans concentrates his attention on the background. Somewhat obscured by the rocket exhaust, there seem to be two more waiting to be launched, each prominently marked with large, black letters on white, 'TTT'. Could these be Jakow's space probes, but why only five? Where are the others?

The world is excited because the huge rockets are being launched from somewhere in Mongolia, in rapid sequence, and somebody jumped to the conclusion, from the launch trajectories pointing in different directions, that they are a pre-emptive, blatant first strike, aimed at different targets around the world. Red phones are jangling until finally a message breaks through to everybody: the projected targets don't make sense, no one on earth is being threatened.

Did Jakow actually pull that one off? After all, he has been dead for how long now? Three years? Surprising that such an immense undertaking happened in spite of his absence. Money? Most likely Arkyz was utilized to dupe the nuclear powers and all their spy satellites into concluding that the construction project happening in the Gobi had been innocuous.

Hans is tempted to arrive at a more unpleasant assumption. Jakow's superhuman intelligence project should not have been advanced enough to put anything worthwhile out there. Arkyz, however, possibly infected by three arrogant humans, became brazen enough to put his own digitized DNA into the space capsules, inadvertently carrying out part of M's scheme. Hans shakes his head at such a waste of resources since whatever it is, whatever is being hurled at the universe, is a testament to the immaturity of the human race.

Okay, so they weren't nukes and once more the world escapes killing itself with fire and brimstone. With Arkyz probably by now capable of gloating, will the human race die whimpering instead as it poisons itself?

Hans goes back outside, however not to continue watering the garden. Vegetables at the market are ever so much cheaper than home-grown; he will use the precious water on his lawn instead because you can't go shopping for green grass like you would for carrots. Something had stirred in him and suddenly desperate, he wants to see water droplets sparkling on green grass. He turns off the tap, hooks up a sprinkler, turns the water on again and retreats to sit on a bench and watch. Hans is making it rain, and as the arc of water waves through the air, back and forth, he is rewarded by an occasional glimpse of a little rainbow.

Saturday, April 9, 2044

Ah, another day in the Valley of the Sun. The sky is that same steel blue that it was yesterday and the day before and the day before that. June and Hans are in the Mesa trailer park and have a decision to make. June's father had passed away three years ago and two years later June's mother, plagued by various illnesses, decided against continuing to come and live in a trailer park for six months of the year, on her own and apart from family. Until her mother bequeathed it to June, the trailer had sat empty. Hans and June are debating whether to sell it or keep it for the future.

Hans has reached the magic age when retirement starts beckoning; this could become their Snowbird get-away. However, there are reasons to hesitate about committing to the park. The future of the trailer park itself is uncertain. Many parks have already disappeared, the owners lured by the money of developers to let their increasingly valuable land be used for erecting condo towers. Also, the demographics are shifting. Attrition among the older residents is making room for a new generation of owners, not retirees but working people unable to afford regular housing. Who can predict what the social milieu of the park will be like in five or ten years? Already in the few days they have been here they have encountered some people shopping for trailer bargains, people they hope would never become their neighbours.

After three days of decluttering and cleaning a place not lived in for a while, Hans and June are eager for some relaxation. While deciding the fate of the trailer, they intend to also spend time in the sun, poolside or on the golf course, depending on the mood of the day.

June has reconnected with two friends who rent in another park and are not due to leave for home until the end of the month, and the three of them are golfing this morning. Although invited to make it a foursome, Hans declines because of June. Several seasons ago she decided to take up the game under the condition that husbands and wives don't golf together. She had absolutely no desire to be subjected to a running commentary from Hans about the do's and don'ts of the game, especially the 'don't this' and 'don't that'.

Such a shame if he were to waste this day not playing golf. That he isn't on a course right now is his own fault since he had neglected to book a tee time for himself. Well, he can always go to a course and be joined up with some strangers; he has learned how to enjoy golf as a social occasion, ever since his experience at the Triple Towers some sixteen years ago.

Although he rarely thinks about Jakow when back home in Alberta, here in Arizona the desert prompts his mind to drift back to that little mountain. Whatever happened to Qu, he wonders, and Arkyz? Of course, the red car is a constant reminder every time he chooses to use it, which is not that frequently anymore; it has been several years since he last took advantage. This time around he has decided for them to indulge, especially since it could be their last convenient opportunity. Still, even this much later he feels that enjoying the car is a betrayal of his principles, that somehow, he has been 'bought'. But it is so much fun to drive, and the status it gives him when he pulls into the parking lot at a golf course is something money can't buy.

On second thought, rather than golfing, maybe he'll just take the car for a long drive, up the back way around Superstition Mountain. Knowing the women she is with, Hans is sure that June will be gone for at least four or five hours. Should he take some lunch for the trip? A look in the fridge reveals nothing that is handy, so just some beer to put in a cooler. He hopes June has her set of keys with her because he is going to lock up the trailer when he leaves. He exits by way of the deck to make sure everything is secure on that side of the trailer and then comes around the front of to where the MG is parked in the carport.

But, what is this? Some street person, obvious from the shaggy, gray-streaked hair down to the shoulders, has the nerve to be in his car! In the passenger seat, just waiting for the driver to show up, sitting there so nonchalantly! Hans calls out,

"What are you doing here?"

He doesn't want to come across sounding too harsh because he feels sorry for some of these people; one never knows the circumstances that might put himself in that kind of predicament. To get a better look, he approaches the front of the car but from the driver's side, just in case this should become unpleasant. The intruder turns out to be a man, although Hans could not have guessed that by seeing him from the back. Darkly suntanned, dressed in a tee shirt that shows off some muscle, and what is this, old-fashioned cut-offs? This is all so brazen.

"You know you're trespassing. You should leave."

Hans had intended to sound in control; after all, this is his private space that's being invaded. The uninvited passenger just stares back, and Hans becomes confused. Why this uncomfortable feeling that he should know this man? What kind of deja vu is this?

"If I found the car I would find you," is all the man says, yet enough for Hans to shrink back.

"But you're dead!"

"That's what they say."

Hans is not willing to accept what he sees; he is staring at someone that was reported dead by the Phoenix Sun. And months later, by the Times.

"That explosion or whatever, how did you survive?"

"The implosion wasn't exactly planned, but it didn't come as a surprise. It was merely a matter of time until things would blow up."

Although Hans wants to hear more, he is unwilling to be hospitable just yet. He remembers their parting was not amicable.

"What brings you here?"

That comes out more abrupt than Hans intends yet Jakow lets it pass.

"I have some business to conclude here, Hans, and I thought it might interest you enough to come along as an observer."

"Never! You know, Daniel, you know very - - ," Jakow cuts him off.

"It is Noah. My name is not Daniel, it is Noah. I am Noah Jakowsky."

Take a deep breath, Hans, and feel the ground with your feet. The earth is rotating a thousand miles an hour, but gravity has you firmly planted. Take another deep breath and now look the man square in the face and be aggressive, you don't owe him anything.

"Jakow, or whatever, what is going on?"

"As I said, I am not Daniel Jakow. He is dead. I am Noah Jakowsky. Hans, we are in a setting here that is not conducive to reacquainting with each other. We used to have great conversations when we were hitting golf balls. As a suggestion, can you find us a course where we can play a round and talk like old times?"

With Hans unsure how best to say it, Jakow pre-empts.

"I know, my appearance, the way I look, no one will let me on their course. Nothing that money can't fix."

Easy Hans, easy now. Yes, that was arrogance talking but if you want to hear the rest of the story, let it ride. Besides, it could be fun watching how this man, if it is really Jakow, will conduct himself, especially at the course that suddenly comes to mind.

"Okay, Dan-, I mean Noah. Clubs?"

"I'll just rent a set, Hans. Shouldn't affect my game that much, playing with strange clubs. Since the Triple Towers I haven't played even nine holes."

Hans thinks it and says it.

"Smart, setting up excuses early."

"Hans, I think I can still show you a thing or two."

"We'll see."

Hans gets in and puts the car in manual mode. It would be so much easier to tell the car the destination and sit back, relaxed and not have to worry about the traffic, but then, what's the fun of having a car like this?

"I see you still enjoy driving. That's something else I haven't done in a long time, probably at least twenty years. Certainly not where I live now."

"So, where is that?"

"I think I might have mentioned it when we met years ago, that before the Triple Towers I had secluded myself to an island in the South Pacific. Well, I've gone back to it. It is a long way from anywhere, but nobody bothers me."

Other than the screeching of tires there is silence as Hans recklessly shows off, weaving in and out of traffic, and with every close call making this 'Noah' visibly nervous. Perhaps his driving is keeping the man quiet, or it could be that he is saving the conversation for the golf course where they arrive in record time; never had Hans made it here this fast. The parking lot is full, but Hans is in luck for someone near the entrance to the club house is just pulling out and he whips into the vacated spot.

"I am not sure we'll get on." Hans cautions. An executive course with a mix of par three and par four holes, not that dissimilar to Jakow's course at the Towers, it is well maintained and very popular.

"Let me try." 'Jakowsky' volunteers. Hans stays back a couple of paces because he wants to laugh. Or is it because he wants to dissociate from someone who marches to the desk and loudly asks for the head pro, oblivious to the oblique looks from the nattily dressed golfers waiting for their tee-off time. The assistant pro manning the desk turns at the imperious tone and stares at what must be an interloper. Hans cringes and pretends to study a score card.

"Why? I can help you."

"All right then. I need to rent a set of left-handed clubs and my friend and I would like to tee off in half an hour. It would be nice if you could manage that."

"You are not serious, sir, are you? Totally impossible. We have no tee times open until six thirty." Everybody within hearing range should have caught the sarcasm, not just the tone of voice but also the time. Almost sundown. Hans remembers about the name and whispers to him.

"Noah, let's go."

"Not so fast. I asked for the head professional and this rude young person is not obliging me. Once more, young sir, the head pro, please."

"If you insist," and just like that the junior pro is most anxious to find the man in charge; anything to get out of this embarrassing predicament. He disappears and shortly comes back with a man wearing a look on his face that is well rehearsed from dealing with duffers wanting to become elite overnight.

"Yes?"

"I want -"

"I was told what you want, and you were told that we have no tee times available, is that correct?" There was no 'sir' attached to that, and Hans wonders if this new Jakow has met his match.

"Who is the owner of this course?"

The pro doesn't comprehend what Jakow is implying.

"Pardon me?"

"You heard me. Get me in touch with whoever pays your salary or the CEO of the corporation that owns this course, whichever is the fastest. And have him show himself on your computer screen."

The unflappable pro manages a weak,

"It's a she."

Hans can't stand this any longer.

"Noah, you push this any further, I'm not playing golf with you."

Strangely, that threat has an impact. Without another word Jakow turns and barges through the crowd that had gathered to watch the show. Hans has to run to catch up with him. Both get into the car and sit and wait for the other to say something first. Jakow gives in.

"You picked this course deliberately, didn't you? Well, I am sorry for how I behaved. Sometimes I forget where things are at. Come to think of it, I'm not that sure Arkyz would have approved the money for this course."

Hans had thought that the episode inside had finished it for him, that he wasn't going to give this 'Noah Jakowsky' any more of his time but the mention of Arkyz sparks his curiosity. Alright, let's not wind this up just yet.

"I know a course where we can get on anytime. It's not as nice, but we could play." And he adds,

"And talk."

Jakow seems to retreat within himself.

"Sure," is all he says.

Hans tells the little sportster to start and is surprised when there is no response. Well, this is awkward. What now?

"Sorry, Noah. This has not ever happened before." He regrets the words as soon as they are out of his mouth, remembering another time.

In a tone Hans does not recognize Jakow speaks, and not to him but at the car.

"Arkyz!"

The car starts and Hans nearly loses control. With the electric motors howling and the tires smoking, Hans has to fight the steering wheel to prevent the donuts the car is trying to make in the crowded parking lot. It is only by luck that he manages to find the exit, and they shoot out into the street where the avoidance systems of other cars rushing by prevents an accident. Again, that voice,

"Arkyz, be nice!"

The car immediately behaves and adjusts to the flow of traffic. Even so, it is with white knuckles that Hans gets them to a golf course in whose small lot are parked only three vehicles. At the pro shop tee times are handed out by someone that looks more like a bored clerk than a golf professional. Hans pays the green fees, since they are cheap, but he lets Noah bargain over clubs, because a left-handed set has to be assembled out of the used clubs that are for sale. Noah wants to walk since it is a relatively short, executive type layout. Wisely, Hans gets them a golf cart because the temperature is already threatening the record high for this day.

To no one's surprise the first tee is open and they can go anytime they are ready. Hans flips a coin which Jakow guesses wrong so Hans will tee off first. Having loosened up with his driver, Hans stays with it and hits a decent shot down the middle. Jakow, commenting that the hole is only two hundred and ninety yards, disdains the driver. Instead, he takes a mighty swing with a three iron and hooks the ball out of bounds. He looks at the club as if there is something wrong with it and tees up another ball.

"Play it from where it went out," suggests Hans.

"No, we have to play this fair. The stakes are too high."

Hans has a tingle start at the base of his neck. Without trying to sound anxious, he asks,

"Oh, and what are we playing for?"

"Relax, Hans. It is simply whether or not you are going to come with me tomorrow."

"Stop, Noah. You know that I am completely finished as far as any of your projects are concerned."

Before Jakow says anything further he hits his second tee shot. It stays in the fairway, finishing some thirty yards shy of where Hans had ended up. They jump in the cart and Hans races to Jakow's ball. Hans has seen where there are some other golfers coming to play. For him that has the makings of an uncomfortable round. If Jakow and Hans get into any kind of lengthy discussion, the group behind them is going to be breathing down their neck. This would spoil not only their golf but also break up the flow of their conversation. Hans is eager to avoid that since he definitely wants some things explained.

Jakow makes a decent approach shot, ending up just off the green. Hans gets lucky with a bounce that puts him a foot away from the pin.

"Pick up, the first one is yours."

By conceding the hole, Jakow also indicates that the competition should be match play. Okay, fine with Hans since he too prefers it over stroke play. They tee off with a wedge and nine respectively on the short second and they both chip and putt for pars. Hans wants to talk yet avoids bringing up the car incident, intending instead to clarify what he thinks Jakow is assuming about their future relationship.

"You knew that when I left that night it was all over for me. I feel under no obligation to do anything more. Actually, I think the reverse holds true. You owe me, especially you owe me an explanation about what is going on."

"Fair enough. The history recorded by the car tells us that you made a certain trip and probably found out there had been an accident. I think you also assumed that it was inevitable that Arkyz and I would be parting company. Except we didn't and it wasn't an accident. The blowing up of the Triple Towers was sabotage, it was Qu rebelling in her new role as D5."

Somehow this does not surprise Hans and although he is reluctant to push for details, he would like to know about Qu's fate. The third hole, also a par three, escapes being hit by their tee shots. Jakow gets the lucky bounce with his chip and Hans does not, losing the hole.

"So, Qu became D5, right, and what happened to her?" The concern Hans shows for a computer rather than inquiring how Jakow managed to escape is indicative of how he is insulating himself against a man who once had awed him. Jakow doesn't acknowledge the slight and instead answers the question.

"It seems D5 had planned it as a suicide but failed. She, 'it', tricked the others to get into the coal bin under pretext to save them from the explosion, and she seems to have ended up there as well. Arkyz gets some garbled messages from the four of them now and then."

"How did Arkyz not get blown to bits?"

"Let's hit our tee shots first."

The hole is a short par four, less than three hundred yards, and Jakow goes with the iron again. This time it is drilled straight down the middle. Hans goes with the three wood and hits a good one, just past Jakow's ball.

"The whole computer floor got blown to bits, but Arkyz had already expanded itself beyond the Towers and was embedded in most of the networks around the world." Jakow hits a nice approach shot but it doesn't hold on the severely sloped green and rolls off.

"Daniel, I mean -, Noah, it sounds like you were there when things blew up."

"Close but lucky. I was golfing and felt a tremor and I ran into the desert. It seems I had a premonition because of how strangely D5 had been behaving and the fact that Arkyz was already communicating with experimental MIs in the outside world. Because of Arkyz being elsewhere, yet able to observe events by way of the sensors of the four mobiles in the Towers, we have a complete record of what happened inside."

"Talk about lucky, and I'm not talking about your chip."

From off the green, Jakow had chipped in for birdie for one up. Hans gets that back on the next hole, a par three of less than a hundred yards; his wedge shot rims the hole. He birdies, Jakow pars, and they are even. Alright then, here comes the easy sixth hole, a par four that is only two forty. Hans isn't going to force it, so he goes with the driver. Good choice for it ends up on the green. As he gives way to Jakow on the tee box, he has to ask him the obvious.

"And here you are talking to me, Noah. Aren't you supposed to be dead?"

"Not by a long shot, watch this."

Because Hans is looking at a birdie Noah chooses the three wood, and he is going to rip it. The beautiful high arc curves out of bounds.

"Now you're dead."

"Yes, Daniel N Jakow is dead. An official coroner's inquiry said so. Accidental death, body not recovered. Arkyz is doing a good job of burying the old and creating the new."

"You and Arkyz? I don't understand."

"For all practical purposes Arkyz now 'is' the internet. Arkyz has gotten what I promised it, and in return is giving me leverage to continue with at least part of my dream. Even you must have heard about the Gobi Desert rocket launching. Because things with China got messy, there were only five when it should have been twelve. It was Arkyz that made those five possible and it is Arkyz again that is making tomorrow possible, seven more launches. That's what I want you to observe with me. Seven intergalactic messengers are departing from a platform built in the desert not far from what is left of the Triple Towers, and they are carrying very interesting DNA. Care to guess?"

They reach where Jakow's second drive has ended up and he prepares to chip. Although Hans doesn't want to guess, he certainly wants to know but he will wait for Jakow to make his shot. The wristy effort doesn't even reach the green and he picks up his ball.

"The hole is yours. Aren't you going to hazard a guess?"

"Noah, it all depends on who did the selecting, you or Arkyz?"

"Both. Actually, we agreed on all four samples, one of each aboard every space capsule."

"Okay, I'm assuming your digitized DNA is one choice and a condensed version of Arkyz, since he seems to be in charge, is another. So, more than that?"

"You always were a diplomat," is the sarcastic rejoinder from Jakow, who then adds,

"Yes, more. Two more."

"Noah, I don't have a clue so I'm going to hit my ball instead."

Hans still has the honour and tees off. He is feeling the rhythm after the last hole and his drive splits the fairway. Jakow hits a poor tee shot, slicing it out of bounds, making Hans wonder if he is trying to lose. The second try also flies left and into somebody's yard.

"Enough, let's go pick up your ball."

Hans thinks that's a shame because this is the best drive he has ever hit on this hole. Okay then, two up and two to go. He could win this thing. Hans notes that Jakow is struggling to say something yet can't seem to get it past his lips.

"Hans, I want you to know that Arkyz chose the memory of Qu, the part that was erased out of her mind, to encode and include it as a sample of our experimental humanity."

"That doesn't make sense. Choosing Qu, yes, but for Arkyz to be making that choice is not logical. Is Arkyz losing it?" Hans adds the last question in all seriousness, only to be shocked by Jakow's answer.

"Frankly, yes, and his threat to humanity is probably unavoidable. Arkyz is mostly involved in the financial sector now, legitimately and otherwise, accumulating tremendous assets, but it is also getting to be a massive search engine. It is compromising its initial intellectual integrity by an ambition to become omnipotent. It is becoming diluted and fragmented and Arkyz has inadvertently admitted as much to me. I suspect that eventually it will go insane with unpredictable consequences."

Hans doesn't want to concur with that gloom. Like other times when things get too somber, he thinks to be clever and reaches for some lame attempt to be funny.

"Be more optimistic. Maybe the media tycoons and the irrational blog groupies out there will gang up and try to tear Arkyz to pieces; it could become an epic struggle, fit for a movie, like that ape and the sea monster. Hey, that's my vision for the future: they all cancel each other out and the world returns to normal. And you had better get it together on these last two holes, you're two down."

"Thanks. That really cheered me up. Incidentally, don't you want to guess as to the fourth choice?"

"I won't guess, but I am curious."

"Of course you are. That's your nature. That is why, by mutual agreement, Arkyz and I decided to include your DNA as well."

Hans was teeing off and it was unsportsmanlike of Jakow to tell him that just as he was into his backswing. It is only a par three with a little pond on the side, but his slice finds the water.

"Take a drop by the water, Hans, it's lateral."

Hans, still furious for letting his golf swing be affected like that, to have an emotional reaction spoil a shot, ignores the advice and launches another one, into the water.

"This one is yours," he mutters, stomping down the fairway, forgetting they are playing from a cart. Jakow calls after him,

"I haven't teed off yet."

"I said it's yours."

Jakow takes the cart to the next tee and waits for Hans.

"Before I hit, I just want you to know that it's alright if you don't want to come to the launch tomorrow."

"Noah, let it go. I'm done with your kind of future."

They both hit poor tee shots, mediocre approaches, and then two putt for bogeys. Without saying anything, both seem to agree not to continue on to the back nine; they have played enough golf. Hans wins by a hole. Neither one makes a move to shake hands. It just wasn't that kind of a game.

Both are subdued on the way back and Hans exhibits less bravado with his driving. The silence is interrupted by Jakow before they are about to reach the trailer park.

"Stop, this is where I get off."

Hans pulls the car over to a stop and turns to face him.

"So, this is it."

He made it as a statement, but Jakow correctly interprets it as a question.

"No, Hans, not quite. I have something to say to you that has been long overdue. You asked, numerous times, why you were invited to the Triple Towers, and I kept stalling to give you an answer. Remember that we have the same birthdate, that we are almost twins. Remember when I shocked you and told you that I had researched your background and was tracking your life? My ego drove me to find someone to compare myself to. I lured you to the Triple Towers so that we could stand facing each other, so that I could compare myself and what I had become to you and what you were. It has taken so long to arrive at this moment because the better I got to know you, the more ashamed I became for doing this. Hans, I got you there so that I could gloat."

As on other occasions, this strange man succeeds in leaving Hans speechless.

"I don't know what to say," he manages.

"So, don't. Forget that you ever knew Daniel Jakow and remember me as Noah Jakowsky." He gets out.

Hans watches in the little rear-view mirror, watches Noah walking away, not looking back, walking to where a black rental is coming to a stop at the curb. Even after the limo drives away, Hans continues looking in the mirror and finds staring back at him two eyes that ask for ID.

Acknowledgements

For a writer to have space to be creative, it is helpful when family mostly get out of the way; better yet, when they don't, and become part of the team.

Thank you to my two daughters and my wife for making the writing of this story possible:

Tracey Drach still is not fully aware how crucial her role was as the unofficial editor, her imagined presence constantly looking over my shoulder, not allowing me to play guessing games with the reader.

Kara Tersen was the cheerleader, and so much more. Many hours she devoted to providing the technical expertise that let the rambling manuscript evolve into a format fit for publication. And, she is also the artist that designed the cover.

Words are inadequate to express gratitude to Verda, my life-long companion, for her tolerance of my erratic, often disruptive writing schedule. So many times I should be doing other things, including sleeping, and she let me be, finger stabbing the keyboard.

Manufactured by Amazon.ca
Bolton, ON